Praise for the C

SHADOV

"Silverman provides us with inside look into the world of talk radio as Carol Childs, an investigative reporter, finds herself in the middle of a Hollywood murder mystery, uncovering evidence that may point to her best friend. A hunky FBI Agent and a wacky psychic will keep readers guessing from beginning to end."

– Annette Dashofy,
USA Today Bestselling Author of Lost Legacy

"Silverman creates a trip through Hollywood filled with aging hippies, greedy agents, and a deadly case of product tampering. Forget the shower scene in *Psycho*; *Shadow of Doubt* will make you scared to take a bath!"

– Diane Vallere,
Author of the Material Witness, Style & Error,
and Mad for Mod Mystery Series

"A thoroughly satisfying crime novel with fascinating, authentic glimpses into the world of talk radio and some of its nastier stars... The writing is compelling and the settings ring true thanks to the author's background as a newscaster herself."

– Jill Amadio,
Author of Digging Too Deep

"Carol is a smart, savvy heroine that will appeal to readers. This is a cozy with a bite."

– Rosemary Smith,
Books for Avid Readers

"Absolutely engaging, I could barely put it down. The characters in the book were well-developed and the plot was chillingly genius."

– Lyn Faulkner,
Netgalley Reviewer

SHADOW OF DOUBT

Nancy Cole Silverman

SHADOW OF DOUBT
A Carol Childs Mystery
Part of the Henery Press Mystery Collection

First Edition
Trade paperback edition | December 2014

Henery Press
www.henerypress.com

ISBN-13: 978-1-940976-53-2

Printed in the United States of America

SHADOW OF DOUBT

A CAROL CHILDS MYSTERY

NANCY COLE SILVERMAN

HENERY PRESS

The Carol Childs Mystery Series
by Nancy Cole Silverman

SHADOW OF DOUBT (#1)
BEYOND A DOUBT (#2)
(July 2015)

To Mom

ACKNOWLEDGMENTS

Writers may be born to write. They may have stories they want to tell, but without the right people in their lives, providing them with the proper structure and support, so many writers would never have the opportunity to pen the stories or write the words that spin around inside their heads. My guess would be sometimes those very helpful people don't even know who they are. Perhaps they are teachers, ministers, priests, rabbis, scholars or friends who along the way offered an encouraging word, suggested a new direction, or just listened. I'm lucky. I've had many such people in my life, and for this book I'd like to name a few.

Thank you, Kendel Lynn, acquiring editor with Henery Press and to all the very supportive people at Henery Press, including Art C. Molinares, Erin George and Stephanie Chontos. Without your talents this book would have remained another lost file on my hard drive. Special thanks to my mother, Ruth Bowman, and to my close friend and hiking partner, Rhona Robbie, both of whom read endless versions of this book. Thanks also to my sister, Marjorie Palmer, who not only read my book but blessed it. She's a minister, and that means a lot to me. Lastly, but not least, I thank my wonderful husband, Bruce Silverman, who, without his support, I could not be me.

Thank you all.

Nancy Cole Silverman

PROLOGUE

"...and finally, I'd like to thank my agent, Pepper Millhouse. Pepper, you've been like a mother to me. Without you none of this would have happened." Amber Marx, barely seventeen, in a voice shaking with emotion, brushed a tear from her eye as she held the award for Best Supporting Actress above her head and nodded in the direction of her agent's table. "Thank you."

Pepper smiled and raised her wine glass as the two exchanged a brief look. Then the actress gathered the skirt of her long lemon-yellow chiffon gown in one hand and pranced off the stage like a gangly young filly.

Pepper knew that *look* was for helping the young actress secure her emancipation from her abusive father, the details of which Pepper had silenced from the press. Most of her fans and the media simply knew Amber as Hollywood's sweetheart, first appearing on the screen at age two as the impossible but adorable baby Ann in the blockbuster *Baby Business*. The camera loved her, her fans worshipped her and the press couldn't get enough of her. There was no doubt in anyone's mind the young ingénue was well on her way.

"I hope she's as happy with you when she realizes you pitched Clarissa St. Clair for *The Lady in White*," Pepper's niece, Samantha, whispered to her as the two sat back down to enjoy the Beverly Hilton's eloquent four-course dinner.

"We all have to grow up sometime, don't we? And if our little Miss Amber is upset, she can get in line. She'll hardly be the first. Besides she'll barely have time once she's finished *The Sorcerer's*

Daughter, and there's already a sequel in the works. So, for right now, what she doesn't know won't hurt her. Unless, that is, you're planning to say something?"

"Me?" Sam laughed. "And incur the wrath of my dear aunt? I hardly think it's my place."

Pepper Millhouse, president of ACT, the American Creative Talent Agency, was easily one of LA's top agents. Among industry insiders she was regarded as a bulldog. She enjoyed bragging that she'd pissed-off more of her fellow agents than remained in the business. Samantha knew she wasn't wrong. Pepper had a target on her back. Any day of the week there were a number of agents, actors and even a few directors and producers who would love to have seen her exit the business in an untimely manner. Preferably in a body bag.

"You think between you and that little flunky of yours you can wrap this up?" Pepper tossed her head in the direction of Andrew Reese, Samantha's pretty-boy assistant, then stood up. "I need to chat with Clarissa for a moment and if I squeeze out now I can beat the traffic home."

"And why should tonight be any different?" Samantha grinned sarcastically. As head of publicity for the agency, her job required the wearing of many hats, the least of which was to appease her aunt.

"Always the sassy one, aren't you?" Pepper cupped Sam's chin in her hand, turning her niece's head towards her. She looked directly into her eyes. "So much like your twin. Too bad she's so much prettier." Patting the side of her face with a dismissive laugh, she dropped her hand, and added, "But we all have to live with our shortcomings, don't we? Ciao."

If Samantha flinched it wasn't detectable. Her smile froze on her face. Her aunt's words, like an assassin's sharp dragger twisted deep beneath her ribs, reminding her she was nothing without her aunt. She owed her everything.

"Ciao." Sam's eyes followed Pepper. Her aunt's small frame, slightly bent in her silver evening gown, weaving between tables crowded with some of Hollywood's biggest names, headed toward the exit. Slowly, Sam raised her hand. Pantomiming a gun, she pointed it in the direction of her aunt and fired. *Pow!*

Pepper leaned against the large double doors to her bedroom and exhaled. It had been a long day and an even longer evening. Everybody wanted something from her, and the only thing she could think of was what she wanted, her bath. A nice warm, bubbly soak where she could forget about demanding clients and the pressures of her job.

Throwing her shoes aside she walked over to the bar, poured herself a glass of red wine and flipped on the CD player. Vivaldi was perfect. Tiptoeing to the bath she stripped off her evening dress, letting it fall to the floor, and reached for her robe. Catching her reflection in the mirror she studied her naked body.

By her own assessment Pepper Millhouse wasn't a bad looking woman. She was of average height and build with dark hair and blue eyes. Running her hands across her stomach the loose skin beneath her grip puckered. She sighed. Then straightening up, she touched her breasts, lifting them slightly and smiled. Her fabulous double D's made up for a lot of the sins of sagging flesh. Forty years ago they had gotten her into as much trouble as they had success. In her day, Pepper Millhouse had been quite the number, a stunner in fact, who had been linked romantically to a number of Hollywood's leading men, all of whom she'd been smart enough not to marry. Rumor was, at one time or another, many of her conquests had been either delightfully under her—or under contract with her.

Pepper dimmed the lights and lit a candle. Leaning closer into the mirror she pushed the skin under her chin back behind her ears. Thank goodness for high cheekbones. She could ward off another facelift for one more year, but no more. Hollywood could forgive anything but age. Taking another sip of wine, she reached for a bottle of light grape seed oil, one of the specialties her housekeeper Arminta had set in a basket next to the tub. She patted it gently onto her face, down her neck, chest, arms and legs. It tingled as she applied it. Glancing back into the full length mirror, she saw that the elixir had been working. Already she could see the skin smoothing, the dimpled effect around her legs and arms, the puffiness that comes with age, diminishing.

She pushed a button on the tub and a cascade of warm water from the elaborate gold faucet flowed into the Jacuzzi. She reached into the basket for a bottle of bath salts and read the hang tag, Lavender Lush # 7. *For best results rub vigorously onto those troublesome areas plus neck and chest then add to tub for a delightful soak.* She took a quick whiff. A lovely lavender lemon grass aroma gave her a momentary lightheadedness. After adding the salt to the water she began to rub her neck and chest as instructed. Her dark hair had already started to frizz from the humidity and pushing it away from her face she noticed a thin gray halo surrounded the base of her hairline. She hated that tell-tale sign of age and made a mental note to make an appointment with her hairdresser. When the tub was full, she sank slowly into the warming bubbles, the scented candle easing the tensions of the day, the music from Vivaldi's Four Seasons: the ideal escape.

A tingling sensation ran up her arms and legs, the bubbles like silk against her skin, warm and pleasurable. Gently she sponged her neck, letting the water trickle soothingly down her chest, suds slipping between her fingers, clinging softly to her body as she massaged her neck and shoulders.

Resting her head upon a bath pillow she closed her eyes and ran her tongue mindlessly across her lips. They were numb. *Too much wine.* Feeling lightheaded, she concentrated on the swelling sounds of the violins. With one sudsy hand above her head, she kept beat to the music, as though she were an orchestral director.

The suds, now like sticky pods against her skin, clung to her, warming with the gradual crescendo of the violins, quietly bubbling, multiplying like a growing colony. She pushed them away and concentrated on the manic plucking of strings, their quick staccato movement now like small bites up and down her legs. She opened her eyes.

Ants! Emerging from within the bubbles were thousands of tiny black spindly creatures.

She was hallucinating. Her head warm, her heart racing, the brisk, rapid tempo of the music bursting the bubbles. Surrounding her body were thousands of crawling black ants.

Frantically she splashed at the suds, her nails scraping to remove the foamy pods that now adhered to her skin like small suction cups. It was hopeless. With each frenzied movement more bubbles broke with more of the insidious black ants now crawling up her chest, into her hair and ears. Her eyes stung, her chest ached, her body burned from the inside out. She tried to pull herself from the tub, but collapsed. Her legs limp, her arms heavy. She had lost all control of her limbs. Nauseous and short of breath, her body slid back against the tub, the beat of her heart mirroring the feverish pace of Vivaldi's final chorus. It was the last thing she heard. Suddenly, like the music, it was over, and her lifeless body slid beneath the water.

CHAPTER 1

My name is Carol Childs. I'm a reporter—or more correctly—I'm a middle-aged mom in transition from my role as a sales exec with KCHC, a talk radio station in Los Angeles, to that of a news reporter. Most of what I do is a balancing act. My daughter Cate is in college, and my fourteen-year-old son Charlie is more preoccupied with sports than he is in need of mothering these days. Thankfully, I have a new relationship in my life, a hot FBI agent named Eric Langdon. He seems to think I've got it all together.

KCHC recently had an opening in their news department and I convinced management to give me a chance. The only problem was KCHC's news director Tyler Hunt, a one hundred and twenty-five pound boy-wonder who considered anybody over thirty-five ancient. He didn't want me for the job but offered it to me on a probationary basis. To him, I was the world's oldest cub reporter in need of a good story. And now, right in front of me was exactly what I needed, a damn good story.

I'd been asleep or at least in that twilight state, floating blissfully when I heard a banging on my front door. Tucked safely in Eric's arms, I was tempted to ignore it, but the knocking was persistent. I lifted my head, careful not to disturb Eric, and peeked with one eye at the clock. It was barely six forty-five.

"Did you hear that?" he mumbled. The soft early morning stubble of his beard tickled my ear.

"No," I said, snuggling back against his chest. "I'm sure it's nothing."

"Nothing's sounding very determined." He sat up and I was suddenly disengaged from the crook of his arm. Without a word I slid out of bed, grabbed my robe and stumbled down the stairs toward the front door. The incessant knocking was getting louder.

"Carol! Carol! Are you home? Please, it's an emergency."

I opened the door to find my neighbor, Samantha Millhouse, barefoot and disheveled in a pair of sweat pants and a stained t-shirt, clutching her cell phone. Her short dark hair, usually so neatly styled, showed evidence of hot rollers on one side while the other was like an untamed bush growing out of the side of her head.

"My aunt died," she said flatly. She sounded more annoyed than disturbed. I tightened the sash around my robe and opened the door wider.

"Pepper?" My voice must have raised an octave. "I just saw her on TV last night at the Silver Screen Awards."

"She's dead!" she said as she stepped inside the door. "Her housekeeper found her, looks like she drowned. I need to use your phone. My cell died while we were talking and I'm going to need to call my assistant, Andrew."

I nodded in the direction of the kitchen. Sam pushed by me. "Arminta said she found her body in the tub. When she came into the house this morning she heard music coming from my aunt's bedroom upstairs. She went to check on her and there she was, drowned."

"Are you okay?"

Sam exhaled and reached for the phone. I watched as she took the receiver off the hook then swung around and looked at me. "You know there was never any love lost between us."

I knew Sam's relationship with her aunt was rocky. It was apparent to me the two didn't get along the day I moved into the complex with my son Charlie. Sam's Aunt Pepper had stopped by with one of her clients, a young starlet named Amber Marx, who happens to be my son's big celebrity crush. For about two seconds I think he thought Amber, not Sam, might be our new neighbor. She was standing outside Sam's place smoking as we came up the walk, trying very hard to avoid the scene going on inside. Pepper was raging. I don't think there was a soul in the neighborhood who couldn't hear her screaming.

I glanced over at the coffee pot on the kitchen counter. In another minute it'd turn on automatically. I needed a cup. "Is there anything you need me to do?"

She looked like she was about to answer when Eric's cell phone rang. I turned to see Eric, standing at the top of the stairs, barefoot with a towel wrapped around his waist looking like he was ready to model for a fitness magazine. He held his cell to his ear and from the serious look on his face I knew the call was from the FBI.

Sam looked back at me apologetically. "I'm sorry, Carol, I thought you were alone."

I glanced up at Eric. *I've got this.* With my thumb and little finger to my head I motioned I'd call later, then turned my attention back to Sam. She was on the phone with her assistant. I could hear her giving instructions on what to do and who to call. I waited for her to finish. I was chomping at the bit to learn more. News of Pepper Millhouse's death was big. I needed to call the station.

CHAPTER 2

Tyler Hunt has a constitution I could set a clock to. I called to give him a heads-up on Pepper's death but he wasn't answering. When I got to the radio station, I saw Tyler heading to the men's room with his newspaper and crossword puzzle, as was his habit this time of day. I raced down the hall after him, but too late. The door swung closed in my face. I debated whether or not to knock, then decided I'd given it my best effort.

After leaving Sam, I verified with the paramedics the circumstances surrounding Pepper's death and interviewed her housekeeper. I'd missed my window of opportunity with Tyler and I wasn't about to go further. If Tyler didn't like me breaking news of Pepper's death in the Kari Rhodes Show, he'd let me know. It's easier to ask for forgiveness than permission. But for now, this was my chance. Without a moment to spare, I slid into the news booth and began my report.

"This just in—Hollywood agent Pepper Millhouse was found dead in the bathtub of her Beverly Hills mansion this morning... this after an eventful evening at the Silver Screen Awards at the Beverly Hilton where her client, Amber Marx, won best supporting actress for her role in *The Long Summer*. In an exclusive report to KCHC radio and this reporter, Ms. Millhouse's niece, Samantha Millhouse, says her aunt's body was found by her maid when she entered the home earlier today and heard music coming from her employer's upstairs bedroom. Paramedics called to the scene report that the initial cause of death appears to be an accidental drowning."

I barely finished my report when Kari Rhodes, KCHC's entertainment reporter, glared at me over the top of her red designer framed glasses and mouthed, *Stay put!*

Already the switchboard was starting to light up. That's the way it is with talk radio. When news breaks, particularly when somebody important dies, listeners pick up the phone and want to talk. Suddenly the airwaves turn into a shrink's couch, allowing fans to phone it in. It doesn't matter who's on the air; it can be some oversized personality with all the empathy of an anteater, but in a city like Los Angeles, where people spend more time in their cars than they do one-on-one with their friends and family, radio's their immediate go-to.

"Dead?" Kari's voice resonated out over the airwaves, full of vibrato. Not a surprise for a former Broadway gypsy who'd sung and tap danced her way into talk radio after blowing her knee out on stage years ago. Her midday show was like a coffee klatch with news and celebrity gossip she dished out like a Jewish yenta.

"Carol, I can't *believe* what you're reporting. Pepper Millhouse dead? Not only am I surprised, but you realize of course, this makes three?"

I stared through the glass that divides the news booth from the broadcast studio. I was stunned. I was prepared for any number of reactions; sadness, surprise, disbelief. What I didn't expect was for her to tie Pepper's death to that of two other people. "I'm sorry," I said. "Three? I'm not following."

Kari stood up and began a slow two-step while playing with the cord to her headset.

"I'm not surprised you don't know. They weren't big names, but names none the less. Older ladies. Their deaths wouldn't draw much of a reaction. But that's the way it is in Hollywood. Death in threes. Think about it. A few years ago it was Ed McMahon, Farah Fawcett and Michael Jackson. It's called a Triaphilia."

"Exactly who are the other two people you're referring to?"

"To start with there was Adel Powers. She was the founder of the ACT agency. She died six weeks ago, and Helen Howard, a senior partner at the same agency, just two weeks ago. And now Pepper Millhouse. You may not have known them, but believe me, I've known these gals for years. Worked with them and…" she sighed, and throwing the microphone cord over her other shoulder, added, "I just don't buy they're suddenly all dead. It's all too curious, and all under frighteningly similar circumstances. Each of them found alone, at home and in their tubs. Now tell me, don't you think there's something to that?"

I was scanning the *LA Times* obits on my laptop when out of the corner of my eye I caught Tyler in the hallway, his hands flattened against the studio glass, looking like he wanted to kill me. I was in trouble, but we were on the air and Kari wasn't about to let me go. She sashayed her skinny body over to the glass partition between us and smiled. I looked at Tyler. *What do you want me to do?*

Tyler shook his head, his expression letting me know the damage was already done. I measured the next words carefully.

"I'll agree, Kari, the circumstances surrounding their deaths are strange, but in reality Miss Powers was well into her eighties." I started summarizing from obits I'd pulled up on the Internet while Kari continued to pace in front of me. "And Miss Howard had been in and out of addiction treatment centers for pain medications. Her obituary says she had a history of heart trouble."

"But Pepper Millhouse was in this studio just last week and she looked to me to be in remarkably good shape."

I glanced back at my notes. Pepper Millhouse was fifty-six, a non-smoker and from what I knew of her through Sam, a workaholic. The paramedic report was preliminary, the initial cause of death thought to be drowning. If conditions were at all suspicious there'd be a coroner's report out soon.

"News like this is always shocking," I said. "As soon as we hear back from the Medical Examiner, I'll have an update."

I felt I'd done my best to address Kari's issues. I stood up and was about to remove my headphones when Kari tapped impatiently on the glass. She pointed at the screener, a pimply-faced intern, who held up a yellow pad. Amber Marx. Line 1. I glanced over at Tyler. He held up five fingers, stared at me like I dare not go a minute over, then turned and walked away.

Meanwhile, Kari's saccharine sweet voice thanked Amber for calling and announced that she'd asked me stay on in the studio with her. "But first, Amber, let me start with congratulating you on your award for best supporting actress last night."

"Stop!" Amber's voice sounded like it was about to crack. "This isn't about me. It's about Pepper Millhouse, and I want everyone to know what a wonderful person she was and what a loss she's going to be, not just to me, but to the entire industry."

I wasn't surprised to hear Amber say how much she'd miss Pepper. There wasn't a supermarket tabloid in the country that didn't have headlines screaming about her troubled relationship with her father. Few had any details but all of them included pictures of her as one of Hollywood's sweethearts. Baby photos from her first appearance on the big screen right up to shots of her on the set of her current picture, *The Sorcerer's Daughter.*

The bright spots in her life were all because of Pepper. She had made her a superstar. But behind the scenes Amber's life was an evolving tragedy, worsened with the recent drowning of her mother on a family vacation while in Mexico.

"And I hope, Carol, you will find out what really happened last night. 'Cause I agree with Kari, something strange is going on. Pepper Millhouse wasn't just my agent. She was like a mother to me."

I didn't say another word.

Kari wrapped the segment with Amber. Together they recapped their relationship with Pepper. Kari credited Pepper with helping her find a new career here in L.A., and Amber went on, sometimes tearfully, about how helpful she had been both professionally and personally.

Their stories made Pepper sound more like Mother Teresa than the Queen of Mean Sam had described. I had heard enough and planned to leave during the commercial break when Kari pointed a long manicured finger in my direction and signaled me to stay.

"Amber wants to talk to you, privately."

I was surprised by Amber's request, and even more so because she appeared to have remembered our meeting in front of Sam's condo. At the time, she seemed so much more interested in my son. I had no idea she knew I worked for the radio station. I figured Sam must have told her.

"How's Charlie doing? Does he like his new school?" Her voice sounded much lighter, at ease.

I was a little uncomfortable with her reference to Charlie. I decided it was best to keep my answer short but friendly. Amber Marx may have only been three years older than my son, but I didn't need to read the tabloids to know she was far more sophisticated. I told her he was doing fine and hoped to go out for varsity football next year.

"That's great. Tell him I'll have to come watch a game sometime."

That wasn't going to happen. I wasn't about to encourage any relationship between Amber Marx and my son.

"You must miss a lot not going to a regular school," I said.

"Not really. I travel a lot. Most kids just read about what I've seen firsthand. Last year I was in Europe on tour. I met the Queen and the Pope on the same trip. Plus I have tutors and there's nothing I can't find online. And I've got tons of fans following my tweets. What's to miss?"

My bullshit meter was beginning to run a little hot. I didn't for a minute believe she was as cool and collected as she wanted me to believe. I congratulated her on her big win last night, reiterated my sorrow for her loss and told her I needed to get back to work, but she interrupted me.

"Look, Carol, I want to thank you for checking into Pepper's murder."

"Murder?"

"What else could it be?" she said. "And when you find the

killer, I wouldn't be at all surprised to learn it's my father. He's had it in for Pepper ever since the emancipation. Without Pepper, I never would have been able to get away from him. He blames her for everything."

She hung up and I sat staring at the phone. *Did Amber really believe her father murdered Pepper Millhouse?* If she did, I didn't have time to wonder. My cell phone buzzed.

Tyler. *I'm waiting!*

It's a straight shot down the hall from the studio to the newsroom. Tyler's office was in the corner, a small space that looked like it had once been a storage closet. Lined against the walls were stacks of newspapers, magazines, maps and periodicals. Tyler's a hoarder. His desk in the center of the room was piled high with more of the same. On the wall behind him were framed photos of some of old Hollywood's legends, black and whites of Marilyn Monroe in jeans and a midriff top pumping iron, James Dean in a tight fitting t-shirt with a pack of cigarettes rolled into his sleeve, and his favorite, Jack Webb on the set of Dragnet.

When I walked in, Tyler's attention was focused on his computer. Silently, I took a seat in front of his desk, crossed my arms and legs and waited, thankful for the stacks of newspapers piled between us. He ignored me. Part of the plan, I figured. I reminded myself I had nothing to fear. He was half my age, barely old enough to drink, and, if nothing else, I represented a good portion of his listening audience. On staff I was his token middle aged, well-educated, woman. He needed me.

"Carol, I don't mean to go all Joe Friday on you, but really, what's it going to take? 'Just the facts, ma'am.' That's all I want. Just sit in that news booth and read the news. Nothing more. Not until I say so. Think you can do that? Just the facts. Just once?"

"Really, Tyler? Joe Friday?" I couldn't believe I was about to get *that* lecture.

"My point being, Carol, is that Kari Rhodes is talent. You're news, and I need you to stick to the stories on the wire. Nothing more, no surprises. Got it?"

"But..." I was about to tell him that I had tried to alert him to the story, short of following him into the men's room that is, and that I had done exactly as he requested. Stuck to the facts. That Kari—being talent—had trapped me. But before I could get another word out of my mouth, he stopped me.

This wasn't good. When Tyler was upset he filibustered. It was his way of letting you know you had screwed up. And I had done the worst of all offenses. I hadn't come to him first with news of Pepper Millhouse's death. It didn't matter that I had tried. In his mind I had committed an unpardonable offense. But before he ever got to my sin of omission, I was about to be hammered. He launched into one of his canned presentations on the tenets of journalism, his belief in a code of ethics that he hoped I, and other members of his team, would follow.

"I think of it as the holy grail, Carol. And while I encourage the on-air talent to mix it up, stretch the truth and have some fun, I stand firm that *my* news department be professional and accurate. Pure and simple. Got that?"

"Yes," I nodded. "Just the facts. But I—"

He held up the palm of his hand making it clear this was not going to be a two way conversation. I nodded again, hoping to look sufficiently humbled so that this lecture would end. But no such luck. He droned on. I counted the number of freckles on his face and wondered at what point in life they'd disappear.

"I mean it, Carol. When you've got a story, you come to me first. I don't like surprises, and I don't want to hear something on the air you haven't shared with me beforehand. You got that?"

"Yes," I said. At last we were getting to the root of my sin. Never, ever surprise Tyler. I was about to stand up. In fact, I was half way out of my chair when he leaned forward with his elbows on the table and looked at me.

"And I don't think I need to remind you, you're still on probation here."

I sat back down. There it was. The unveiled threat. My probationary status as a reporter was for six months. I was forty-years old and four months into reinventing myself as a reporter. If I wanted to keep my job, I didn't dare do anything that might give Tyler Hunt reason to fire me.

"You don't need to remind me."

"I hope not, Carol, 'cause this is number one." He held up one finger and repeated himself. "One!"

"Only one?" I held up my index finger, closed one eye, and smiled, hoping to reduce the tension between us. Things like this had worked for me in the past. "Like in baseball?"

"Three strikes and you're out." He said it like an umpire. He wasn't buying my attempt at humor.

"Three strikes. Got it."

I was anxious to get out of Tyler's office. I stood up, about to leave without saying another word, when he glanced back at his computer.

"Just a minute, I have something for you." He scratched out a note on a yellow pad. "You want to cover breaking news so much? I got one for you. The city's been looking for ways to cut back on water usage. UCLA has just installed new waterless urinals in the men's room at Pauley Pavilion. They're launching a new campaign, Pee Green." He thrust the sheet of paper in my direction and smiled. "See what you can do with this."

Pee Green? In less than an hour I had gone from reporting the death of one of Hollywood's biggest agents to checking out waterless urinals. I snapped the paper from his hand, thankful to finally leave his office.

CHAPTER 3

I was headed north on Veteran Boulevard toward the UCLA campus when I heard sirens and caught the sight of red and blue lights flashing in my rearview mirror, closing in behind me. I pulled to the side of the road as three of LA's finest swept by me at speeds twice that posted.

Screw the urinals! Putting my foot to the floorboard, my red Jeep groaned beneath the strain as I fell in behind the brigade. I followed them onto campus, past Rieber Terrace and Hedrick Hall, to a spot the Campus Police had cordoned off with yellow crime scene tape. After parking my car, I grabbed my reporters' audio kit, which included my recorder, headphones, mic and press ID, and ran in the direction of the crowd. My reporter's nose had picked up a scent. This was going to be big.

Campus security was forbidding entrance to the area, but students had already started to congregate. Curious onlookers, some on bikes and others with skateboards in their arms were standing two and three deep behind the yellow tape. I pushed forward and was about to try and talk my way through the barrier when I spotted Eric. He was standing with a group of agents inside the security perimeter. They were easily identifiable in their blue FBI windbreakers.

For the last month Eric had been working a missing person's case with LAPD and the UCLA Campus Police. A young college coed had disappeared. It didn't take much beyond the sight of a stalled construction crane and a group of workers idly standing by, all grim faced, to know what had happened. My stomach sank. This was every parent's worst nightmare. I grabbed my cell and punched in Eric's number.

"Hey, I'm on the other side of the tape. Can you get me in?"

Eric's head bobbed up and I could see him looking around. He spotted me, smiled and waved. "I can, but there's not much to see. We got the body out a few minutes ago."

"The girl?" My throat tightened as I asked.

"Yeah, looks to be the one we've been looking for, 'bout eighteen, brunette."

"No foul play?" I interrupted.

"No, it's more like she went out for a walk after dark, maybe didn't know where she was going. Probably decided to take a short cut across the construction site back to the dorms and fell into a hole."

I scribbled furiously into my notepad. I was about to hang up and see if I could find a few students to interview when Eric asked me to hold on.

"There's someone here you're going to want to talk to. She gave us the lead on the location of the body. I'll send her back toward the Student Union Building. You can't miss her. Look for a woman wearing a long skirt and a cowboy hat. Her name's Misty Dawn. You can thank me later."

"You can count on that." As I hung up I was already thinking of ways to make up for Sam's unexpected interruption this morning. However, I'd have to get creative. Eric lives in the marina on a boat; not that that's a problem, but just the thought of sailing makes me queasy. Plus Charlie was due back home tonight after staying with his father for the weekend. Any chance of romance would have to be put on hold until my son was out of the house again.

"You must be Carol." I heard the woman's voice before I saw her sitting on the planter box in front of the Student Union. She was exactly as Eric had described, wearing a long buckskin skirt and a straw cowboy hat. Her long, graying blonde hair, trimmed with colorful beads and Indian feathers, was pulled into a ponytail that fell over her right shoulder.

"Misty?" The woman stood and walked slowly toward me, her full-figured gait slightly uneven, her shoulders lightly bent. I estimated her to be somewhere in her late-sixties. "Agent Langdon said we should talk regarding the discovery?"

I extended my hand, but rather than take it she touched a pentagram she wore on a beaded macramé necklace around her neck. Rubbing the pendant between her fingers and her thumb she stared in my direction through cloudy blue eyes. I could make out the beginnings of cataracts blurring the iris and moved my head slightly side to side, but she stared straight ahead. I wondered how she had recognized me.

"Ahh. No wonder he wanted me to speak to you. Tall, blonde and pretty." Her voice was a little too loud.

Passers-by turned their heads. I sensed she was a regular figure on campus, one of those oddballs who make a public place their home. She stepped uncomfortably close and peered into my face.

"He's quite taken with you, Miss Childs, and he's not one to do so easily. But then again, you're a bit smitten yourself. No surprise there. He's quite the catch."

I felt my checks flush. I didn't need some university mall psychic counseling me on my romantic endeavors, particularly in broad daylight.

"Oh goodness. I've embarrassed you. Well, don't worry, sweetie. I'm not going to say anything, and he didn't either, other than, you know, we should talk about the girl." She pointed back in the direction where the young coed's body had been found and shook her head.

"You see what I have is a gift. Some think I'm crazy. Others call it witchcraft, or think I'm psychic. You imagine whatever you like." Putting her gnarled hand on my shoulder she leaned closer to my ear and whispered, "But just between us girls, your Agent

Langdon's quite good between the sheets, isn't he?"

What? I pulled my head away and stepped back. "Perhaps we should stick to the facts about the girl." I pointed to a more secluded area next to the building and suggested we move. "You helped the police find the body?"

"Indeed I did. For the past two weeks I kept hearing something. I wasn't certain what it was. At first I thought it might be a deer or even a baby's cry. They actually sound a lot alike you know." She made a baby-like whining sound. I noticed several more people on the mall quicken their pace as they passed. I tried not to make eye contact and focused back on her.

"The girl," I said.

"Oh. Yes, the girl. Well, the breeze swept her voice away. Whoosh! And it was gone. Just like that." She gestured with a wide sweeping movement of her arms. I took a step back to avoid being hit and looked at her sternly. She exhaled, sounding a bit annoyed, then continued. "And then, finally, yesterday, I was planting some of my special herbs. I've got these really wonderful seeds and—"

Ummmmm. I cleared my throat, gently as possible. "We really do need to stick to the subject."

"You're right." She sighed. "Anyway, I was here at the university's garden, digging holes, right over there, like I said, for my herbs." She pointed in the direction of the south campus and for a moment I thought she might head off in that direction. I stepped in front of her. She wasn't going anywhere.

"And?" I said.

She sighed, knit her brows and put her hand to her mouth. She was clearly distracted. I wondered how she was able to remain focused on anything that wasn't right in front of her, much less an elusive voice she claimed to be channeling from beyond.

"The missing girl," I said. This time a bit more emphatically.

"Yes, of course, the missing coed. Well, that's when I realized it. The girl was buried in the pilings. Suddenly her voice, or actually her message, it all became very clear. So I called the police and, here we are."

"Just like that?" I had never interviewed a psychic before. I had no idea how they knew the things they claimed to know. Short of Eric's claim Misty helped the FBI find the body, I remained a skeptic.

"That's all there is to it." Again she gestured broadly with her hands. "No hocus pocus or dishes flying around. Not like in the movies. Only a voice or image in my head and then it's a matter of finding the physical evidence.

Of course the police do that. I simply supply them with leads. Works sometimes, though not always. But in this case, I'm glad it did. It'll bring some closure to her folks."

I thanked Misty for the interview, took down her contact information then dug into my bag for my phone. I needed to call Tyler and give him the who-what-when-where concerning the missing girl. Misty stopped me.

"Would you mind standing still for a moment?" Putting her hand on my arm I felt a chill at her touch. "There's something I need to do." She walked around me, looking at me as though I were a statue. Her clouded eyes scanned my body, like I might be prey. "Whatever you do, don't move."

I felt like one of those bugs mounted on a specimen board in a biology class, pinned to the mat.

"Why?" I asked. "Is there a problem?"

"There this aura, a dark energy around you. You haven't felt something?"

"No." I was annoyed. "And I—"

She held her hand up in front of my face, close enough that I could see the creased lines on the palm of her hand.

"Please, you need to stand very still."

With one hand over my head she waved her palm as though she were mixing the air above me. Then with the other she made a huge sweeping motion from the top of my head down each side of my body.

"Be gone!"

I didn't know if I were embarrassed, humiliated or frightened.

People were rushing by and looking at me. I wanted to move, but I couldn't. My feet felt glued to the pavement.

She repeated the motion, again and again, then stood back, caught her breath and looked at me, or maybe she thought she was looking through me. I couldn't be certain. Her cloudy blue eyes had a distant look. I doubted she could really see me at all.

"There," she said, clasping her hands together. "It's done. But I don't know for how long."

"What's done?" I asked.

"I removed the negative energy field from your aura." She grabbed my hand, squeezed it, and stared into my face again. "It was creeping all around you, like an angry gray mass. I don't know why, or for how long, but I do know death is very close to you. You need to be careful."

She dropped my hand and, without saying goodbye, headed off in the direction of the botanical gardens. She vanished into the crowd, leaving me dumbstruck.

My phone rang. It was Eric and he sounded anxious. I could tell from the background sounds of car doors slamming and engines starting, that he was on the move. I glanced back at the construction site and saw dust rising as vehicles, one by one, left the scene.

"You get the interview with Misty?"

"I did. What a trip, huh?"

I wanted him to say Misty Dawn was a fraud. Something that would help me laugh off this psychic prediction she had made that death was all around me. But I knew better. The fact Eric had turned me on to Misty, and made certain I'd gotten the inside scoop on how they'd found the body, made her not only credible, but all the more creepy.

"She's as close as I've seen to the real thing. But I can't talk right now. I just wanted to touch base. I'm going to be out of pocket for a while. I'll call."

I hung up the phone, wishing we could have talked more. I wanted to tell him about Kari Rhodes' crazy theories of threes, that

Pepper Millhouse had not been the first person in the agency to be found dead in the bathtub of her home, but the third. And how Amber Marx had called the station, going on and on about how much she loved Pepper, then told me off the air she believed her father had killed her.

Most of all, I wanted him to say something to make me laugh about Misty so that I could forget about her spooky prediction. But for now, Eric was headed somewhere off the grid and I needed to get back to work.

I called Tyler. If I had any hope at all of avoiding strike two, I needed to get the missing coed's story to him fast. If he heard it from some other source first and then realized that I'd been right there on the campus, it would be strike two for sure.

Tyler answered on the first ring.

"How's it coming with that urinal story?"

"I've got something better."

"Better?" He sounded like he wanted to bite my head off.

"That missing coed at the university? They found her." I paused momentarily for effect's sake. "I've got an interview with a psychic who helped the FBI, an exclusive."

I thought I might have heard a groan.

"A psychic?"

"The Feds credit her with helping to find the body. They think she's the real thing. Story's great."

I expected Tyler to show some degree of enthusiasm. After all, the story of the missing coed had made national news. The FBI had been called in and nearly every news media outlet in town had been counting the days since the girl's disappearance. Best of all, I had beaten them all to it. No other station had even gotten wind of the discovery, much less had an interview with the psychic responsible for locating the body. My story was an exclusive. I was prepared to file a report that, in my mind, might even win some national award. I was already counting the accolades. Instead I got nothing. Not the smallest bit of excitement.

"Get me the story, and don't forget—"

"I know. The waterless urinals. Can't wait."

"Just the facts, Carol. You're still on probation."

CHAPTER 4

Tyler was an obnoxious boss but he was also sensitive to my role as a working mom and allowed me to work a split shift, for which I was indebted. Afternoons, I'd leave the station, pick up Charlie from school, then race home to get an early dinner on the table and a head start on his homework before returning to work. Most days I barely get back in time for my evening shift. Often Samantha looks in on Charlie, which gives me peace of mind, and no doubt is why he's doing so well with algebra. Sam's a genius with equations. I'm at a loss for anything beyond basic addition and subtraction.

This afternoon I got an earful from Charlie as he jumped in the car. Usually as I pull up, he hands me a list of things we need to do, most of it revolving around his budding athletic career. He's convinced he's going to grow up to be an NFL quarterback, and there's no telling him otherwise. Today, after hearing about football practice, I shared with him the news of Sam's Aunt Pepper's death. I wanted to let him know that Sam might not be around tonight, but I was wrong. As we headed up the walk toward our condo, my arms full of groceries for tonight's dinner, Sam's cat sprang from behind her front door and came to roost in a tree in the center of the courtyard.

"Mom, isn't that Samantha's cat?"

"I'm not sure." The black and white cat flashed by so fast that I could hardly get a good look. I nearly dropped my bags and with it our quick-fix dinner for the evening.

Charlie grabbed one of the sacks before it could fall and

together we stared up into the big oak to get a better look. Sam's housebound feline was never allowed outside, but clinging to the tree and looking very unsettled, was, if not Bossypants, his look-a-like. The cat hissed.

"You better tell Sam her cat's out and ask if she'd like to come for dinner. There's something I need to talk with her about."

"You going to ask if she did it? Killed her aunt?"

"Charlie!"

"Well, she could have. She's always saying so. Or maybe she had someone do it for her."

"Go!" I waved him off in the direction of Sam's front door. I knew he had reason to believe that Sam might have *thought* about killing her aunt. On numerous occasions we had both heard her threaten to do so.

Last fall we had been sitting outside on the porch. I'll never forget the scene. I was attempting to help Charlie with his math homework when Sam came up the steps to the courtyard—an open atrium we all share beneath the large oak tree. She looked like she'd been out all night. Her dark hair was mussed and covered her face and in her hands were a pair of little strappy sandals. I thought she might be crying and was afraid she was about to stumble on the walk. I rushed over to help her.

"You okay?"

"Why? You thought maybe I was drunk and coming home from a party? An all-nighter perhaps?"

"No, you look—"

"Like I've just emerged from hell, then?" She stopped and pushed the hair out of her eyes. They looked strained. She exhaled, deeply, trying to compose herself. "'Cause that's how I feel. Like I've been cleaning up after the Queen of Mean in her dirty little courtyard and I can't get the stench off me."

I had no doubt that Sam's reference to the Queen of Mean meant her aunt and I might have been shocked had I not come to expect such statements from her concerning Pepper. Since moving in next door to Sam I had heard many stories about her unsavory practices. There was nothing Pepper Millhouse wouldn't do if it meant money on the table.

But even Sam was surprised by Pepper's most recent transgression. Standing beneath the oak tree she described the scene at the agency like something out of a slasher movie. One of Pepper's long term clients, Kim LaSalle, had stormed into the office with a butcher knife, screaming she was going to kill Clarissa St. Clair for stealing her husband and then Pepper for setting it all up.

Sam swore me to secrecy.

"Not a word of this gets out, Carol. If the tabloids ever learned what happened, it would ruin Kim. She might never work again. I can't let that happen. She's too fragile. This is strictly off the record. Besides, I've got a much more benign version of the story for your station, and if I've done my job and covered this all up, you'll have the exclusive."

I was happy to hear that. But I wasn't happy to learn that Sam was once again cleaning up one of Pepper's dirty tricks. I could see from the exhaustion on her face that she'd spent the last twenty-four hours trying to contain the latest crisis. Pepper had used Kim's husband, Dek De Convero, also one of her clients, to boost the chances of Clarissa St. Clair being cast in an upcoming movie with Dek by creating a mock affair between the two of them.

Sam explained that her aunt wanted to generate enough buzz in the tabloids so that the casting agents for *Lady in White* might take Clarissa seriously. Evidently Pepper didn't think it was a big deal. Kim would get over it and later Pepper planned to fix everything by throwing one of her big parties at Millhouse Manor. Maybe even stage some big recommitment ceremony for them. But Kim was having none of it. Dek had a history of affairs, even an illegitimate child stashed away somewhere and Kim was going crazy. Then yesterday, she stormed into the agency. She came after Clarissa and Sam. She said if she hadn't come between them Kim might have killed her. Fortunately, the security guard was able to calm her down and get the knife away from her.

It was no wonder Sam looked so spent. I helped her over to the table where Charlie and I were sitting and offered her a chair. Charlie was deep into his math homework, but I could tell he had been listening. She smiled at Charlie and pointed out a mistake in his work, then looked back at me.

"So the official story, Carol, is that Kim LaSalle suffered from a reaction to some medications and has been taken to a local hospital for observation. But between you and me, I wish she had killed my aunt. 'Cause let me tell you, she could have saved me from doing it. One day, I promise you, I'm going to kill that woman myself. You just wait and see. And when I do, it's all going to be mine: her house, the agency, everything."

I was thinking about that conversation when Sam walked into the house with Charlie. She was dressed exactly as she had been earlier this morning, in a pair of wrinkled sweats and a t-shirt. The only difference was that now she was wearing a headset on her head, her phone obviously recharged. She was in the midst of a conversation. Putting a finger to her mouth she looked at me, shook her head and smiled.

"You don't need to worry. I've got everything under control. Everything's exactly as it's always been. Nothing's going to change. It'll only get better. I'm in charge now." Then pulling the headset off, Sam flopped down at my kitchen table. "You got anything to drink? This has been the day from hell."

Considering how Sam's day had started I wasn't surprised. I walked over to the bar, uncorked a bottle of merlot that Eric and I hadn't finished the night before and, filling two wine glasses, placed one in front of her.

"To my anniversary!" she lifted the glass to mine.

"Your anniversary?"

"Quite the coincidence really. Ten years with the Queen of Mean and suddenly she keels over the same day. How's that for special?"

"I'm not following."

"Today would have marked my tenth year with the agency. And the best part of that is the automatic bonus that kicked in. Believe me if Pepper had thought she was going to die she would have taken the money with her. But fortunately for me, she rubberstamped it last month. It was automatically deposited into my account today, and believe me, I've already spent it. Ordered myself a big screen TV. I had it delivered this afternoon, part of my victory celebration. And hey, guess what?" She laughed. "There's a Laker game on TV tonight. Charlie, you wanna watch?"

I looked over at Charlie. While there may have been no love lost between Sam and Pepper this celebration was over the top. Even for Sam.

"Charlie, why don't you go check on Bossypants? See if you can't get him to come down out of that tree. I'll start dinner."

Charlie shrugged his shoulders giving me that teenage whatever-look then turned around and walked out the door.

"Are you alright?" I sat down and put my hand on Sam's before she could take another sip of wine. I could appreciate her sarcastic humor. We'd bonded over stories about our dysfunctional bosses in the past, but this concerned me. "What's going on?"

Before she had a chance to answer, her phone rang. Looking annoyed, she glanced at the caller ID, pushed a button and sent the call to voicemail. "It's been like this all day, one call right after the other. Believe me, the sharks are circling and everybody wants a piece of the agency. I haven't done a thing but assure people everything's going to be okay. But trust me, our contracts are iron-clad. I'm ready for this. Nobody's going anywhere. It's all going according to plan."

"Plan? Exactly what do you mean by plan?"

"Carol, when the president of a company dies there's always a next in line. And that's me. You know that. It's pretty much the same with every business, and certainly that's the way with the ACT Agency. I've got carte blanche. If Adel Powers and Helen Howard were still alive, it might be different. But they're not. So I'm it. And I've spent most of the day, excuse me, no, all of the day, assuring clients and scavenger agents out there that things at the ACT agency aren't about to change. You wouldn't believe what people are saying."

"You mean that your aunt may have been murdered?"

"Murdered? Really? Is that what they're saying?" Sam scoffed. "Actually, I was referring to the swarm of agents trying to steal my clients out from under me. They're all spreading rumors the ACT Agency is done. Things like that happen all the time. But murder? Where did you hear that?"

"The Kari Rhodes show. It's all she's talking about."

"I'm not surprised. I'm hardly the only one in town overjoyed with the news of Pepper's death. I'm afraid I was too busy ordering my big screen TV to listen." Sam took a sip of her wine and smiled at me.

"Sam, this is serious. Kari's saying Pepper was murdered. And not just your aunt, she thinks Adel Powers and Helen Howard were murdered, too."

"The old ladies?" Sam put her wine glass down and turned it slowly by the stem, staring at it. "Now that is a stretch. I can believe Pepper, but Adel and Helen? I don't think so."

"But Kari does. And now she's got a number of listeners who are calling in to talk about it, including Amber Marx."

Sam leaned back in her chair, her hand on the stem on the wine glass, twisting it. "I suppose that's to be expected. Poor thing's really devastated. I had to send my assistant, Andrew Reese, over to stay with her just to keep her calm."

I didn't have time to tell her what Amber had told me about her father before Charlie walked back into the room. He had a big smile on his face and the cat was in his arms, purring quietly. The rescue had gone seamlessly. The two appeared to have developed a very close relationship. He sat down at the table with Bossypants in his lap. "Did I hear you say something about Amber Marx? What's she doing these days?"

"Finishing up a movie, and not that your mother would want you to know, but she's been hanging out at the beach in Santa

Monica. She bought a place down there. You should get your mom to take you. I'm sure she'd love to see you."

Sam winked at me. She knew Charlie was a big fan and constantly fishing for information about Amber Marx. She also understood I was less than wild about his infatuation. I gave Sam the evil eye, then turned to Charlie. "Take that cat out of the kitchen, now. Then go wash your hands. I'll start dinner."

I waited until Charlie had left the room, then got up from the table and started taking the fixings out of the bag for supper. "Amber thinks her father murdered your aunt. She told me so off the air."

Sam reached for the wine bottle and poured herself another glass. "That's great. Now I'm no longer the number one suspect."

"You?" I slapped a box of noodles on the counter and stared at her.

"Oh, come on, Carol. If people think Pepper was murdered who do you think they're going to think did it? They'll say it was me. I'm the perfect suspect. Everybody knew I hated her. On more than one occasion I threatened to kill her and now that I'm running the agency, it's not going to take much for anyone to think I did. But they'll never prove anything."

"Just what would there be to prove? You were at the awards show last night. You couldn't possibly have murdered Pepper."

"The problem is, Carol, I'm not about to put on a sad face. I'm not sorry and everybody knows it." Sam leaned across the table and lifted her wine glass for a toast. "To Pepper, may she rest in peace."

I turned my back and started preparing dinner. I wished Sam would be a little less sanctimonious and more concerned about her reaction to Pepper's untimely death, if only for appearances sake. Her cavalier attitude worried me and I didn't feel comfortable toasting to it.

"Don't worry, Carol, the police don't arrest you just for saying you'd like to kill someone. They actually have to prove it."

CHAPTER 5

The following day I listened to Kari Rhodes as I drove to work. She was hyping her theory that Pepper Millhouse's death and that of her business partners was no accident. I yelled back at the radio. "This is ridiculous! You don't even have a coroner's report yet. What are you saying?" I must have looked like one of those crazies I see every day on my commute to and from work, pounding on the steering wheel, screaming at the radio like an idiot.

"In fact, folks, I'm convinced we're looking for a serial murderer. There's not just one agent who died, but three! And all of them, as far as I'm concerned, under dubious circumstances: home alone, at night, in their bathtubs. Can you imagine? Give me a break. Just how long is it going to be before we know the truth? These women were murdered."

I could picture Kari, a hungry vulture squatting on her barstool, dressed in black, her headphones slightly askew, stretching her skinny little neck across the console to the mic. I knew she wouldn't let go of a story like this. It was exactly what her listeners tuned in for: tabloid gossip.

"...and you can take it from me, I knew Pepper Millhouse. She was a vibrant, attractive woman, exercised daily, was a respected member of our community and involved in a number of charitable organizations. Believe me, this woman didn't accidentally drown. She had enemies. And someone close to her, someone who understands the business, stands to profit not only financially but professionally by her death, they know this was no accident. Believe me, somewhere, someone is celebrating."

I didn't like where Kari was going with this story. Sam wasn't a Hollywood star or a public figure. Kari didn't dare mention her by name, but it was clear to anyone who knew the agency that Kari was talking about Pepper's niece, Samantha Millhouse.

And I didn't like that I was beginning to have my own doubts about Sam.

The idea that Sam might have murdered her aunt was absurd. How could I even entertain such an idea? She was my neighbor, my friend, the source for so many of my insider industry news leads, not to mention the woman who looked in on my son while I worked evenings. Sam certainly wasn't a serial killer.

But the person I was really angry with was Tyler Hunt for his double standard. One for reporters, like me, who were told to stick to the facts and another for KCHC's larger than life show hosts, or talent as he liked to call them. For them it was a no-holds-barred circus atmosphere. Anything goes. As long as the switchboard lit up with callers, it was fair game. Kari Rhodes was taking full advantage. Making Pepper's death sound like a cold, calculated murder. All before the coroner had even ruled on the cause of death.

My stomach soured. I reached to change the station hoping music might help to settle my nerves, when the phone rang. It was Eric.

"Hey, I'm sorry I couldn't stick around yesterday. I did catch your report on the missing coed. Nice quotes from the psychic by the way. How are you?"

"Fine. That is, if you can call sleeping with one eye open normal." I shut off the radio. I considered telling him about Misty's strange psychic prediction. It had kept me up all night, but I began with Sam and how Kari Rhodes was turning Pepper's death into a real whodunit. "And not just Pepper. She actually believes there's a serial killer going around murdering ACT's agents. She thinks it's someone close to them, and I don't even want to tell you the thoughts I have swimming around in my head about Sam."

"Samantha?" Eric sounded surprised.

"Yes, Sam. Kari hasn't actually put her name with the murders yet—she doesn't dare—but she might as well have. She describes the killer as someone close to the agency with a personal vendetta and money and position to gain. I can see this turning into a real witch hunt and I don't like it."

Eric scoffed. "Carol, I highly doubt Sam's a serial killer. There's probably nothing more to this than Kari trying to create some big mystery to keep her audience engaged."

I knew Eric was right. I needed to take a beat. Kari was just doing her job and I had mine to do.

"All the same, I've got a call into the coroner's office. The sooner I can put an end to this nonsense the better it'll be for Sam. But there is something about Pepper's death that does bother me."

"What's that?"

"Amber Marx. She called the radio station yesterday, right after the news of Pepper's death broke. She was terribly upset. Pepper wasn't just her agent. To hear her tell it they were close, like mother and daughter. After she finished up with Kari she asked to speak to me, off the air. She told me she thought her father might have killed Pepper."

"Did she say why?"

"Only that her father blamed Pepper Millhouse for everything. Amber lost her mother last year, and after she died it was Pepper who helped her to emancipate herself from her father. Could be motive."

"Maybe." Eric didn't sound convinced. "Tell me you're not sleeping with one eye open because of that."

I backed off. In hindsight, Amber's accusation sounded more like a tabloid headline. *Star Screams 'My Father Did It!'*

"No. Of course not," I said. "It's that psychic of yours, Misty Dawn. It was something she said."

I expected him to laugh. I wanted him to laugh and put my jangled nerves at ease. I needed him to say she was strange. But he didn't. Instead Eric explained that on occasion the FBI used psychics, sometimes successfully and while he didn't necessarily believe in them there was no explaining how they knew what they did.

"What did she say?"

"She said I was in danger. That I had this death aura all around me and then she did this strange thing with her hands. She claimed she'd removed it. It's crazy, but it's kind of got me looking over my shoulder."

He paused. I was waiting for some witty response, something to allay my fears, but none came. "Could be because you were working the missing coed case, or there's something to Pepper Millhouse's death. I don't understand how she knows what she does, but do us a favor."

"Us?" I liked the sound of that. The thought of us soothed my nerves.

He laughed softly. I imagined his lips against my ear and felt a warm rush from my loins all the way up the back of my neck. Misty was correct about one thing. Eric and I did have chemistry. "I'm sure you'll be fine. Like I said, you're working on cases that deal with death. Some of it's bound to rub off on you. But just the same, lock your doors. I'll be back next week. Miss you."

The first thing I did when I got to the radio station was to call the Medical Examiner's office. If the coroner didn't have anything and Pepper's death was due to natural causes, there was nothing to be concerned about. Kari's theory about a serial killer would be pointless and my worries about Sam totally unfounded. Unfortunately, I came up empty handed. The coroner's report wasn't ready and results weren't expected for another twenty-four hours. I was disappointed, but at least I wouldn't be supplying Kari with proof of Pepper's murder, or evidence of foul play. Thankful that Kari wouldn't be able to depend upon me to validate her theory of murder, I grabbed a handful of news stories from my in-basket and slipped into the broadcast booth.

I was wrong about how I imagined Kari to be dressed. She

wasn't in her traditional black garb, which might have been appropriate for doing what she had earlier announced was a memorial show to Pepper Millhouse. Instead she was wearing a long, colorful sarong that tied around her neck and hung like a shapeless drape on her skinny body. The reason for her costume change was six-foot-four and drop dead gorgeous.

His name was Dek de Convero, and he was Kari's mystery guest for the next hour. I'm not starstruck, but I'm probably no different than any other middle-aged, heterosexual woman. Dek is a superstar and from the news booth I had a front row seat to the adjoining studio and could eavesdrop on their conversation before they went on the air.

"So this afternoon, Dek, as part of my tribute to Pepper Millhouse, in addition to your professional relationship with Pepper I'd like you to share with our listeners a little about your personal relationship."

Dek smiled broadly. With his deep dimples and thick curly hair, the man's reputation as a lady's man was undeniable, but his answer was totally gallant. "There are some things, Kari, a gentleman just doesn't discuss about a lady, and Pepper was quite a lady. I'm sure you understand."

"Of course, but you and Pepper did share a past, a very amorous beginning in Hollywood. Certainly you could share some small story with us." Kari looked like a flirtatious schoolgirl, leaning toward him on the barstool, her chin cupped in the palm of her hand as she spoke.

"I'm not going to deny that we were lovers. We were both young, we were great friends and for a time, yes, we were romantically involved. But I'm happily married now and I don't see the need to bring up the past."

"Of course not. And how is Kim? Will she be going to Spain with you for your next project, *Lady in White?*"

For months the tabloids had been full of rumors that Dek and his wife, actress Kim LaSalle were separated. Photos of Dek and Clarissa St. Clair were splashed across their covers along with a very angry looking Kim LaSalle beneath headlines that read, "I'll kill her!"

"No. I'm afraid it's only cast and crew."

"And your leading lady? I know there's been a lot of speculation, but perhaps today we can formally announce just who that will be."

"I doubt that'll come as much of a surprise. Certainly many in your audience already suspect."

"Sixty seconds, Miss Rhodes." I looked up to see Kari's on air director with his hand in the air, his finger about ready to cue me. In the background the station's ID was just wrapping up. *KCHC... Chick Radio... LA's first all-female talk station ....where your news and your views make a difference.* Then, "Five, four, three, two..."

Ordinarily I wouldn't have noticed anyone coming in or out of the studio during my broadcast. Tyler frequently barges in with last minute changes, sometimes replacing one news story for another, but this time I nearly stumbled over my words when the door opened. I glanced up, my eyes momentarily frozen on the image. There standing in the doorway was Clarissa St. Clair. She looked radiant. She was dressed in a short, white, nearly transparent organza outfit. Her long dark wavy hair nearly down to her waist framed her delicate features and hung loosely over her milky-white bare shoulders.

I had to remind myself to concentrate as she entered the room. Out of the corner of my eye I spotted Dek. He stood up, smiled, and extended his hand. There was no denying the effect she had on him. No wonder Kim LaSalle wanted to kill Pepper Millhouse for putting the two of them together. I would have wanted to kill her, too.

CHAPTER 6

Charlie and I could hear screaming as we came up the walk to our condo. My first reaction was that it had to be a wild animal, a screeching owl, since we have a few in our neighborhood. Then I realized the sound was human. I looked at Charlie and motioned with my index finger to my lips to be quiet.

On the street I had noticed a brand new Aston Martin with personalized plates, Amber ♥ HW. That could only mean one thing. The high pitched shrill belonged to Amber Marx.

"I don't believe you! Pepper wouldn't do that. She was like a mother to me. You're lying."

Seconds later, Amber brushed past Charlie and me, pushing her long blonde ringlets over one shoulder as she stomped down the brick walkway like an angry child. We both stared back over our shoulders as she made her way toward the car with the keys in her gloved hands. She looked out of sync in her heavy Doc Martins and short sassy skirt swinging over long, pale legs. As she reached the car she gave one last look back toward the condo and flipped us the bird.

"What was that all about?" Charlie looked like he'd just been struck down by his idol. I squelched a smile, delighted to see her image tarnished in his eyes.

"I haven't got a clue, but I bet Sam does." I nodded in the direction of Samantha's front door.

Standing in the open doorway of her condo was Sam. Hoisted onto her hip, and looking as though he might have been trying to escape, was Bossypants. She patted him lightly on the head as she hollered. "I take it Amber didn't stop to chat?"

"What's up with her?" Charlie looked back over his shoulder. Behind us we could hear the Aston Martin's fine-tuned engine roar like an angry lion as Amber sped away.

"Let's just say the girl's got some issues. But I'm glad I caught the two of you. I've been home all day re-hanging some old photos. I could use some help." Sam backed away from the door. Behind her the floor was strewn with pictures, books, old record albums, and scripts that had been removed from the wall to accommodate her new big screen TV. "And if it's okay with your mom, Charlie, there's another Lakers game on tonight. I can order us a pizza if you like."

Sam looked at me for approval, but Charlie was already through the door before I could answer.

"Amber's upset." Sam shifted the cat from one hip to the other and patted him on the head. "She seems to think Pepper promised her the role in *The Lady in White*."

"But Clarissa got that role. It was announced today on the Kari Rhodes Show. Certainly she knew that."

"Welcome to my aunt's world of dirty little tricks. She left that lovely chore to me. Just one of the many reasons I'm delighted she's dead."

I glanced nervously over my shoulder. "I really wish you wouldn't talk like that. At least until the coroner's ruled on Pepper's death. Kari Rhodes is making way too much of this right now, calling for a police investigation. Believe me, you don't need that."

Sam shook her head, walked back inside and put Bossypants down. "Truth is, Pepper never wanted Amber to have that role. She pitched Clarissa. It was Clarissa's turn. That's the way Pepper was. She enjoyed pitting people against one another. She did the same with my twin sister and me."

Sam stooped down, picked up one of the photos on the floor and handed it to me. It was a graduation picture, two sisters in cap and gown smiling at the camera. In it they looked very much alike, dark hair, straight white teeth, attractive. Sam's parents weren't in the picture. They had died several years before in an airplane crash, and Pepper had become their legal guardian. "That was taken right before we went to work for my aunt. She treated us like some social science experiment. Good twin, bad twin, that type of thing. It's no wonder Sarah left the agency."

I didn't know the details behind Sarah's sudden exit from her aunt's business, only that one day she left, announced she intended to be an actress and signed with a small talent agency somewhere in the valley. Sam took another photo from the bookshelf and showed it to me.

"Amazing what medical science can do, right? You'd hardly recognize her as my twin."

"Wow! That's your sister?" Charlie jumped up off the couch, his head between ours, staring at the photo of Sarah. She was dressed, or maybe just painted into what looked like a hot one piece bathing suit, and spread across the hood of a cherry red 1973 Chevrolet Camaro. "What a babe!"

"Charlie! I thought you were watching the Lakers?"

I snatched the photo from Sam's hand and hid it behind my back. At which point, Kobe Bryant hit a three pointer and the screams on the TV diverted his attention back to the game.

Sam laughed, retrieved the photo from behind my back and returned it the bookshelf. "My point being," she said, "is that what's between my sister and me can only get better with my aunt out of the picture, and so will the agency. I couldn't have planned it any better, and, believe me, I'm delighted to have her gone."

"No doubt, but still, why didn't Pepper tell Amber about Clarissa? I mean, if she was so duplicitous and uncaring, what'd it matter?"

"Pepper wanted to test me. She thought I was too weak-willed to handle it. When we first got word about *Lady in White*, Amber had just started filming *The Sorcerer's Daughter*. It's the third in a series of four films she had agreed to do. Behind her back, Pepper liked to refer to her as her little cash-cow. Bragged she could probably get a total of seven maybe eight movies out of the franchise, and she wasn't about to upset that. So she pitched Clarissa. I'm sure she thought it would have been too chancy for Amber to take a project in between. Particularly given everything Amber had just been through with the death of her mother and the emancipation proceedings."

"So when did you tell her?"

"I didn't. The night of the awards show I was going to tell my aunt she needed to do it. That it was her deal."

"And she never told her?"

Sam shook her head. "No. She died instead. And that little scene out there on the patio with Amber was her reacting to the news."

I picked up a framed photo with Pepper standing with Amber and Clarissa. The shot must have been about ten years old, the girls maybe seven and nine. Clarissa was taller with long dark hair down to her waist, Amber smaller and very blonde, her hair in pigtails.

"Amber's had a problem ever since her mother died. The last year's been different, or maybe difficult is a better word. We were all required to keep an eye on her. I was pushing for her to take some time off, but my aunt never would have allowed that. Amber was guaranteed income. Pepper planned on working that girl until she wasn't useful to her anymore. That's just the way she was. Maybe now it'll be different."

"What do you mean?"

"I'm in charge now. Amber can take a break and get the rest she deserves. My aunt never would have allowed it, but I will."

Sam handed me a stack of loose photos of Amber in her first films; a small round cherub with short blonde curly hair, a pubescent teen and present day, Hollywood's Sweetheart, a budding, young ingénue. I sorted through them then stopped. Posing with Amber was a face I recognized, and not from the screen, but because I knew her.

"That's Misty Dawn. Why is she in this photo?"

"You know Misty?" Sam chuckled. "You didn't tell me you were into psychics, Carol."

I explained how I'd met Misty when I had reported the story about the missing coed at UCLA.

"I'm not surprised to hear she's working with the Feds. She's got quite the following, and she's an old friend of my aunt's. Pepper gave Misty her start in Hollywood, reading for her clients. She's become the Psychic to the Stars, but lately she's been working as a story consultant on *The Sorcerer's Daughter*. Did she read for you?"

"I wasn't there for her to read." I didn't want to tell Sam how Misty had managed to pick up on my relationship with Eric. That she appeared to know more about my sex life than I was comfortable with, particularly with my son in the room. I switched the subject, but in the back of my mind I wondered if maybe Eric was right, that Misty's warning to me did have something to do with the stories I was working on. There was death all around me: the missing coed, Pepper Millhouse, the old ladies at the agency. That had to be the reason for her warning.

"You know, she's usually right on about those things. I don't know how she is with the police, but when it comes to relationships she's never wrong."

"Good to know." I placed the photos back on the shelf and glanced over at Charlie. The game was tied. I hated to drag him away at such a crucial point.

"I can order pizza," Sam volunteered, then went over to the bar and poured herself a glass of wine. "Like one?"

"No, I've got to get back to work."

"That's what I like about you, Carol. We take things seriously; with us it's not a game. That's how it was with my aunt. But you know what's going to be the big difference around the agency with my aunt gone?"

I shook my head.

"People. My aunt enjoyed using them. She used them like playing cards. For her everything was a game. And as long as she was winning she was happy. She didn't care about anybody but herself. She'd collect clients like playing cards. She'd pair them off like she did Dek and Clarissa and then discard them like she did with Kim LaSalle. After a while, they were all just worthless pieces of paper, pictures in frames like these here." She picked up another photo, a group shot of Pepper with Dek and Kim. "But with me it'll be different. It's not just a game. I like to hold onto my people. They're more than playing cards in the deck. I don't discard them, I take care of them, and when I can make a play it's a win-win for everyone."

"I hope you can do that."

"Believe me, with my aunt out of the way there's no reason I can't."

Charlie let out another whoop in support of the Lakers and rolled back on the couch with Bossypants in his lap. The cat screeched, jumped and ran into the bedroom.

"You sure you don't want to order that pizza?"

"No," I said. "And Charlie has homework." I didn't ask her to check in on him. It didn't feel right, not tonight.

CHAPTER 7

I didn't know what happened to Pepper Millhouse, whether she had simply gone home the night of the Silver Screen Awards and died of a heart attack, or been drowned in the bathtub of her house by some serial killer targeting little old agency ladies. Nobody did. There was no proof, just lots and lots of questions. The coroner's report was being detained for reasons they wouldn't say and in its absence Kari Rhodes continued to rant. She was now referring to the death of Pepper Millhouse and her two business partners not only as a triaphilia, but as the Hollywood Bathtub Murders. She even had theme music created for a special update, a ninety second sound bed with drums and horns that played out like a national security alert. The whole affair was much more dramatic than I ever thought possible. But even more curious was Sam, who was amassing new toys. In addition to the big screen TV, new items were beginning to arrive, things like, a king sized mattress, area rugs and a treadmill. Then there was the knock on my door.

Sam needed my help. "My aunt had a will and there's going to be a reading tomorrow. My sister Sarah's going to be there. I need moral support. Could you come with me?"

I didn't think that sounded out of the ordinary, and I actually did want to meet Sam's twin. We drove together to Beverly Hills where the meeting was scheduled to take place inside Pepper's attorney's office just west of Rodeo Drive on Wilshire Boulevard.

The posh tenth floor corner suite, with a white-on-white décor, had floor to ceiling panoramic views of the city and ocean that on any other day might have been captivating. But when the elevator doors opened my eyes were riveted on Sarah. She was standing in the center of the room, waiting with her small, white pooch poking his head out from her designer handbag.

I did a double take. She looked more like a wax figure from Madame Tussaud's than an actual human being. She was dressed in a short, tight, red sharkskin sheath dress that looked as though it might fit a Barbie doll, cut to reveal her bulbous cleavage. I nearly burst out laughing. Sarah Millhouse was a joke, the extreme opposite of Sam, who was as barebones as it gets when it comes to fashion and makeup.

I waited for Sam to introduce me, but instead she whispered something under her breath about not being ready to deal with this. She exited in search of a ladies room, leaving me alone with her sister and her obnoxious purse-pal. The dog looked in my direction and yipped as I approached.

"I'm Carol Childs, Sam's friend," I said, extending my hand.

"You mean the reporter?" She didn't bother to take my hand. She looked mildly distracted as she squinted at me, her eyes giving me the once over. "You look more like you should be on TV than radio, but then beauty and talent don't always go hand in hand, do they?"

Her backhanded compliment, reminiscent of something I knew Pepper might have said, stung. She turned her back to me and walked over to a magazine rack on the wall and selected something to read.

"Do you suppose we'll be long? I have a manicure appointment at one. I really hate to miss it. I broke a nail on the way over."

I couldn't help myself. I replied, "Maybe you should call 9-1-1. Better yet, Cedar's isn't far, perhaps you might try the emergency room."

Sarah sighed dramatically and stared at me, as though it was beneath her to say another word.

She didn't need to. Our silence was broken when Sam reappeared. With her was her aunt's attorney, Rodger Matteson, a distinguished looking gray haired gentleman, who looked as though he might have come directly from a tanning booth. I couldn't imagine a more perfect man for the role of Pepper's attorney. He was dressed in an expensive looking three piece suit with a matching baby blue tie and pocket square that set off his even bluer eyes.

"Mr. Matteson!" Sarah squealed and dropped the magazine she'd been reading on the floor. Then trotting across the room in her spiked stilettos she pushed herself between her sister and the attorney and pressing his arm beneath her own, squeezed her breasts against his chest and planted a kiss on his cheek. "It's so sad to see you again under such circumstances. My poor dear Aunt Pepper. It's just awful."

Sam looked at me and shook her head. Sarah was a cliché, a bleach blonde hottie who tried too hard. Personality-wise the sisters were extreme opposites, as far apart as the North and the South Pole. I waited for Sam to introduce me, but before she could say anything, Matteson linked his arm beneath Sam's, and with a sister on either side, led the way to his office.

I followed, like a third wheel, entering a large corner suite with two story arched windows and floor to ceiling bookshelves that gave the room a sense of grandeur. In the center of the room Matteson's desk, a huge inlayed wooden affair, was bathed in sunlight with two very expensive looking hand-carved antique leather chairs placed in front of it. The entire set up looked imported from a European castle. Sarah took one of the chairs and Sam the other. I sat slightly to the back of the room on an overstuffed, white couch and settled in for what I thought might be a pretty extensive reading of Pepper Millhouse's will.

"Well, ladies, what we have here is surprisingly simple." He held up two sheets of paper and smiled almost apologetically.

Two pages? That's it? Based upon the fact Pepper Millhouse was easily worth ten million dollars, something was amiss. Sarah's purse-pooch started yapping. Matteson stood up, backed away from his desk and with a cautious eye trained on the mini-beast, held the will up in front of his face like a flyswatter, and laughed nervously.

"But then, that was Pepper, right? She made changes like she did her wardrobe, seasonally." Matteson paused as though he were waiting for a laugh, and when none came, cleared his throat and loosened his tie. "Of course, over the years your aunt must have had half a dozen different wills. But, I can assure you, this is the last one, although, it was a bit of a surprise."

He paused, reached for a glass of water on his desk, swallowed hard then continued.

"You see...about two weeks ago Pepper barged in here quite unexpectedly and presented me with this document. It's a handwritten will." He put the papers back down on the desk, then pulled his hands away as though he thought the dog might be about to bite him. "She said she'd been thinking about it and wanted to take care of it right away."

Again he glanced from twin to twin, as though he were trying to get a reading from each of the sisters before he continued. From my perspective they were both getting impatient. Sarah was squirming in her chair and Sam, oddly enough, was staring out the window as though the entire ordeal bored her.

"And you both know how persuasive Pepper could be when she wanted to get something done. There was never any waiting around, not with our Pepper. In fact, she had both Dek de Convero and Clarissa St. Clair with her and appeared to be in quite a hurry. Told me she wanted to change her will, right then and there, and insisted my secretary, Miss Larson, and her two clients witness it. You'll see their signatures on the bottom here. It's all in order."

I don't know what Sam was thinking, but right about now I was beginning to imagine that simple will or not, things were not going to go down smoothly. Matteson reached into his pocket for his glasses. Putting them on, he glanced back in my direction, the look on his face like he was seeing me for the first time. I smiled, finger waved apologetically for the lack of our introduction, then shrugged.

If Sarah could bring a dog, certainly Sam could bring a friend. He sighed dismissively, the look on his face affording me less recognition than he had given the dog. Then without so much as a nod he looked back to the will. I wanted to snarl.

"I, Pepper Millhouse, being of sound mind and body, do hereby declare this to be my Last Will and Testament and do revoke all other Wills and Codicils heretofore made by me. To my niece, Miss Samantha Millhouse, I leave my estate, Millhouse Manor, its furnishings and all my personal effects, including my jewelry, my wardrobe and my new Mercedes Sports coup, plus my stock portfolio. I also appoint Samantha Millhouse as chief operating officer of ACT."

"What?" Sarah leapt to her feet. Her small dog tumbled from her bag to the floor. "Move, you stupid mongrel." She kicked the animal away and reached for her sister's throat. "You! You did this!"

Samantha pushed her sister away and screamed back at her. "Me? The only thing I did was work my butt off, and where were you?"

"Oh, yeah, right! You couldn't wait until she died. Everything you did was so you could get control of the agency. You even bragged about it."

"And why not? She was a dreadful, controlling bitch who made a lot of people's lives miserable. Now she's dead and I can make it better, not just for me, but for a lot of people. I'm thrilled."

"I'll bet you're thrilled. All the way to the bank."

"Well, I deserve to be. Where were you? Out getting your boobs done, or cheeks, or whatever the latest fad was."

"How dare you! I'll get you for this. You twisted her mind against me, got her to change her will, and stole my inheritance." Sarah grabbed her purse off Matteson's desk and looked like she was about to leave, then turned and screamed back at Matteson. "There's no way Pepper did this! Sam tricked her and then she killed her and I'm going to prove it."

"Please, ladies." Matteson held up one hand, waiting for Sarah to compose herself. "There's more."

"More? What more could there possibly be?" Sarah folded her

arms beneath her ballooning breasts and even from behind her I could feel the heat of her stare as she waited for Matteson to complete the reading.

"To my niece, Miss Sarah Millhouse, I leave *one dollar* to be paid by her sister Samantha Millhouse from the funds derived from my estate at such time as she deems appropriate."

"Appropriate!" Sarah slapped her bag on Matteson's desk and screamed at her sister. "You killed her! And I'll bet you killed Adel Powers and Helen Howard, too, just to make certain there wasn't anyone in the way. But you won't get away with it. I'll make sure of it. You just wait!"

Sarah grabbed her bag off Matteson's desk, and not seeing the little dog inside, yelled for the missing pooch. "Wally! Wally, where are you?"

The dog, nervous and trembling, was hiding beneath a huge ficus in the corner of the office. Sarah trotted over to him with Matteson behind her. She grabbed the small, frightened animal by the scruff of his neck just as he was about to lift his leg. Turning around, she caught Matteson by surprise. Wally relieved himself, squirting a stream of yellow directly down the front of the attorney's expensive silk suit. Matteson jumped back, a look of horror on his face. Frantically he tried to brush the urine from his jacket while Sarah hurriedly stuffed the small dog back inside her bag.

"I'll get you for this, Sam. You just wait and see. You're going to spend the rest of your life in jail." Then, like a scene out of a bad movie, she stomped out of the office.

I was stunned and more confused than ever. I wondered if Sam had any idea that Pepper's will would leave her everything. Maybe that's why she wanted me here. Maybe it wasn't just for moral support or because she thought her sister might go ballistic, but because she wanted me to have the story. She had done as much with insider industry news before. Kim LaSalle's slasher attack was hardly the first. I stood up and stared at Sam. She was on her feet hugging Mr. Matteson like she'd just won the lottery.

She smiled at me from over his shoulder and gave me a thumbs-up.

The only thing I knew for certain was that Sarah wasn't going to go away without a fight, and that the fallout was going to be horrendous. I could imagine the headlines. None of this was going to be in Sam's favor. Worst of all, I was starting to feel like I was in the middle of something, maybe the wild card in a game Sam was playing to win.

CHAPTER 8

I picked up the phone to call ahead to the station as I left Matteson's office. I wanted to get hold of Tyler right away. I knew Sarah Millhouse would be hot to talk to anyone about what had just transpired with Pepper's attorney and, if that someone was Kari Rhodes, I wanted to make certain Tyler heard the story from me.

He answered on the first ring, putting me on speaker. I could hear the heavy typing of his fingers flying across his computer keyboard, lightning fast, just like his mind. "What ya got, Carol? I'm busy. On the air in five."

"Pepper Millhouse had a will."

"That's not news. All rich people have wills. What else you got?"

"The only surviving members of her family were her nieces, twins, Samantha and Sarah…"

"So what? I've got other stories on my desk. I'm on deadline. You gotta do better than that."

"She left everything, I mean everything, millions, her house, her jewelry, her car, her business, all of it to Samantha, and—"

"Okay. I'm listening." The heavy clicking of his fingers on the keyboard stopped. "Text me the name of the attorney and don't forget, I need—"

"I know, boss, *just the facts*." I gave him my best Jack Webb impersonation. I expected a laugh, or at least recognition that I was coming to him first as he had instructed, but I got nothing, just a stern reply.

"The autopsy report, Carol, you have that yet?"

"No. But I'm on it." I had already tried to call the coroner's office several times this morning, but to no avail. I told him I'd call back as soon as I got it.

"Good, 'cause until you do this isn't much more than fill for Kari's entertainment report."

The phone went dead. I was beginning to think if I didn't find something more newsworthy concerning Pepper's death I'd be doomed to cover waterless urinal stories for the rest of my career, or even worse, reading station IDs and doing traffic updates. I picked up the phone and tried the coroner's office again. By now I was actually hoping Pepper Millhouse had been murdered. Just not by my neighbor.

By the time I got to the radio station Kari had already updated the Hollywood Bathtub Murder report with news of Pepper's will. Embedded with the edgy new age sounds from a symphonic keyboard was the story: *Hollywood Agent leaves millions to favored niece...* And with her on the air to discuss the incident was Sarah Millhouse.

Sarah wasn't physically in studio with Kari. That would have worried me. She was so irate when she'd left Matteson's office I feared she might have attacked me, if she saw me. If for no other reason than because I was her sister's friend, guilty by association. Fortunately, she was there in voice only, patched in via a phone line.

"So, you're telling me you had no idea?" Kari sat vulture-like in the dimly lit studio, dressed in a loose fitting black caftan with her elbows on the console, her skinny neck and small head tucked down beneath her pointy shoulder blades as she leaned closer to the mic. "Absolutely not a clue?"

"Not one," Sarah said. "And let me share with your listeners that I'm not only devastated with the loss of my dear aunt, whose death I find highly suspicious, but that I'm absolutely convinced what happened at her attorney's office this morning is part of something even bigger, a conspiracy maybe."

Sarah was doing a good job convincing Kari's listeners that she considered what had happened to her was criminal. She sounded like a victim, her voice thin and strained. Not a surprise after the outburst I'd just witnessed inside Matteson's office. Her throat had to be raw from screaming.

"I can imagine what a shock this must be for you, to suddenly find that you've been disinherited."

"Actually, Kari, if I might interrupt, that's not what's important here. What is important is that I don't believe my aunt's death, nor those of her business partners, was accidental. Not at all. I think they were murdered."

No! I wanted to scream, call a time-out, knock on the glass between our studios, anything to get Kari to stop Sarah before she labeled Sam a murderer, much less a serial killer. But there was nothing I could do. Tyler would have my job if I interrupted her broadcast. He had given Kari free reign, and she was doing exactly as he paid her to do, hyping the story, getting people to call in, interacting with her listeners. The switchboard was already beginning to light up.

"Sarah, before you say anything you might regret, let me remind you, we've yet to actually see a coroner's report. We've no way of knowing beyond speculation how it is your aunt died. However..." She glanced over at me and smiled. "Maybe Carol might be able to shed some light on the matter. She's been following the case. Carol?"

I hadn't expected to be called into the conversation, but this was my chance. Tyler could hardly blame me. I looked at the clock. Kari's show was due for a station break in eight minutes. I had time on my side. If I stretched out my response I could keep Sarah from verbally accusing her sister on the air. All I had to do was keep talking.

"Yes, Kari, it is slightly unusual for a report to take so long. I've really no idea why. We usually can get results back within seventy-two hours, but then again, things can get busy with the Medical

Examiner. They examine about sixty-five hundred bodies a year."

I pulled up the LA County Coroner's web page and started to read from it, citing obscure facts I knew would take up time. "State law requires that anyone found to have died of sudden, violent or unusual causes be examined, unless of course they were older and ailing, like Helen Howard, who, as you well know was well into her late eighties or Adel Powers, who had a history of medical problems."

My delay was working. I had managed to drag out my report and Kari's on-air director, a tattooed Gen-Xer with glasses stood up. With both hands in the air, he indicated we had less than ten seconds to station break. I was just about to wrap the report when Sarah screamed.

"I don't need to read an autopsy report! And after this morning, I'm through pretending this could be anything but murder and that my—"

Do you suffer heartburn, leg tremors or night sweats...

It was perfect timing, down to the split second. The commercial cut Sarah off before she could officially point an accusatory finger at her sister. I was about to breathe a sigh of relief when Kari surprised me and invited Sarah to stay for the next segment. I picked up the phone and redialed the coroner's office for the sixth time that morning. Still there was nothing. A prerecorded greeting expressed sympathy for my loss and asked me to leave a message. I left my name and hung up.

I couldn't blame Kari for what she was doing. The story was just too good to pass on. Her listeners were loving it. It had everything Hollywood loves: murder, mystery, money and now the battle between the nieces, the good twin versus the bad, and the switchboard was a constant barometer signaling just how much the public was eating this up.

Listeners can be very opinionated. Some called to say they thought Samantha Millhouse was the bad twin. She had everything to gain. She had manipulated her aunt, turned her against her sister, then openly claimed how much she hated her. There was little doubt in that camp that Sam had killed her aunt, and some who even believed she had killed her aunt's business associates as well. Others said they didn't think there was a connection between the death of the old ladies at all, and that Sarah was the murderer. They believed that once Sarah had learned about her aunt's will, she plotted to kill her, and maybe even framed her sister. As for the old ladies, the cause of their death was yet to be determined, and the timing, purely coincidental. There was no end to the possibilities or the accusations. As soon as one light on the switchboard dimmed another took its place. Finally Kari returned to Sarah.

"Well, you've heard from the court of public opinion, Sarah. What do you have to say?"

"Kari, what I want your listeners to understand is that this has never been about the money, not for me anyway. I'm sure to many Pepper Millhouse was a rich woman, a very successful talent agent, but to me she was my aunt, my father's sister, the only surviving member of my family other than my twin. She was my guardian who saw me through college, my mentor, my ally. I'll never forget her."

I listened as Sarah went on about her relationship with Pepper. Her voice cracking as she talked about how, after her parents died, Pepper had stepped up and overseen their education.

"Not that we ever lived with my aunt. My sister and I were in college, but she was there, financially. She gave us our start, our first job at the agency after graduation."

"But you didn't stay with the agency. You went out on your own. You even hired a competitive agent to represent you."

"What else could I have done? My sister pushed me out of the agency, exactly like she did Adel and Helen. She turned my aunt against them, got Pepper thinking they were old and useless, and then she turned her against me, too. Tried to convince Pepper I was ungrateful. It's the only reason my aunt would have ever cut me out of her life."

Several fans called to support her. Some saying they had seen her in a recent made for TV movie about a blonde bombshell, about as bright as a two watt bulb, who joins a protest against an oil company and convinces them to embrace alternative energy. It was as believable as the story she was telling about being pushed out of the agency, but with a higher moral cause making her, if nothing else, a likable character.

"Sarah, certainly you understand how this looks. Your aunt suddenly dies and leaves everything to just one of her two nieces. One who was with her to the end and another who has gone off and is actually under contract with another agency. It's only natural that people will talk. They're going to wonder about each of you."

"All I can say is that my aunt would never have done this. The last time I saw her was at her birthday, and she told me she was sorry I'd left the agency, that she wanted me back in her life. My aunt was a very generous person. I believed no matter what she'd take care of us. I knew if anything ever happened to her, she'd divide things equally. We were family."

"You don't think that perhaps something might have happened that caused her to change her mind?"

"The only thing that happened to my aunt was my sister. Sam never made any secret about how much she wanted the agency, and behind my aunt's back she said things that were terrible about her. Everybody knew Sam hated Pepper."

"You sound pretty convinced."

"Wouldn't you be? I think it's oddly coincidental that my aunt and her business partners all died within six weeks of each other and that Pepper left everything to my sister, including the agency. Beyond that I have no comment."

No comment! Sarah might as well have hung the noose right around Sam's neck. I didn't think there was a listener tuned to the station who didn't think Sam was guilty.

CHAPTER 9

It had been eleven days since Pepper's body had been found in the bathtub of her home, and still the coroner had yet to rule on an official cause of death. I was beginning to think that because of Pepper's high profile and the obvious rivalry between Sam and her sister, this case had simply been blown way out of proportion. Despite Sarah's finger pointing at her sister, Amber's wild accusation about her father, and Kari's idea about a serial killer, there was no proof of any malicious activity. I was beginning to have my doubts the coroner would find anything. With the lack of any new evidence, even Kari's updates on the Hollywood Bathtub Murders were starting to wane and Sam had wisely piped down in her criticism of her aunt. She returned to work and was immersed in the day-to-day activities of running the agency. Things started to look like they might return to some form of normalcy. Sam even found time to bring over a pan of homemade lasagna for Charlie and a thank you gift for me: bath salts for helping her through what she was now calling a seriously rough patch.

Then I got a call from Dr. Gabor at the coroner's office.

"Officially, Ms. Childs, I'm only allowed to share with you that the results of the autopsy I performed on Ms. Millhouse indicate she was murdered." In a very thick Hungarian accent Dr. Gabor apologized. He explained the police had ruled the exact cause of Pepper's death to be classified, and consequently could tell me nothing more. "It appears there's another, possibly related, investigation going on."

"Another investigation?" I felt my heart skip a beat. Certainly

Pepper's death wasn't going to be tied to that of the old ladies?

"Yes, and again this is off the record. I'm calling you, Ms. Childs, because you work for KCHC, and I'm a fan, not only of the station but of Kari Rhodes. I thought you should know—between you and me anyway—that as far as her theory of threes goes, she may not be so far off. I'll not say more, only that the police are looking into it."

My hand started to shake as I scribbled notes on a pad in front of me. This wasn't just speculation, not anymore. This was real. Somebody had actually killed Pepper Millhouse and not just Pepper but maybe her two gray-haired mentors as well. I hoped that somebody wasn't my neighbor.

"Was Pepper Millhouse drowned? Can you at least tell me that much?" If Pepper had drowned there was no way Sam could have done it. She was clear across town at the awards' ceremony. As for the others, I had no idea.

"No. That would have been much too easy to determine. Drowning is the eighth most popular form of homicide we get around here. Our Ms. Millhouse it appears died from respiratory failure. Would you care to take a stab at the other causes?" Dr. Gabor chuckled.

"No," I said. "But if drowning is number eight, perhaps you might share with me—off the record, of course—just which of the other forms of homicide was used to kill Ms. Millhouse."

"Ahh. A reporter with a little morbid curiosity, are we?"

"Not at all. Just a reporter hoping to find the cause of death. Off the record of course."

I had heard the coroner had a ghoulish manner and enjoyed shocking reporters with some of the more gruesome details of his job. Perhaps if I pushed him, just a bit, he might share with me the cause. I crossed my fingers.

"Between you and me, Ms. Millhouse appeared to have applied an herbal rub, a toxic substance if you will, that targeted her cardiovascular and central nervous systems. It would have created a chemical reaction within the body, causing the cell membrane to modify and sodium and potassium ions to inhibit repolarization."

"I'm sorry, Doctor," I stopped him midsentence, my voice pleading. "Could you please be a little less technical?"

"In short, Ms. Millhouse probably never knew what was happening until it was too late and by then she would have unable to do anything about it. She would have died within fifteen minutes of exposure. The overall sensation would have been excruciating; a feeling of being flayed from the inside out." I sensed delight in his response and cringed. It sounded like an agonizing death.

"Do you know yet what kind of toxic substance it was?"

"We're looking for a particularly quick acting poison that leaves very little evidence in the body. It takes a little time to screen for these things, hence my delay in determining the cause of death. But my guess is we'll find it's a naturally occurring toxin from an organic substance, most likely a plant, probably Aconitum from the Ranunculaceae family."

"Excuse me, Doctor. English please. I'm afraid I'm not up on my Latin. Is there a generic name? Something I might be more familiar with?"

"Devil's weed, monkshood, wolf's bane, blue rocket. Goes by half a dozen different names. We call it the queen of poisons. But again, Ms. Childs, I must warn you, we haven't had this conversation. This is all off the record. You can't use any of it. Now if you'll excuse me. I'm in a bit of rush." He paused as though expecting a drum roll. "People are just dying to meet me."

With Pepper Millhouse's death officially ruled a homicide, I had no choice but to make it my lead story at the top of the hour. I, of course, went to Tyler first, exactly as he had requested, and filled him in on the autopsy results, or those I could report anyway. My report fell right in the middle of the Kari Rhodes show.

"The Los Angeles County Coroner's Office announced this morning it has officially ruled the cause of death for Hollywood agent Pepper Millhouse to be a homicide. Ms. Millhouse, whose body was found in the bathtub of her home on the evening of the Silver Screen Awards, is believed to have been murdered. The exact cause of death is pending further investigation."

I finished my broadcast, muted the mic in the news booth and decided to stay in the studio, curious to hear what Kari would do with the news. I was hardly surprised. She smiled and, as if I had given her the story exclusively, bowed her head with her hands folded prayer-like in front of her chest and mouthed the words *thank you*. Adjusting her headphones, she began her assault.

"Well, I have to say, I'm not surprised. Haven't I said all along I didn't think Ms. Millhouse's death was accidental? Mark my words, we're going to find that Adel Powers and Helen Howard were also murdered, and like I've said before, I for one am not going to be surprised to learn it's someone close to or maybe even involved in the agency."

The little yellow pulsating lights on the phone indicating callers started to light up and with them the acid in my stomach. I couldn't sit back and listen as Kari went on with her good twin bad twin theory, setting Sam up as the murderer and Sarah as the wronged twin. If Sam really was guilty, I needed to find out. And if she wasn't, I needed to find the killer. I was about to get up and leave the studio when Tyler buzzed me on the inside studio line.

"You have a hysterical caller on the line. She says it's an emergency, a matter of life and death."

I picked up the line and knew before I heard the voice on phone it had to be Sam.

"Carol! You've got to help me. The police are here." Sam sounded panicked. In the background I could hear deep voices, the sound of furniture being moved, and what sounded like the cat screeching. "I can't believe it. They're telling me the coroner's ruled Pepper's death a homicide. They've got a search warrant. They're here to look for evidence."

"Evidence? What kind of evidence?" I couldn't imagine even if Sam was guilty she'd be stupid enough to hold on to any kind of evidence.

"I don't know. I'm not thinking clearly. What do I do?"

I took a deep breath and exhaled. "Call an attorney? You must have one."

"The agency used Mr. Matteson's firm for just about everything, but I think my sister's gotten to him since the reading of the will. I don't trust him."

I didn't doubt that. Based on the situation between the two sisters I wouldn't put it past Sarah to try solicit any favors from Matteson.

"Just keep your mouth shut. Don't say anything or go anywhere. I'll call the station's attorney. He'll know what to do."

I first met Mr. King about a year ago when I worked in sales. I had inherited his account from a young, fresh faced sales exec. She couldn't stand the man and for good reason. The King, as he liked to call himself, was a balding, short, wide-bodied womanizer who chased anything in a skirt. He was also a brilliant legal mind, a lawyers' lawyer, who despite his giant sloth-like appearance was the go-to guy for media and KCHC's own on-air authority. King was the expert for anything legal and highly sought after for his opinion, whether it concerned a congressman who had been caught with his pants down or a constitutional interpretation of the law. He was The King, an obnoxious old flirt who constantly liked to test the waters, and he was also the best person I could think of to help Sam.

I picked up the phone. "Mr. King, I need a favor."

"For a pretty lady, who perhaps might repay me with a lovely dinner, and...?" he paused, the implication obvious.

"That's not gonna happen," I said coolly. It never failed; if nothing else, King was as persistent as he was harmless in his pursuit. "But this favor may have something to do with a high profile murder case you might find interesting."

King paused and cleared his throat. I knew I had his attention.

"I'm listening," he said. "Just who are we talking about?"

"Pepper Millhouse."

"Ahh, finally a little sex and violence."

"You knew Pepper?" I don't know why I was surprised. The King knew everybody.

He chuckled. "A gentleman never talks."

Thirty minutes later I was outside Sam's house. The police had left the front door open. Standing alone in the middle of the living room was Sam. She was barefoot and dressed in a pair of loose-fitting capris and a t-shirt. The expression on her face was total disbelief. I walked in and stood next to her. All around us, everything she owned was being tossed. Clothes, books, autographed scripts and photos were piled in heaps on the floor. The room was drafty. Furniture had been turned over, the drapes swept back from the walls and windows opened. Nothing was left untouched.

"Do you know what they're looking for?"

"I haven't got a clue." She shook her head then loud enough so that the officers could hear, added, "Certainly they know I was at the Silver Screen Awards Show with my aunt the night she died. And that she went home alone. I must have had three thousand witnesses."

"Sam! Don't say anything." I took her hand and nodded in the direction of the kitchen. Maybe there we could at least sit down and wait for Mr. King. But the kitchen was even worse. The countertops and the table were covered with pots and pans. Things were pulled out of the cabinets and cereal boxes were opened, their contents spilled onto the counter.

I cleared a space at the table, we sat down, and I pulled her hand away from her face. She was biting her fingernails. I had never seen her look so distraught.

"This is all my sister's doing. She's behind this; she's setting me up. The police should be checking her place, not mine. You just wait and see. She won't stop until I'm in jail, and she has everything."

I squeezed her hand. "It's going to be okay," I said.

I don't know why I said that. Even I was having doubts about Sam. She had been so damn cavalier about Pepper's death, going on about how she didn't care and how great it was now that the agency was hers. After witnessing the animosity between Sam and Sarah, I was on the fence. If it wasn't Sam, maybe it was Sarah. Or like Sam had said a thousand times, Pepper did have a target on her back. A lot of people would've liked to see her dead.

"We're going to need to bring in a dog." A cop stood in the hallway and hollered in our direction.

Sam glanced down the hallway then back to me.

"Where's Bossypants?" I asked.

Sam shrugged, the look in her eyes a thousand miles away. I gathered if the cat was still in the house he was probably in the bedroom, maybe hiding under the bed. I considered rescuing him, but wrangling a frightened cat under the present circumstances didn't seem like a good idea.

"She's got a cat," I hollered.

"Cat's got a problem then," the cop hollered back.

This wasn't going to be good. And when the dog arrived, the cat did what cats do; it hissed and shot through the living room like a rocket. It was a scene out of a cartoon. A screeching black blur-of-fur bolted from the bedroom and through the living room looking for an escape, and spotting the open front door, slammed into the screen. I'm certain Bossypants didn't realize the screen was closed, but just the same, the poor animal came crashing into it with such a thud that it shook the door, just as Mr. King was about to ring the bell.

From the look on King's face he must have thought there were shots fired. Quickly he jumped back, crouched down and took cover. Tripping over his own two feet, he fell off the front step and toppled into the planter.

If it hadn't been such a serious situation, I would have laughed out loud. Sam hurried to pick up the cat. He had rolled into a ball in the corner of the room and was dazed. I ran to the door to help Mr. King and offered him my hand, but he refused. He was disoriented.

Slowly lifting his bulky frame to his feet he brushed the leaves and dirt from his overcoat, then adjusted his glasses and checked his pockets, and patted his comb-over back into place.

Without a word to me he nodded and stepped over the threshold, then asked to see the search warrant. Sam nodded toward the coffee table where the warrant lay atop a stack of scripts like an unpaid bill. I whisked it off the table and presented it to him.

He held the document at arm's length, looking both over and through his glasses as though he weren't certain which angle was better. Then sighing dismissively, he turned and picked his way carefully through the maze of clutter, working his way toward Sam's bedroom.

"They'll never prove I did it," Sam said.

"But they're not going to have to, right?" I wished she wouldn't talk like this.

"You know what my sister did. This is all her fault." Sam looked at me, her eyes steady on mine. "Like you said earlier, I shouldn't say anything. Not until I've spoken with my attorney."

I chalked up the craziness of our conversation to stress and offered to get her a glass of water. But before I could do anything we heard voices coming from the bedroom. King appeared first, his portly body walking duck-footed ahead of the officers. He looked directly at Sam.

"Please don't say anything, Miss Millhouse."

Behind him, two officers appeared. In the hands of one was a large brown paper bag marked evidence.

"Miss Samantha Millhouse. You're under arrest for the murder of Pepper Millhouse. You have the right to remain silent..."

"Arrest!" I looked at Mr. King. This couldn't be happening. Sam handed me the cat; he purred restlessly against my ribs as the police pulled Sam's arms behind her back and handcuffed her. "Wait! Sam, please. Tell them you didn't do it. Tell them the truth. Tell them your sister's setting you up, that you hated Pepper but that you didn't—"

"Carol, stop! Right now." With his back to me King stepped in front of Sam. "Miss Millhouse, whatever it is you might be thinking of saying, I need to ask you to remain quiet. Can you do that?"

Sam nodded.

"But this isn't right. It's a mistake." I tugged at King's coat, the cat still under one arm. "Please, you've got to do something."

He reached down to the coffee table, grabbed a script and pressed it in my hand, then told me to be quiet.

I looked at the officers and back at Sam. I wanted to tell them this was a set up. I could think of at least two other people in addition to Sam's sister who would have liked to see Pepper dead. Why weren't they being arrested? Or at least questioned? What about Amber Marx's father? Or Kim LaSalle? And Sarah, she had as much to gain as Sam with Pepper's death. But I couldn't tell them anything. King's back was to me, like a wall, blocking me while he talked to Sam.

"Miss Millhouse, these gentlemen are going to take you downtown. I'll meet you there, and we'll handle this."

I watched as the officers lead Sam out the front door. "Don't worry, Sam. Everything's going to be fine." I looked at King, my eyes searching his. *It will, won't it?*

"We'll talk later," he said.

CHAPTER 10

It's never good to have to report on friends. In fact, with reporters it's an unwritten code, something akin to what doctors and lawyers do when it comes to treating and defending their own. They don't. And for just that reason I worried Tyler would hijack my story if I came to him first with the news of Sam's arrest and broadcast it himself, like he had Pepper's will. I was too close, and he knew it.

I also knew my choices were simple. Either I went to Tyler with news of Sam's arrest, knowing he would take the story himself or, even worse, pass the information on to Kari. In such case the scuttlebutt against Sam would continue to stack up, and in the court of public opinion she'd be found guilty long before she ever stepped foot in a courtroom. Or I could risk it. Even if it meant I'd be doing traffic updates for the remainder of my probation it'd be worth it. I could wait until Tyler was out of the studio and include the news in my next report.

I decided on the latter.

I slipped into the office and pulled a Tyler, feigning a sudden need to visit the ladies room, thus avoiding him altogether. I knew he'd be too busy to notice. The station was scheduled to carry a UCLA basketball game, and he was rushed with last minute details before heading out to Pauley Pavilion. I figured if he heard the story he'd call to complain. I could tell him we were the first to get the news, I had it exclusively, that by the time I got back to the studio, he'd left for the game. He could hardly find fault with that.

But it didn't work out quite so smoothly. I had figured wrong. Tyler was running late; I caught him out of the corner of my eye as he headed past the big studio window with his backpack and baseball cap on just as I had begun my broadcast.

"Police have arrested Samantha Millhouse, niece of the Hollywood agent Pepper Millhouse, who was found dead in the bathtub of her Beverly Hills mansion last week."

Tyler backpedaled until he stood in the center of window, and like a college proctor with his arms across his skinny chest, scowled at me. I responded with a slight salute of my left hand. Not that I meant it to be offensive (left-handed salutes are considered as such) but I'm left handed. I wasn't thinking. However, I could see he thought I'd done the equivalent of flipping him off. In quick response he held up one finger, then two. Our eyes locked. *Yeah, I know, two strikes!* With a thumb and pinky to his face he mimed, "Call me!" then disappeared.

I refocused my eyes on the story in front of me.

"Evidence believed to be linked to the murder was removed this afternoon from the niece's house. Samantha Millhouse was arrested without incident..."

Half a dozen times during the broadcast I wanted to stop and say how bizarre this all was. That I knew Samantha Millhouse, she was my friend and neighbor, a woman I trusted to look in on my son while I worked evenings. A person I welcomed into my home and whose cat I fed when she was out of town. I wanted to let my listeners know the stories I had heard about Pepper Millhouse, a.k.a the Queen of Mean. That any number of people wanted to kill her. But that would have been unprofessional, and like Tyler said, my job was *just the facts, ma'am*. Just the facts.

I finished my broadcast and was about to leave the studio when the internal phone line on the console started to blink. I glanced at it and debated whether or not to answer. It was well past seven p.m. All of KCHC's staff was long gone and the evening hosts, Dan and Deb, had been preempted for the game. I was alone. I picked up the line.

"KCHC News. May I help you?"

"Carol? It's Misty Dawn. We need to talk. It's urgent." Her

voice sounded ragged, her breathing irregular. I could hear her moccasins shuffling in the background as though she was in a hurry. "Something's happened. I need to see you. Can you meet me at the university's gardens?"

"Now?" I was stunned to hear Misty's voice. My hand went cold on the receiver.

"Please, Carol. I've been listening to the station, the reports about Pepper Millhouse—the will and now Sam's arrest. You know how Sam carries on about her aunt."

I pulled the phone away from my head and stared at it. I felt as though a presence had morphed through the line and was sitting in the studio with me. "I didn't realize you were aware I knew Sam."

"*Really*, Carol? You're wondering that *now?* Isn't it enough that I know all about Eric and...Oh! By the way, he's coming home soon. You should get that red teddy of yours ready. He likes that."

"What about Sam?" I asked pointedly. I was determined to keep the conversation away from my personal life.

"I think I can help."

"Are you telling me you know who the killer is?"

"Oh, heavens, if it was only that easy. No, but I may have information, something that might prove helpful."

"Then perhaps we could discuss this on the phone. There's no way I can leave the station. Not now. I'm alone and due back on the air within the hour."

"Oh dear, I'm afraid that really is a problem. You see, I need to see you tonight, before someone else dies."

"Dies!" I wasn't sure if I'd said that as an expletive or a question. Only that as the word escaped my lips the lights flicked in the studio. Or perhaps it was just my eyes. I wanted to think so. I took a deep breath and exhaled. "Whose death are we talking about?"

"Don't worry. I'll come to you. Be there in a few."

I called and alerted KCHC's night security guard Jake and told him I was expecting a visitor. I considered telling him that Misty Dawn was a little odd then dismissed the idea. Radio stations get their fill of strange personalities. I asked him to show her to the employees' lounge, then call me.

I had barely finished perusing the news stories for my next update when Jake buzzed. Misty had arrived and was waiting for me. I glanced at my watch. *What'd she do, fly?* It was less than five minutes since we'd spoken.

I grabbed some wire copy for my next report and headed down the hall toward the employees' lounge, then stopped when I got to the door.

Sitting at one of the small round café tables in the corner was Misty. She looked like a fortune teller. On her head, instead of the straw cowboy hat she was wearing the last time I saw her, she had on a colorful shawl that hung to her shoulders, decorated with all kinds of beads and crystals. Laid out in front of her were at least a dozen clear plastic baggies with all sorts of crusty looking seeds and weeds. Some of which, I worried, might not be legal.

"I see you've made yourself at home," I said.

"Not quite. I need a little tea first." She reached into a knapsack and took out a small cup, then patted each of the small baggies in front of her as though she were feeling, or maybe looking, for one in particular. Finding it, she took out a pinch of something and sprinkled it into the cup. "Do you mind?" She passed me the cup and nodded to the hot water tap next to the sink.

"Not at all." I filled the cup and handed it back to her.

"Will you join me?"

"I have my own, thank you." I reached into the cabinet for a box of chamomile tea, something to calm my nerves. Silently, with my back to her, I fixed myself a cup, then turned and raising my cup to hers, took a sip.

"Pepper Millhouse has been reaching out to me."

I nearly choked.

"Pepper Millhouse is dead," I said. I took a small step backwards towards the kitchen counter. "What do you mean by reaching out?"

"Why, talking to me, of course. What else?"

I slowly took a sip of my tea. If Eric hadn't vouched for this odd woman I'd think she was one step from a mental institution.

"She's been talking about the poison. She's very concerned about it."

"The poison?" Now she really had my attention. I wasn't sure if I was more surprised to hear Misty say she'd been in communication with Pepper Millhouse, or that she actually knew Pepper had been poisoned. Either way, I was shocked. The Medical Examiner had been quite clear the police wanted to keep that fact quiet. My reports, as well as those of the other news outlets had only said that Pepper's death had been ruled a homicide.

"Umm... This really is a good cup of tea. You sure you won't let me make you one?"

I shook my head and put my hand protectively over the top of my cup and leaned farther back against the counter.

"You don't know what you're missing." I watched as she took another sip, closing her eyes, savoring the tea like a fine wine. Then taking a deep breath she opened them and looked at me. "One really has to be extremely careful with herbs. They can be tricky, even poisonous."

I didn't say anything. I watched as she placed the cup back on the table and stared at it as though it had magical powers. I waited for her say something and when she didn't, I cleared my throat.

"Harrumph, Pepper? Poison?" I said gently. "Would you care to tell me what it is you know? You said it was urgent."

She sighed and sat back in the chair, eyes now wide open, her face relaxed. "First, you have to understand, I was very surprised to hear from Pepper. She and I weren't exactly chummy. I was the one who discovered Amber Marx and introduced her to Pepper. Her mother, poor woman, was a client of mine. I used to read for her. Psychic readings, star charts, that kind of thing. You'd think Pepper would have loved me for that, but with Pepper it's more about 'what have you done for me lately?' You know the type."

I glanced at the clock. I didn't have time to get into Misty's history with Pepper. I was due back on the air in thirty minutes.

"So exactly why is it you think Pepper's talking to you?"

"I suppose because she's upset."

"Why?" I asked skeptically.

"Because she's dead. Why else?" Misty's posture straightened; she looked directly at me like she was surprised I'd ask.

"I see." I took another step back and glanced at the clock again.

"You don't see anything at all. That's the problem. And don't be so patronizing." Misty pointed a finger at me. I feared I had upset her, and she'd start rambling again. I didn't have time for that. I softened my voice. "I'm sorry, Misty. I'm in a bit of rush. You said it was urgent we meet. That other people might die if—"

"It's your aura," she blurted. She wrapped her hands firmly around the cup, her knuckles white. "You're the conduit. At first when I saw that dark energy field all around you I didn't get it. But now I do. You're the connection. You know who the killer is. Or you will very soon. And Pepper thinks so too."

"Me?" I hit myself in the chest with my fist, knuckles to the sternum. "Why would I know?" I paused and thought for a second. "Does Pepper think Sam did it?" I held my breath. I could feel my heart pounding against the palm of my hand.

"That's just it. She doesn't know. Whoever it was wasn't in the room with her when she died. That's why she needs someone close to the case who can find the killer."

"What about the police? Last I checked that was their job."

"You have to understand, Pepper wasn't particularly pleased the police took so long to realize Adel and Helen were murdered."

"Wait a minute. You're telling me, Adel, Helen, and Pepper, they're all connected? "

She scoffed. "Don't look so surprised. On some level you had to have known. Anyway, you'll have the evidence soon enough, when the coroner's report is released, or perhaps sooner."

Misty relaxed her hands around the cup and slowly took another sip of her tea. I considered most of what she was saying might have come from Kari's show.

But the fact that she knew Pepper had been poisoned frightened me.

"What about you? Aren't you supposed to be clairvoyant, or whatever? Can't you find the killer?"

She put her cup down again, and smiled. "I'm too close. The older I get, the harder it is to read someone I know."

"I didn't realize there were limitations," I said.

"Plus my hearing's not what it used to be."

I choked back a laugh and thought about calling security. Was this a joke? A clairvoyant with aging issues? I decided I'd play along.

"So what is it she wants me to do?"

"Why solve the crime, of course. I suspect you're already very close. You probably just don't know it."

I wondered if by close she meant maybe sitting right in front of me. I glanced at the bag beneath her feet and back at the clock. It was getting late. If I was going to call Charlie I needed to call before ten p.m.

"Oh, sweetie, it's not me. Is that what you're thinking?" She smiled at me as though to apologize for reading my thoughts.

I didn't say a word.

"And you mustn't worry about your son. He'll be fine. But you do need to keep an eye on him." She stood up from the table and started packing her things. "You know how willful boys are. Always thinking they're invincible. Anyway, I can see I've done my job here tonight." She hoisted her bag onto her shoulder then looked at me again. "This was good, right? Let's do it again soon."

I watched as Misty appeared to almost float out of the room. I swear her feet didn't touch the floor. I didn't hear the shuffle of her moccasins or the shaking of her beads, and if I had been drinking anything but chamomile tea, I would have had to blame it on the effects. As it was, I'm still not certain.

CHAPTER 11

I got to the courthouse first thing the following morning. Mr. King told me he'd meet with me before Sam's arraignment, but he was nowhere in sight. I checked my voicemail, mostly to assure myself that Tyler had received my message that I'd be covering Sam's arraignment.

We hadn't connected the night before, and I figured Tyler might still be miffed that I hadn't come to him with news of Sam's arrest. I'd left messages everywhere: his office phone, cell phone, email, even on the yellow pad on his desk. In red felt pen I'd written, *At the court house. Samantha Millhouse arraignment, nine o'clock, Carol.* I wasn't taking any chances he'd assign the story to anyone else.

"You have no new messages." I took that as a positive sign and breathed a sigh of relief. Tyler may have called two strikes against me, but I wasn't out yet. I still had my job. Or at least I did until he called and told me otherwise. Either way, I was operating on the premise that it's easier to ask for forgiveness than permission.

While keeping a lookout for Mr. King on the plaza, I bought a cup of coffee and picked up a copy of the *LA Times*. The paper had the story of Sam's arrest on the front page which didn't surprise me. Kari's show, the nightly news, and the late night entertainment reports all had news of Pepper Millhouse's death, and the subsequent arrest of her niece was everywhere.

King had assured me that today's arraignment was just a formality, a reading of the charges against Sam. He explained they would be entering a plea of Not Guilty, and a date for a preliminary hearing would be set. Nothing unusual, he said, with the upside being that with a little luck the prosecutor would agree to bail. Since Sam had no previous convictions, and the evidence the police had gathered against her was largely circumstantial, King was hopeful bail wouldn't be an issue. If all went well I expected to be filing an on-air report for the KCHC morning show from the steps of the courthouse, and Sam would be home before lunch. Then she and Mr. King could begin to unravel this nightmare.

But there was a snag.

I could tell by the way King walked toward me, his small balding head sunk between his heavily rounded shoulders, that something was terribly wrong.

"What's the matter?" I tossed my coffee cup in the trash and rushed toward him.

"I don't have time to get into it now. I've just left a meeting with the District Attorney. You need to prepare yourself."

"Why? What's happened?"

"Follow me." He moved toward the entrance of the building. A beefy looking security guard blocked my entrance. Flashing his ID the guard cleared King in matter of moments, fast-tracking him through to the lobby, while I was left standing barefoot on the other side of metal detector holding my shoes in my hand. "I'll explain later, but for now the best thing you can do is your job. You're a reporter, Carol, and Sam's going need you to be a damn good one today."

I watched as King disappeared into the elevator, heading up to the Superior Court on the eleventh floor. I wondered exactly what it was he wasn't telling me.

Samantha walked into court between two sheriff's deputies. She was dressed in the black sheath dress I'd pulled from her closet yesterday and given King to take to the courthouse. At the last minute it had occurred to me she might need something. Still, she looked awful. Her dark hair straight and stringy, her eyes puffy. She shuffled toward King, bent with her arms and wrists folded across her hips like a wounded animal.

I had no idea if Sam knew I was there. The room was crowded with spectators who wanted a front row seat for the proceedings. It would have been almost impossible for her to see me seated in the back of the room.

"His Honorable Jonathan Spence." A court bailiff walked to the center of the courtroom. We all stood, waiting for the judge to enter from his chambers behind the bench, then took our seats.

"Miss Samantha Millhouse, I see here you are represented by counsel."

"I am, your honor." Sam's voice was faint, lacking its usual confidence. The judge asked her to speak up, explaining the court reporter needed to be able to hear her to record her response. "Yes, sir." She replied in a slightly stronger voice. "I am represented by my attorney, Mr. King."

"And your attorney, has he explained to you the charges filed against you for the murder of Pepper Millhouse?"

She nodded.

"Again, Miss Millhouse, I need you to speak up."

"Yes, he has, your Honor."

"And the additional charge of first degree murder for the death of Ms. Helen Howard?"

If I'd been standing I would have had to sit down. I couldn't believe what I was hearing. Additional charge? I glanced around the courtroom. Reporters on either side of me scribbled furiously into their notepads. No wonder Mr. King wanted me to be prepared. Tomorrow's headlines would be a disaster for Sam. For some people just reading that someone was charged with a crime was enough to convince them of their guilt. Kari Rhodes would have a field day with this, prosecuting Sam to the full extent of the electronic media.

"I have, your Honor."

"Then I will read the charges as they have been entered. Miss Millhouse, will you please stand?"

I watched as King helped Sam to her feet, putting his arm around her as the judge read the charges.

"Samantha Millhouse, you are being charged with first degree murder in the deaths of Pepper Millhouse and Helen Howard."

My chest tightened. This was really happening. My friend, my neighbor, my big story; it was all tied together, and I was in the middle of it all. Misty's premonition was right. Like some strange mystic curse, there·was death all around me.

"Are you prepared to enter a plea?"

A silence came over the courtroom. We all leaned closer to the bench, waiting for King to respond. "We are. My client wishes to enter a plea of not guilty."

"Let the record show that the defendant, Miss Samantha Millhouse, has entered a plea of not guilty to charges of first degree murder in the deaths of Pepper Millhouse and Ms. Helen Howard. At this time, Miss Millhouse, I—"

"Your Honor," King interrupted. "The defense would like to request the court consider bail."

Before the word bail was out of his mouth the lead prosecutor Bryan Scott shot to his feet.

"Your Honor, the prosecution believes Miss Millhouse is a threat to the community and requests that bail be denied. During a search of Millhouse's residence investigators found evidence believed to have been used in the death of Pepper Millhouse and Helen Howard. In addition, your Honor, it has come to our attention there are circumstances surrounding the death of another business partner in the ACT agency, a Miss Adel Powers."

Suddenly I had a vision of Misty, huddled over her tea cup looking at me with those milky white eyes of hers. Her voice rang in my ears. *Of course they're connected....* I shook my head. Why would Sam want to kill Adel? The agency's founder was frail and close to ninety. Why bother? According to Sam, Adel didn't come by the office that often, and when she did she frequently fell asleep in the lobby. Eventually Sam painted over Adel's parking space and later had the signage over the front door changed from Adel's

Creative Talent Agency to simply ACT. She thought it sounded less hokey, but I wasn't about to share that piece of information with anyone. None of this made any sense. Sam couldn't possibly have murdered Adel.

"We're requesting an investigation into the death of Adel Powers based upon possible links to the murders Miss Samantha Millhouse has been charged with today. In addition, Your Honor, at the time of the search of the accused's home we also found travel brochures to countries like Croatia, Dubai, Taiwan, all of them with no extradition treaties with the U.S. For this reason, The District Attorney believes Samantha Millhouse is a flight risk and should be held without bond."

I felt numb as I stood on the steps of courthouse filing my report amid a sea of reporters all doing the same. It felt surreal to be reporting Samantha Millhouse had now been officially charged with first degree murder in the death of two—possibly three—women. I couldn't believe this was my neighbor, and I had no idea how I'd explain this to Charlie.

I wrapped up the story and held on the line for Tyler. His voice was edgy.

"I don't want to see your face around this station today. I'm not going to get into a long lecture with you on the number of things you've done to piss me off or why it is I shouldn't fire you right now. I'm just going to tell you. Don't screw this up. I'll give you the story. You can follow it to the gates of hell for all I care, but you mess up, you're done. I'll see you Monday morning. Have a nice weekend!"

The line went dead. I felt a twinge of uncertainty as I listened to the dial tone. I wasn't sure if I should feel vindicated or screwed. All I knew is that Tyler had granted me the story, and while I was devastated for Sam, something about it made me very happy. I was still trying to figure that out when a text came through that put a definite smile on my face.

CHAPTER 12

Fish on Friday? Finally! Eric was coming home. His text said it all, code that he had the weekend free and would be over as soon as he finished work. I smiled. We enjoyed our little secret code. Dating an FBI agent added to the intrigue.

I typed back. *Just what the Pope ordered. Six p.m.*

This was perfect. Tyler had banished me from the station until Monday morning, punishment for not coming to him first with the news of Sam's arrest. The upshot being, he'd not only given me Pepper's story but also a much needed day off and reason to celebrate. For the first time in a long time I had a day to myself. With Eric coming over I was determined to focus solely on our budding romance.

I wasn't going to think about Sam. I wasn't going to let her arrest or even Misty's strange prediction mess with my head and ruin my evening. I put it all aside and set the stage for romance. I made dinner, lit candles and dribbled rose petals from the front door to the bedroom and into the bath where I put out bath salts and a silver ice bucket, with a chilled bottle of champagne.

By six p.m. I was dressed to kill, wearing a long lacy blue negligee. I had almost opted for the red teddy Eric liked so much. But because Misty had mentioned it, I felt it was somehow tainted. I didn't want her to be any more part of my love life than she already was. So I tossed the red teddy aside and went with the blue.

I also selected the best of my jazz CDs and loaded the player. Kenny G was playing in the background when the bell rang. Standing at my front door dressed in jeans, a blazer with an open collared shirt and holding a chilled bottle of champagne was Eric.

"I missed you." He stepped inside the room, took me in his arms and kissed me. "I thought we should celebrate."

"Celebrate?" I warmed to the faint smell of his cologne. "Anything in particular?"

"You."

Slowly he slipped his hands around my waist, his lips to my neck, pulling my body to his until the straps of my negligee fell from my shoulders. I smiled. I could drown in Eric's kisses. Somewhere between the front door, the stairway and the bedroom upstairs, we undressed each other, leaving a trail of clothes in our wake.

Later, dressed only in our robes, we retreated to the kitchen and ate dinner by candlelight. Feeding each other, dabbing morsels from the corner of our mouths with small kisses like young lovers.

"What's that?" With our heads together, Eric nodded to the rose petals leading up the stairs.

"You didn't notice before?"

"With you looking like you did when I came in, I wasn't looking at the floor." He laughed. "Any other surprises?"

"Only dessert." I said.

I grabbed his hand and without another word led him upstairs to the bathroom. The candlelight from small hurricane lamps that lined the bath flickered as we entered the room. I filled the tub and sprinkled baths salts into the water. Eric smiled, uncorked the bottle of champagne I'd left conspicuously chilled in the ice bucket and handed me a glass of bubbly. Loosening my robe I let it fall to the floor and in my best Venus de Milo pose, toasted my glass to his.

"To fish on Friday," I said. Clinking my glass to his, I slipped into the tub.

Eric got in behind me. I leaned back against him, his chest warm and sudsy against my body.

"I like that you're home," I took a sip of champagne. "Any particular reason you can talk about?"

"The FBI's been called in to check out Pepper Millhouse's murder. I'll be leading the investigation."

I turned my head and looked at him. I wasn't surprised. I should have expected it; with all the talk of serial murder and poison, of course the FBI would be called in. This was exactly the type of crime they did investigate.

"Well, at least now you'll be able to prove Sam didn't poison anyone."

Eric paused. I could tell something I said bothered him.

"What's wrong?"

"You said Pepper was poisoned. We haven't released that information. How did you know?"

I turned my head away from his and began to rub the suds up and down my arms. *Damn, I'd let that slip.* I should have known better. Even with Eric I probably shouldn't have revealed I knew the cause of death.

"You mean because it was classified?' I asked playfully.

"It's information we haven't revealed to the general public."

I winked. "Agent, are you asking me to reveal my sources?"

He kissed my shoulder. "I think you've already revealed much more than that." He ran his hand along the side of my legs, the warmth of his touch and the bubbles, delightful.

I smiled.

"My source, Agent Langdon, is off the record, at least for the moment. But I will tell you I'm not the only one who knows Pepper Millhouse was poisoned."

"You're not?" With his lips softly to my ear Eric teased, nibbling on my lobe. I could tell he was trying to change the subject. He seldom talked about work, and I knew would never share the details involving an open investigation.

"No, I'm not." I leaned forward, trying to break his spell. "But the person who does is someone who claims to know you very well." I rubbed more of the suds up and down my arms and waited for him to respond. He looked at me quizzically. He had no idea. "It's that crazy psychic friend of yours, Misty Dawn."

"FBI consultant, Carol, not friend, but I will give you that she is strange." Eric took a sip of champagne then squeezed the bath sponge, drizzling warm suds down my back.

"Do you know she actually believes she's in communication with Pepper Millhouse? In fact, I'm not so certain she didn't poison Pepper. Have you seen what she carries around in that bag of hers? She claims herbs, but—" I stopped myself and looked away. Good God, I was sounding just like Misty. I took a deep breath and refocused. "According to my source, Pepper Millhouse was killed with a plant toxin. Aconite, from monkshood. If anyone knows plants and poisons it'd be Misty."

"Misty? You actually think Misty Dawn is a serial killer? I'm pretty certain if she's working with the FBI she's been vetted, probably more than once."

"Well, if you ask me the woman's crazy."

"Why? What's going on?"

"For starters, I think she's stalking me. She showed up at the station last night and claims Pepper told her I might be able to help. Plus she knows about my son. She knows about you, about us."

Eric smiled, took another sip of wine and leaned back against the tub.

"Oh, you mean that she thinks you're hot for me?"

"She said that?" I splashed a handful of water over my shoulder.

"You're not?" Eric laughed. I sensed he was trying to lighten my concern. "I don't think Misty's someone you need to be concerned about, at least as far as being a serial killer goes. I'm sure she's just trying to help."

I leaned back against Eric and began playing with the bubbles. Maybe he was right, but my mind just wouldn't let go of the idea.

"I just can't believe the police found anything inside Sam's house that would connect her to the murder."

"You know I can't talk to you about anything we're working on." He put his hands around my shoulders and gently pulled me back against him, his lips against my ear. They were warm and suggestively bothersome. "Maybe we should work on something else."

"You're making it very difficult to concentrate," I said. I reached for my wine glass and took another sip. "I mean if Pepper was poisoned with some sort of plant toxin Sam would've had to know something about plants. Believe me, she doesn't exactly have a green thumb. Cactus couldn't survive her gardening skills. Whoever did this would have needed knowledge of toxic plants and been able to mix the poison into something undetectable." I stretched my leg out in front of me and traced the drain with my big toe.

"I thought we were going to have dessert." Eric pulled me closer to him.

I could feel he was getting aroused, but my mind wouldn't stop racing. What was it the police took from Sam's house? Whatever it was they had put it in a brown paper bag marked evidence. They had been in the bathroom. My eyes followed my toes to the end of the tub. There on the ledge were the bath salts.

"Oh my God! Stand up!"

Grabbing for the water wand I stood up and stumbled out of the tub. Eric tried to break my fall, but too late. I slipped to the floor. The wand in my hand twisted wildly like a water snake. Cold water sprayed everywhere, my hair, the windows, the walls, Eric.

"What's the matter?" Eric yelled.

"The bath salts! They were a gift from Sam!"

"Carol, stop! Turn off the water!"

I looked up at Eric from my position on the floor. He was standing in the tub, drenched. Streams of soapy cold water were dripping down his chest and legs.

"If these were the same bath salts that killed Pepper we'd be dead by now."

"You're sure?" I reached to turn off the valve, my wet ringlets matted against my face.

"More than certain." He grabbed a towel and dried himself off.

"I guess this means we're going to have to table dessert." I said, apologetically.

He stepped out of the tub, tucking the loose ends of the towel about his waist. "For a while."

CHAPTER 13

Monday morning Sarah Millhouse was back on the air again. But this time it wasn't just radio, she was on TV, and with her she had Andrew Reese, Sam's assistant. They appeared to be making the rounds. The early morning television talk shows were all running promos, hyping her appearance. *Disinherited twin speaks out. Sarah Millhouse believes agency was targeted. Stay tuned for more on the Hollywood Bathtub Murders.*

I was in the kitchen nursing a cup of coffee when the local Channel Five segment came on. Sarah and Andrew, dressed in matching black turtlenecks, were sitting on tall barstools opposite the morning show host. They looked a little too coordinated and a bit uncomfortable as the camera focused in for a welcoming shot, catching Sarah in her micro mini skirt trying to cross her legs.

"I'm sorry, I just hate that I've been put in this position." She laughed nervously, almost falling off the stool as she pulled at the hem of her skirt. "What I mean to say is that what's happened to my aunt and the agency is unbelievably frightening. And now with all the suspicion surrounding my sister, well, it's just all so overwhelming."

Sarah dabbed her eyes with a tissue, Andrew leaned over and squeezed her hand.

"What Sarah's trying to say is that with Pepper's death, the tragic loss of our founders, Adel Powers and Helen Howard, and now with her sister's arrest—" Andrew stopped and cleared his throat. "I mean, with her sister unavailable to us, it's been a very difficult time. But thankfully Sarah's been able to step in and help pick up the pieces."

I nearly choked on my coffee as I stared at the TV in disbelief. *Sarah overwhelmed? Was he kidding?* She'd set this all in motion. If Sam was hearing this right now she'd go ballistic.

I turned off the TV, not wanting to hear any more. Instead, I picked up the phone and called the coroner's office. I still needed to get the results of Adel Powers' autopsy. If it came back positive for murder it'd be one more murder charge against Sam and I needed to know as soon as possible.

"Is Dr. Gabor in? This is Carol Childs with KCHC. I'm investigating the Hollywood Bathtub Murders."

"I'm sorry. Dr. Gabor doesn't take calls until he's finished in the lab. If you're looking for the results of an autopsy you can access it via our website." The officious voice on the other end of the line sounded as though she were about to hang up. I quickly opted for a friendlier approach.

"Actually, he and I spoke earlier. He did the autopsy on Pepper Millhouse. He told me if I had any questions I could call back, that his assistant would be sure to put me through."

I crossed my fingers and waited for her reply.

"He doesn't like to be disturbed, Miss Childs, particularly by reporters. If you like I can transfer you to his voicemail."

"It's more urgent than that. It concerns an autopsy for Adel Powers. Her body was exhumed last week. I assure you, it's extremely important."

"If it's as important as you say he'll call you back. He generally returns calls between four-thirty and five."

"But he must take a break. Coffee? Lunch? I really have to see him."

"He usually breaks about ten-fifteen for coffee. If you like, I'll tell him you called."

"Don't bother. I'll be there. Ten o'clock, sharp."

I looked at the clock. It was almost nine a.m. With a little luck I could shower, dress, and cut through traffic in time for Dr. Gabor's coffee break.

The coroner's office is a large old fashioned, red brick building located in downtown Los Angeles. With its wide center staircase reminiscent of years past, it appeared out of sync with L.A.'s more modern architecture. I parked the car, raced up the steps and with very few moments to spare was met in the lobby by a young woman who looked like she expected me. She introduced herself simply as Lindy. The nameless voice I'd spoken with earlier on the phone finally had a face. She asked me to wait, then disappeared through a set of swinging metal doors.

Moments later a large man with a mop of wavy dark hair appeared at the same doorway, arms folded across his bulky frame. He stared at me through thick lenses that made his eyes look like saucers. I assumed this was Dr. Gabor. He was dressed in a blue pinstriped suit, not scrubs or a white lab coat as I had expected, and looked more like Liberace than a forensic pathologist. He gestured for me to follow and with a thick Hungarian accent said, "Come 'vit me."

He proceeded ahead of me down a long neon lit hallway with gleaming white floors. The sound of his shoes echoed a sense of urgency. I did my best to keep up, but even with my long legs I was several steps behind.

"You must be Carol Childs, the green reporter from KCHC?" I glimpsed a dimpled smile on the side of his face as he turned his head to look over his shoulder at me.

"Green?" I quickened my pace trying to close the gap between us.

He ignored my question and lengthened his stride. "You know," he said, "I used to practice medicine before I came to this country. Studied geriatrics. But my patients kept dying. Would you like to meet a few of my new ones?"

I didn't answer. His broad shoulders shook. He was having fun at my expense. I prayed he wasn't planning a detour through one of the double doors that lined the hall. Any of which I was certain would make me witness to an autopsy.

Finally, we came to the end of the hall. He stopped in front of a small office door, waited for me to catch up, then went in ahead of me and settled himself behind his computer. He smiled as I entered the office. I noticed a half-eaten Reuben sandwich and a pickle on the desk in front of him.

"Would you like a bite?"

I shook my head.

"I'm in a bit of a hurry. I'm due on the air at noon and I was hoping we could discuss the autopsy for Adel Powers beforehand."

"Oh, yes. She came in this weekend. The body was exhumed Saturday. I performed the autopsy on Sunday. You know that old expression, 'No rest for the weary'? Bodies in, reports out. I finished up the autopsy this morning. I was just about to send my report off to the DA."

"And the cause of death?" I asked anxiously.

"It's right here." With the sandwich in one hand Gabor twisted his computer monitor in my direction. "She was poisoned. Like the others. Although with no blood or urine samples it's trickier to find the cause in a body that's been exhumed. Fortunately we knew what we were looking for. We were able to get tissue samples that screened positively for the poison. In fact, I'd say we got lucky."

"Lucky?"

"Ms. Powers' granddaughter brought in a bottle of bath salts she believes her grandmother was using the night she died. Seems once she heard about Pepper Millhouse and Helen Howard's deaths—how they also died in the bathtubs of their homes—she got curious and went looking for something that might tie the three together. It's exactly like that the police recovered from Pepper Millhouse's home."

"Bath salts?" I felt a chill run down my back. I was right. The poison had been hidden in the bath salts. "Do you still have it?"

"Absolutely. Care to see it?"

He put the sandwich down, stood up, walked over to the door and with his large hand on the door handle paused as though he intended for me to follow him. I squeezed the arms of the chair I was sitting in and prepared to stand. Damn it, if I had to watch him pull bloody innards out of a cadaver I was going to do it. But before

I could get to my feet, giving me that large Liberace grin, he reached for a box marked evidence from within a narrow bookshelf next to the door. Returning to the desk he placed the box in front of me and pulled out a see-through plastic bag.

"Take a look."

I stood up and with the tips of my fingers on the outside of the bag tilted it toward me. Inside was a small, white apothecary jar with an ornately designed logo, Lavender Lush #7. I sat back down. It was very similar to the bath salts in my own bathroom that Eric and I had used Friday night. The only difference was that it appeared someone had added the number seven in black felt pen to the label.

"So this is it then? Adel Powers, Helen Howard and Pepper Millhouse, they were all killed with poisonous bath salts, like this one here?"

He nodded, took a bite of his sandwich, swallowed and said, "Appears so. Whoever did this chopped up bits and pieces of the monkshood plant and mixed it in with the bath salts."

"So anyone could have done it?"

"I'm afraid that's not for me to determine, it's up to the police. But it didn't take much, a little knowledge of the poison, gloves and access to the jars."

Access to the jars. I tabled that thought. I'd have to trace the origins of the jars later and figure out who had access. Meanwhile I listened as Dr. Gabor went on about how he'd nearly missed the poison, how difficult some poisons can be to detect.

"In fact, if it hadn't been for the District Attorney requesting an autopsy, we would have missed it entirely. Hate to say it, but we probably miss a lot. Particularly when you consider that with older people we don't always do autopsies. If they've had a heart condition like Pepper Millhouse did, or they've been under a doctor's care we just don't bother, and you, Miss Childs, wouldn't be here right now."

"Would you do me a favor?"

He took another bite from his sandwich then placed the plastic bag with the bottle back in the box. "What would you like me to do for you, Miss Childs?"

"Could I get a copy of the autopsy report you send to the DA?"

"It'll be posted on the website by end of day. Reporters have a special access code."

"Yes, but it'd be helpful to me if maybe I could get a copy now."

"So the green reporter from KCHC can have the results first. Is that what you'd like?"

I nodded.

"I'll email a copy, but, much as I enjoy your company, Miss Childs, I will, by five o'clock, post the results of Adel Powers' autopsy report on our website. So whatever it is you plan to do, you best hurry."

I thanked Dr. Gabor and hurried out of his office.

I knew once the coroner's report was released every news outlet in the city would be scrambling to report Adel Powers had been murdered and looking for the cause. Sam would be in the news even more than she already was now. But with a few hours lead time, maybe I could find out where the bottles of bath salts had come from and who had had access to them. With a little bit of luck, I might be able to lessen the blow of the report, maybe even cast a shadow of doubt as to whether or not Sam was really guilty. I wanted to talk to her, but to do that I needed to get hold of Mr. King, and fast.

As I left the coroner's office I picked up my cell and called Mr. King. I shared with him the results of Adel Powers' autopsy. We both knew it would only be a matter of days before Sam would be back in court again.

And this time, with the prosecutor adding to the charges against Sam to include the death of Adel Powers, it would be for a triple homicide, premeditated murder. If I was going to do anything at all to help Sam escape life in prison, or even worse the death penalty, I needed to act fast.

"This doesn't bode well for your friend, Carol, and I'm sorry to tell you, but I have even more bad news. I spoke with Byron Scott from the prosecutor's office his morning. They're required to share with us what evidence they plan to introduce at trial. I'm looking at the list of items the police took from Sam's house now, and I don't like it. It includes a bottle of bath salts believed to be contaminated with the same type of poison used to kill Pepper Millhouse and Helen Howard, and with what you just told me about Adel Powers, probably her too. Plus they found a plastic bag of dried plant cuttings by the front door. We won't know what that is until they get the results back from the lab, but it's suspicious. Also they found a pair of overalls, some gardening tools and a mortar and pestle that the prosecutor plans to introduce as evidence. He'll say she used them to grind up the poison and mix in with the bath salts."

"That all could have been planted, particularly if someone, like her sister, wanted to set her up."

"I'm afraid there's more. And it doesn't point to the sister, much as you might want it to. The police searched Sam's office. They confiscated her computer. It appears she had been surfing the Internet for information about poisons, particularly plant poisons, and they've got emails."

"Emails?" I couldn't imagine even if Sam were the murderer that she'd actually leave a trail or write anything down, that would have been too obvious.

"It's pretty contentious stuff actually. Sam certainly didn't pull any punches when it came to letting her aunt know how much she didn't like her, or what she thought of her management style. I could accept that maybe she had a rocky relationship with the woman. But in one email she even refers to Adel Powers and Helen Howard as Pepper's Pathetic Posse right in the subject line. Describes them as decrepit old stragglers and suggests Pepper, 'do us all a favor, send them off on a one way cruise, just get rid of them. I don't care how you do it just get them out of the office. They're dead weight.'"

"I'm not buying this. Not for a minute. Sure, Sam might have said she hated her aunt and in an emotional state even threatened to kill her, but write it down? I don't think so. To me it smacks of a set up. It's got to be her sister."

I gave King the four-one-one on Sarah Millhouse, telling him everything I knew, and what I thought put the burden of guilt squarely on her shoulders.

"Look, none of this would be difficult for Sarah to do. Up until a year ago she worked at the agency and now she's traipsing around with Sam's assistant, Andrew Reese. Tell me that doesn't look odd?"

"I need more than odd, Carol."

"Then get me in to see Sam. I need to find out what she knows about the bottles of bath salts, where they came from, who had access, that kind of thing. And I need to see her before five o'clock today. Before the coroner releases the results of Adel Powers' autopsy and the whole world starts to look at Sam as a serial killer. I have to find something to take suspicion off her. If I don't, and soon, she'll be judged by the court of public opinion long before she ever goes to trial. You've got to help me."

By the time I got to the radio station Kari Rhodes was wrapping up the first segment of her show with Sarah Millhouse. It seemed like Sarah was everywhere; there was no escaping her. In addition to the morning television talk shows, her picture was even on the front page of today's edition of the *LA Times*. And now, this afternoon, she was back on the air, in the studio with Kari Rhodes, and with her were Andrew Reese, Amber Marx, and Clarissa St. Clair.

I nearly bumped into Andrew as he was exiting the studio. I stepped back and let him pass before entering. He looked like a young man in a hurry, probably under orders from his new boss, Sarah, to ensure none of ACT's remaining employees mutinied before he'd had a chance to assure them she was in charge.

I walked through the studio, into the news booth and sat down. Sarah glanced in my direction, smiled then whispered something in Kari's ear. She knew I was on to her.

During the commercial break I skimmed the news reports. So

far it was a light news day. A water main had broken in the valley making a mess of traffic and a fist fight had erupted between stalled motorists. I checked my email and found that that Dr. Gabor had followed through and sent me a copy of Adel Powers' autopsy report. I saved it and closed the file. No way did I want word of Adel's autopsy to slip out until I'd had a chance to speak with Sam. It'd be one more nail in Sam's coffin if the news broke on the Kari Rhodes show, particularly with Sarah in the studio. I couldn't let that happen.

I glanced back into the broadcast booth. Clarissa and Amber sat at the other end of the console with their large purses plopped on their laps, compacts, makeup and candies strewn out on the counter in front of them. They were giggling like schoolgirls as they crouched over their cell phones, texting and sharing photos while they exchanged makeup. I was catching bits of their conversation and might not have paused long enough to listen had I not picked up that they were talking about Dek de Convero.

"And this one with Dek was taken on his boat." I watched as Clarissa held her phone up for Kari to see.

"Are you topless?" Amber grabbed the phone from Clarissa and stared at it.

"You're not supposed to see that." Clarissa wrestled the phone back.

"Well, I did. I'll bet his wife doesn't know."

Sarah Millhouse had caught the same conversation and snapped the phone from Clarissa's hand. "You need to pick that up, now." She pointed to the pile of cosmetics and cellophane wrapped candies on the table. "In case you've forgotten, we're here for a purpose."

Amber stood up and began scooping their belongings into her bag and Clarissa's as well. Whispering something into Clarissa's ear she looked as though she was about to leave.

Kari leaned over and placed a hand on top of hers. "Just a few minutes more, Amber, I promise."

"Then you better start with me." Amber slumped back down

on the stool and shoved the headphones over her small ears. "I need to get out of here; this place is claustrophobic."

If I hadn't been there I wouldn't have believed this was Hollywood's sweetheart. Before the station break she had spoken eloquently about her relationship with Pepper Millhouse and how much she would be missed. But this was a total transformation. The girl in front of me was pouting and red-faced, like a child angry to have been told to pick up her things.

Kari smoothed the situation. She started with Amber as promised and congratulated her on her most recent award as Best Supporting Actress for her role in *The Long Summer* and ended with news about her finishing *The Sorcerer's Daughter.*

"And now Amber, what's next?"

"A little R&R as Pepper used to say. I've bought a house at the beach and I think I'm going to learn to surf. How's that for fun?"

"And for you, Clarissa? Next stop is Spain and your new film, *A Lady in White...*"

I felt my phone buzz. I looked down to see a text from Eric. *Two more bodies. Call me. ASAP.*

CHAPTER 14

Two more bodies. I couldn't get out of the studio fast enough. I stood up, threw my headphones on the desk and rushed out of the news booth and into the hallway, looking for an exit, anywhere where I might be alone. I pushed through the heavy security doors at the end of the hallway to a small, isolated smokers' porch. I didn't want to risk anyone overhearing my conversation. I leaned back against the metal door as it shut and dialed Eric's number while I tried to catch my breath, my lungs filling with the stale smell of tobacco.

"What's happening?"

"I'm about to call an emergency press conference. The police got word this morning about an incident in North Hollywood and called us in. A Miss Broderick and her male companion were found dead in the woman's bathtub. Someone from her office called North Hollywood division when she didn't show up for work this morning. And guess what?"

"I don't need to guess. She works for the ACT agency, and they were soaking in the same type of bath salts that killed Pepper Millhouse."

"You got it."

I wanted to tell Eric right then about the autopsy report for Adel Powers, but there wasn't time, he'd already hung up. I felt an icy chill run down my back. Misty Dawn was right. Death was all around me. There were now five bodies.

At that moment I should have gone to Tyler Hunt. I should have done a lot of things that morning, like come in extra early and try to patch over our differences concerning my most recent infraction regarding Sam's arrest. I certainly should have told him I had a copy of Adel Powers' autopsy report. At least that's how Tyler would have liked it. But I was hesitant to give him a heads up. I knew he'd give the story to Kari, and she'd spin it. The idea of listening to her broadcasting news about Adel's death, particularly as I headed out to a scene in North Hollywood where two more bodies had been found, just wasn't acceptable to me.

Instead I pounded on the door to the men's room where I knew Tyler would be and hoped for the best.

"Got a lead on the Hollywood Murders. I'm headed out to the scene now. I'll call."

I heard a toilet flush, but didn't wait around. I was out the double doors to the lobby before Tyler could protest.

By the time I got to North Hollywood a coroner's truck and another large van marked FBI were parked in front of a small fifties bungalow. What looked like it had once been a quiet tree-lined street was now alive with activity. Police cruisers, unmarked FBI vehicles, media vans and their TV crews were all parked cattywampus, as though they had descended upon the area in a great hurry. Overhead a helicopter signaled the presence of police activity. Neighbors concerned for their safety cautiously poked their heads out from behind closed doors, and seeing the presence of the press slowly began picking their way between parked cars and gathered behind us.

Hanging my microphone on a stand in front of the house I huddled with a group of reporters behind yellow crime scene tape and called Tyler. He answered on the first ring, sounding impatient. He had obviously picked up on the press briefing and started barking orders at me like a cub reporter.

"You set to go? What do we know?"

"The police discovered two more bodies and called in the FBI—looks like it's a possible connection to the Bathtub Murders— and I have an exclusive report from the coroner's office on Adel Powers. She was poisoned like the others."

I knew now was the time to break the news on Adel's autopsy. With the discovery of two more bodies it only made sense to do it right away.

"I'd like to wrap up with the coroner's report on Adel. If it's all connected, it means the body count for the Hollywood murders just jumped up to five."

"Hold on," Tyler said.

The excitement in Tyler's voice was palpable. I could hear a series of clicks as he plugged my call into the station. In the background Kari's whiny voice asked how long did he think this *interruption* would be. I choked back a laugh. Even if I had wanted to, I couldn't have planned this any better. Kari and Sarah were being bumped off the air. Sarah would have to find another time to continue her libelous campaign against her sister.

My heart beat faster as the sound effects for KCHC's breaking news was followed by Tyler's voice.

"We interrupt this broadcast with a special report from North Hollywood where KCHC reporter Carol Childs says the FBI has found two bodies they believe may be connected to the Hollywood Bathtub Murders. Carol."

"Thank you, Tyler. I'm standing in front of the house police were called to this morning. Inside they've found two bodies. This appears to be a very fast breaking story, and we understand the FBI has been called in and is preparing to brief the press on their findings."

Before I could say anything more, Eric appeared from within the house. Looking drawn, with his jaw clenched, he walked over to the stand of microphones and introduced himself.

"I'm Special Agent Eric Langdon with the FBI. I'm here to conduct an investigation and will answer a few brief questions following this report.

"At approximately eleven forty-five this morning the North Hollywood Police Department received a call from an employee with the ACT talent agency saying he was concerned one of their staff, a Miss Heather Broderick, had not shown up for work.

Because of an open investigation involving the recent murders of several of ACT's principals, the police dispatched a cruiser to this location where they discovered the bodies of two people, a man and a woman, in the bathtub of the home."

Instantly the sound of cameras clicking and reporters shoving and shouting crowded the air.

"Why is the FBI investigating?"

"Does FBI think this is a serial killing?"

"Please." Eric raised his hands. He glanced at me momentarily then back to the crowd. "The two people whose bodies we discovered inside the house this morning appear to have died under circumstances *similar* to those we've seen with the Hollywood Bathtub Murders. In each of those incidents investigators found a bottle of bath salts, labeled Lavender Lush #7, that was later determined to be the cause of death. Today we found another bottle of Lavender Lush #7 next to the bodies, and for that reason the FBI has been asked to join a task force to investigate. In the meantime, I've called this press briefing to alert the media and to ask for their help in informing the public about the danger of these bath salts."

"Agent, are you saying the bath salts are poisonous?"

"Why type of poison are we talking about, Agent? Do we know?"

"Are we looking at product tampering? Something like we saw with the Tylenol scare back in the eighties?"

Eric stepped away from the microphones and glanced back at the house momentarily before answering.

"Let me begin by saying we don't believe there is any risk to the general public. Unlike the Tylenol scare, the bath salts we're concerned with do not appear to have been sold in any retail store. Lavender Lush #7 looks to be a privately labeled product, most likely homemade and produced on a very small scale. The victims we're investigating were also not randomly selected like they were with the Tylenol murders. They all appeared, with the exception of the man we found with Miss Broderick this morning, to have worked together. Most importantly, I want to make this very clear, we do not believe we're dealing with some random assassin or that there is any danger to the general public."

Again the sound of cameras clicking and the press hollering with questions filled the air.

"Agent, do you think Samantha Millhouse, the woman arrested last week for the murder of her aunt, Pepper Millhouse, and her associate is responsible for these murders?"

Eric shook his head. "I'm not here to comment on anyone's guilt or innocence. What I am here to do is ask for the media's help to keep the public informed."

Eric held up a colored Xeroxed photo of one of the bottles of Lavender Lush #7. It looked like it was taken from one of the crime scenes. The bottle was open, sitting on the edge of a tub. A few grains of salt appeared scattered at the base of the jar.

"What we're looking for are small white apothecary jars labeled Lavender Lush with the number seven handwritten in black felt pen next to it. Like this one here." He pointed to the photo. "If you, or anyone you know, have a bottle, please don't open it, touch it, or do anything to expose its contents. Instead, place the bottle in a plastic bag and bring it to your nearest police station. We have pictures available and appreciate your help. Please make sure you get one before you leave. Questions?"

Immediately reporters began jostling for position, pushing their mics closer toward Eric while screaming questions.

"Does the FBI have any idea how many bottles they're looking for?"

"Do we know what kind of poison it was that killed these people?"

"Right now were investigating a number of leads. As to how many bottles there may be, we just don't know. What we do know is that the bottles found contain an extremely fast acting, toxic substance, but at this time due to the sensitivity of the investigation we're not prepared to identify the exact type of poison used. Next question." Eric pointed to a reporter standing next to me who read from his notepad.

"Agent, you said that the two people in the house 'died under circumstances *similar to* those we've seen with the Hollywood murders.' Was there anything different about today's crime scene?"

"There were two people in the tub today, a man and a woman. Both Miss Millhouse and Miss Howard were alone when they died."

Eric looked as though he were about to finish when another investigator appeared from within the house. He was wearing gloves and the blue jacket marked FBI. He approached Eric and whispered something in his ear.

"I'm sorry. I've got time for just one more question." Eric nodded at me.

"Agent Langdon, can you tell me who it was from the ACT agency that called the police this morning?"

He glanced back at his notes. "Andrew Reese."

Andrew Reese? My shoulder still hurt from bumping into him as he flew out of the studio. There was no way Andrew would have known Heather Broderick hadn't come into work unless *maybe* Sarah had told him. I made a note to question him later, but right now Tyler's voice was coming through my earphone; we were live and on the air.

"Carol, if these bodies are indeed tied to the other bathtub murders that would make a total four dead, but before we went on the air a few minutes ago you told me there might be a possible fifth victim."

My throat felt dry. I swallowed hard.

"Actually, Tyler, we may very well be looking at a total of five homicides. I spoke with the coroner this morning. He had just completed an autopsy on Adel Powers, the founder of the ACT Agency. He told me they discovered evidence of poisoning exactly like that now known to have caused the deaths of Pepper Millhouse and Helen Howard."

"If I might interrupt, Carol, I have in front of me a copy of the coroner's report provided exclusively to KCHC and I can see where the name of the poison has been blacked out. Fortunately, however, via another source we've been able to learn that poison used was aconite, a plant poison, commonly known as devil weed, or monkshood. Stuff grows right here in southern California."

I couldn't believe Tyler had accessed my email, read the autopsy, and was using my notes to reveal the name of the poison. I was furious. The name of the poison was still classified. Even Eric had refused to identify it in the press conference.

"And I have to say, that while I appreciate that the FBI is always worried about copycats, I, for one, am all for public awareness."

"Excuse me, Tyler. You make this sound like there's been some type of cover-up going on. I think the FBI made it very clear that—"

"What? That no one else may be in harm's way? That they don't believe the public to be at risk? That this is a contained situation? My God, Carol, how many more innocent people have to die before we can agree there's someone out there harvesting this stuff and putting it inside bottles of bath salts? Who knows how many people have bottles exactly like this at home?"

"I think what Agent Langdon was trying to say is that Lavender Lush #7 is obviously a small privately labeled item and that the victims, unfortunate as it is, appear to all have been deliberately targeted."

"I disagree. And I find the name, Lavender Lush #7, highly coincidental. Did you know there were seven victims in the Tylenol case? That they were all killed when cyanide was slipped into capsules people thought contained acetaminophen? I'm sure when the Tylenol case first came to light that the FBI reported it was a contained situation as well, isolated to one store, one area. But we found out differently, didn't we? And now, here we have five victims all using the same bath salts tainted with aconite, one of the deadliest poisons in the world. So, my question, Carol, is this, could there be seven potential victims?"

"Certainly you're not saying because there were seven deaths in the Tylenol case and there's a number seven handwritten on the bath salts that you think there's likely to be two more murders?"

"Could be. My advice is people need to be careful. Who knows how many more victims we may have? Maybe two. Maybe three. Maybe more."

Alarm bells were going off in my head. Tyler was pushing this story over the top. He had marginalized the facts and was sensationalizing the events for the benefit of growing the number of listeners to the station. I could imagine him sitting back and smiling with the phone lines on the switchboard lighting up. I had to end this interview fast before he completely discredited everything the FBI had done that morning.

"I think, Tyler, we need to remind people if they find they have a bottle of Lavender Lush #7 they should do exactly as the FBI asked: wrap it in a plastic bag and take it to their closest police station. In the meantime, we'll continue to stay on top of this story and investigate. This is Carol Childs, live from North Hollywood."

CHAPTER 15

When I got back to the office there was a note taped to my computer screen. Tyler had obviously taken a page from my playbook. Written in large red letters on a sheet of yellow paper torn from his note pad he had written, *See me. ASAP. No excuses!*

Grabbing the note, I crushed it in my hand, marched down the hall and stood in his doorway like a soldier. I was either ready to face a firing squad or do battle. I wasn't sure which.

Tyler didn't bother to look up. His fingers continued to fly nonstop across the keyboard.

I waited.

"So how does it feel?" he asked.

My stomach roiled. I wanted to yell at him that he'd exploited the story. He had used me to do exactly what the FBI didn't want to hear happen on the air. We had created a general sense of panic. And not just about the bath salts. Listeners were calling in from all over the city frightened that bits and pieces of monkshood might be mixed into any number of their household products. Worst of all, I feared Tyler had done irreparable damage to my relationship with Eric. I doubted he would ever share a lead with me again. I measured my words carefully.

"What do you mean, how does it feel?"

"To crack a story that puts your best friend in the crosshairs of the prosecution for a serial murder of three, maybe five people. And to be the only reporter in town to have revealed the name of the poison found in the bath salts. Nice work, by the way."

"I didn't reveal the name of the poison. You did. And you knew it was classified. "

"Just doing my job, Carol." He nodded to the chair in front of his desk then looked back to his computer screen. I took two steps into his office and stood with my arms folded across my chest.

"Aconite, deadly stuff." He glanced up at me, oblivious to my anger and pointed to his computer screen. "Never heard much about it before today. In fact, I'll bet a lot of people didn't, but I'll bet they're sure to be talking about it now."

"How could you do that?" I stepped closer, putting my hands on his desk. "You stole that report off my computer."

"It says right here that in addition to being used as a poison that the Chinese use it as an herbal remedy. And get this, witches believe it actually helps them to fly. But that's not the point, is it?"

Tyler's eyes met mine, his look telling me to back off. I took my hands off his desk and crossed my arms.

"The fact is, Carol, that FBI boyfriend of yours didn't mention it deliberately. Not a word about it in his report." He nodded again to the chair. "Why don't you sit down? We need to talk."

"About what? The facts maybe?" I refused to sit; standing over him even though there was a desk between us made me feel more powerful. "Isn't that what you're always preaching to me, Tyler? Just the facts, Carol? You knew the name of the poison was classified and we couldn't use it. It was blacked out of the entire report. Just how do you explain reporting it? You may have ruined us with the FBI."

"Oh, I very much doubt that. Besides aconite wasn't blacked out in your notes."

"So you're going to put this on me?" I glared at him. There was little more I could do.

"Sit down, Carol. We need to talk." This time Tyler wasn't asking. This was a demand.

I sat down. I needed this job and, dammit, this story needed me. If I had any hope of clearing Sam's name, I had to make this work.

"Just so you know, I don't have any problem being the first to report on the nature of the poison and you shouldn't either. That's what we do. If we didn't do it some other station would have. It's a race and today we won. You should be happy."

"But you blew the story out of proportion, trying to make it sound like there's some connection between the Tylenol murders from years ago and these bath salts. You know that's ridiculous."

"Do I? The only thing I know for certain is the FBI is investigating and that they're withholding information. Valuable information the public has a right to know."

"This is a murder investigation, Tyler. They always leave something out. Some clue that will help them identify the real killer."

"Maybe, or maybe there's something about this case and the Tylenol murders they don't want the public to know. But the truth is, Carol, it's an old argument; need-to-know versus right-to-know. And it's why this little romance between you and Agent Langdon is doomed."

I bit my tongue and looked away. I didn't want Tyler to see the concern on my face. I was already worried what Eric would think when he heard the report.

"Law enforcement and reporters, Carol, we're on opposite sides. For them, it's what they think we, the general public, need to know: how much, when and who knows it. But for those of us in news, it's always going to be the right to know. You may think I sensationalized the story, but I just helped you fill in the facts. Gave people what they have a right to know. If you don't like that, you're probably not in the right business."

"I think you could have handled it better."

"Like you did with the autopsy report for Miss Powers? Weren't you withholding that until after Kari's show?"

I didn't answer. I looked away.

There was an awkward silence then Tyler said, "I have something you need to see. Something I found in Kari's office."

I glanced back at Tyler. *Really?*

"Not that I was snooping."

"No. Of course not," I said sarcastically. Leaning back in my chair I folded my arms in front of me. "Why would you do that?"

"Because I was looking for cigarettes when I found this."

Tyler gave me one of his quick geeky smiles then disappeared beneath his desk. Moments later he resurfaced, his face red. In his hand was a small bottle wrapped in Kleenex. He placed it on the desk between us, carefully turning it around so that I could read the label, Lavender Lush. It was exactly like the bottle I had at my house.

"Look familiar?"

My eyes went from the bottle to Tyler's. I wasn't about to tell him that less than forty-eight hours ago Eric and I had been soaking in a tub of Lavender Lush from a bottle exactly like the one sitting in front of me now.

"Where did you get that?"

"Like I said, I found it in Kari's office. It was in a basket where she throws all those promo items she gets from her Hollywood parties."

I grabbed another wad of Kleenex—I wasn't taking any chances—and held the bottle by the top. With the tips of my fingers I twisted it around so that I could clearly see its markings on both the front and the back of the bottle. The packaging looked like some homemade specialty gift, a small white apothecary jar with an ornately designed logo complete with little lavender flowers cascading about the edges of the label. I looked at Tyler.

"May I have this?"

"No, I don't think so." He placed the bottle back below his desk and told me we were done for the day. "Carol, I hope you appreciate I helped you today. Not many reporters get the lead on a big story like this. Don't disappoint me."

CHAPTER 16

Five bodies and not one phone call. Not from Sam's attorney or from Eric, not even a text message. It was past midnight and I drove home in complete silence, checking my voicemail like an addict.

The day had gone from bad to worse. It began with Sarah Millhouse spilling her heart out on the air like some vanquished queen grateful to have been returned to what she believed was her rightful position as the head of the ACT Agency. And it ended with Tyler Hunt sabotaging my report on the deaths of the two victims in North Hollywood, revealing the name of the poison. It was no wonder Eric hadn't returned any of my calls.

I was too keyed-up to sleep. Frustrated that King hadn't gotten back to me about Sam and worried Tyler might be right about my relationship with Eric. Maybe it was doomed. Or maybe I wasn't cutthroat enough to be a reporter. Either way, as I pulled into the garage beneath the condos, I decided it was time I did a little detective work. I'd worry about my love life and my job later. Right now, I needed to find out where the bottles of bath salts had come from, and if Sam couldn't talk to me, I could at least go looking.

It was past midnight as I entered the courtyard and hurried toward Sam's front door. A full moon sent splintered light beneath the leaves of the big oak tree and shadows danced with a cool breeze in front of me like some alien presence. Fumbling with the lock, I glanced nervously over my shoulders, half expecting to see Misty in the shadows. Finally, I felt the lock release in my hand and gave the door a shove. It opened with a thud. I nearly fell inside.

Grabbing the door for balance, I took a deep breath.

Even in the dark I could tell Sam's place was a mess. I flipped on a light to get a better look. The cops had done only a cursory job of cleaning up. Things looked like they had been tossed back with little care or thought as to their order. Stacks of books and photo albums were strewn on tables and onto the bookshelves. Bigger books appeared to have been haphazardly placed atop smaller books, and a large pile had fallen to the floor.

I walked over to the bookcase and picked up a photo album. The spine of the book had broken, the pages ready to fall out. I put it back on the shelf and looked around. I didn't know exactly what I was looking for. But if the cops had found enough evidence in Sam's condo to charge her with the murder there had to be something else, something I might find that would explain why Sam had a bottle of Lavender Lush #7 in her condo. She couldn't have known it was poisonous. In my mind, it was more likely Sam was an intended victim, or that maybe she was being set up. Whatever it was, I needed to find something to prove it.

I started with the bathroom. If the cops had found the bath salts under the sink, maybe I'd get lucky there too. But the cabinets were empty. The police had taken everything, makeup, creams, toiletries; the only things left were a few stray bobby pins, towels and sheets. In the bedroom there was nothing. The curtains on the wall had been pulled back from the window, the mattress striped and turned. I moved on to the kitchen. The cabinets were in complete disarray. Dishes, glasses, pots and pans had been jammed back in with little regard to any semblance of order. Sam would be furious. She was a stickler for keeping things neat. I was about to give up and declare my late night snoop a failure when I remembered I needed to check for cat food and opened the door to the pantry.

Unexpectedly a large open canister of kitty kibble fell to the ground, and a rat the size of a large hamster jumped out and raced across the floor. I shrieked and, grabbing a broom, swatted after the creature, but he was too fast. I looked down at my feet. Spilling out from the cabinet in front of me was a trail of cat food leading all the way into the living room.

I took out the portable vacuum to go after those pieces that had rolled into the living room when I noticed a snapshot laying on the floor in front of the bookshelf. It must have fallen from the album when I placed it back on the shelf.

I took the album from the shelf and before I could even open it more photos fell from my hands and onto the floor. Whoever had put it back had stuffed them into the sleeve without thought to their contents. I picked them up and began sorting through them. Even in the dim light I could see they were all photos from a birthday party. Pictures of Pepper Millhouse and her guests wearing party hats, toasting with champagne, cutting the cake and laughing. I stopped when I came to a photo of Pepper with Adel and Helen. They stood arm in arm, smiling for the camera, the date on the photo, December 14. In just six weeks they'd all be dead.

With a sense of urgency I sat down cross legged on the floor and began flipping through the pictures. There had to be something here. Pepper's parties were all elaborate affairs. Sam would work weeks ahead organizing them, going over guest lists, menus and talent. Nothing was ever left to chance. Pepper loved themed events, well planned out and with souvenirs to commemorate the occasion. She would never let her guests leave without a parting gift. Staring at the photos it occurred to me, as though the thought had come out of thin air. *Lavender Lush had to have been a party favor!* It all made sense: the victims and the connection to the agency. The evidence was right here in front of me. Somewhere in my hands there had to be a picture of the party favors. If I could find the right photo, something showing the bath salts, I could prove Pepper's party was the distribution source. This was where the bottles had come from.

I flipped through the pictures quickly, like playing cards. I'd know what I needed when I saw it. Most of the stack was useless, but I paused when I came to a photo of Dek de Convero and his wife Kim LaSalle with Pepper. They were all smiling for the camera.

Pepper had her birthday cake in hand. Dek had his arm around his wife. There was a slight space between them, but nothing unusual. If it had been me, after what Pepper had done to nearly break up my marriage, I wouldn't have been standing there smiling for the camera. I would have wanted to kill her. But Hollywood, like politics, makes for strange bedfellows. I decided I'd keep the photo and stuffed it into my bag. As far as I was concerned, Kim LaSalle was still a person of interest.

There was another curious photo of Pepper's housekeeper, Arminta, and a baby, and a group shot of Pepper cutting her birthday cake, but still nothing that showed the bath salts. Then another photo did catch my eye. This one of Sarah Millhouse and Misty Dawn—my number one and two suspects—their heads together, smiling. They looked like they'd both had a little too much to drink. I stared at the photo, curious about their connection and was about to put it aside when my cell buzzed.

I glanced at the flashing screen. Caller ID was blocked. Hopeful it might be Eric, I picked up, anxious to share with him my theory about the bath salts. "Hi." I smiled in anticipation.

"Carol! I'm glad you picked up. I've been so worried. Those young people, the ones the FBI found dead in the tub this morning? I warned you there'd be more, and believe me I'm worried this may not be the end of it."

"Misty?" I put my hand on my chest. My heart was pounding. Outside a sudden breeze caused some branches to brush against the living room window. Their scratching sounded as though someone were trying to get in. I stood up and with one hand pulled back the drapery. The courtyard was quiet. Gray dappled shadows from the moonlight danced beneath the big oak tree. Inside the room was beginning to feel claustrophobic. "It's one-thirty in the morning. Why are you calling me now?"

"We need to talk. About the bottles the FBI found. They're mine."

"Yours?"

"I suppose I should have put the two together when Pepper

died, particularly after both Helen Howard and Adel Powers passed away in their baths. Poor dears. But then, why would I? It's not like I go around making poisoned potions."

I wasn't so certain. I gripped the phone tighter. "But they were your bottles, right?"

"Of course they were mine. That's what I'm trying to tell you. Lavender Lush is one of my better products. Marvelous for the skin. Soothing yet stimulating with a bouquet of lavender and musk, a bit of an aphrodisiac, but then you already know that."

I thought I heard a giggle.

"Misty." I stopped her, my voice deadly serious. "Did you make up the bottles of Lavender Lush for Pepper's birthday party and is that why you think there might be more deaths? Because you know there're more bottles out there?" I was pushing her. She had to know something.

"Oh, goodness, Carol, there you go again. Thinking I've done it. After all our conversations and that lovely soak in the tub with your handsome young agent friend, you should know better."

"Misty." I wasn't going to let her lead the conversation back to my personal life. "That's not why you called."

"No, it's not." She sounded more focused now. "I wanted to make sure you got my message."

"What message?" I was tempted to look at my cellphone for some evidence of a missed call, but I knew better.

"About the bottles of Lavender Lush. They were party favors. I've been messaging you non-stop since I first realized the bottles the FBI found were mine. Unfortunately I'd no way of knowing if you'd picked on my thoughts. I had to call. But now that I know you realized the bottles were party favors, and I've told you they were mine, my work is done here, at least for tonight. I think we work very well together. Don't you?"

I didn't answer. I glanced down at the stack of pictures in my hand from Pepper's party. I felt a chill run down my back. If this wasn't a confession it was pretty damn close. If Misty hadn't made up the poisonous bottles of bath salts perhaps she knew who did.

Maybe she was testing the waters to see how much I knew.

"Oh, and one more thing, I keep getting this vision of you. You're looking for something, a picture maybe. Don't worry. You'll find it. You're very close. Ciao."

I shoved the phone back in my pocket and took one last look at the pictures in my hand. I was about to put them back on the shelf when I saw it.

Misty was right. As if by magic, or perhaps Misty-power, there in my hand was a photo of Kari Rhodes and Pepper Millhouse. A candid shot of the two of them together with Pepper's hands on Kari's shoulders, her lips puckered, while Kari leaned in for a Hollywood kiss. But what caught my attention was the bag Kari held in her hand. A goodie bag, and from the top of it I could see the bottle of Lavender Lush.

Finally, I had proof. Kari had been given a bottle of Lavender Lush at Pepper's party. No doubt Sam, too, had brought a bottle of the bath salts home, maybe several bottles. Later, she'd given me one. She probably hadn't even noticed the difference in the labeling, that some had been marked with a black felt pen, the deadly number seven. She had no idea the poison they contained.

I wanted to talk to Eric. I had so much to tell him. I wanted to let him know about Misty's call and that I found where the bottles of Lavender Lush had come from and how Tyler had commandeered my report and leaked the name of the poison. But most of all, I wanted to tell him how lucky we were, that Sam had mixed up the bottles of bath salts she'd given me, and kept the bottle marked Lavender Lush #7 for herself. That she couldn't possibly be guilty. But he wasn't returning my calls.

CHAPTER 17

The next day Tyler Hunt startled me. I had just started my newscast when he walked in on the Kari Rhodes show and with him, nearly causing me to stumble through my lead story, was Eric. His eyes quickly scanned the room and meeting mine, looked away before I could get a read on why he was here. If it wasn't for the fact that I was on the clock and reading from a stack of news stories I might have been rendered speechless.

I glanced over at Kari for some clue as to his presence and got nothing. Per her usual mid-day break Kari was ignoring me, sitting on her stool, reading some Hollywood tabloid and nibbling away at what she considers lunch: a handful of sunflower seeds, a couple pieces of dried fruit and a bottle of some vile looking green glop she swears by. When Kari caught site of Eric, she nearly slid off her perch. The scene was almost comical. She caught herself, ran her hands through her hair and smiled coquettishly. Eric has that effect on women. Tall, cool, with a certain cadence to his walk that could cause a woman's mind to wander. Tyler on the other hand, with his red hair, stovepipe pants, and high top tennis shoes, is more like a cold shower. I had to choke back a laugh. Not an easy thing to do while in the midst of a broadcast.

When I finished my report I took my time stuffing my notes and my reporters' pad into my bag. I was curious to hear how Tyler had convinced Eric to come to the station, particularly after yesterday's broadcast. I didn't have to wait long. Before I reached the door Tyler was tapping on the glass to the news booth.

"Carol, would you come in here, please? There's something I need you to do."

Despite the mind numbing commercials that played in the background I could hear the blood pulsating in my ears as I walked past Eric from the news booth and into the studio. I had no idea what I was getting into.

"I called Agent Langdon here today because I realized that we actually had a bottle of Lavender Lush right here at the station." Tyler smiled and nodded for me to take a seat.

"Really? And he agreed? After *you* accused the FBI yesterday of down-playing the importance of the investigation?" I looked at Tyler then back at Eric. "I'm surprised he even took your call. I got the feeling the FBI might not be returning any KCHC calls ever." I put my bag on the floor and sat down across the console from Eric, my eyes searching his. He remained pokerfaced.

"Relax, Carol. I'm certain Agent Langdon understands how things between the press and those charged with protecting our national interests can be, shall we say, less than cozy. We all have our jobs to do. I have mine, you have yours, and Agent Langdon his."

Taking the bottle of Lavender Lush Tyler had shown me last night, he placed it on the console, directly in front of Kari. "Recognize this?" he asked.

Hugging herself with her skinny arms across her chest, Kari leaned in closer and squinted at the bottle. "It looks similar to the one the FBI found with the young couple in North Hollywood. I saw a picture of it in the paper."

"Only this bottle's not marked with the number seven," I said. "Like the bottle from yesterday, or those found with the other Hollywood bathtub murders." I started to reach for the bottle, but Eric held his hand up and shook his head. *Don't.* Again I searched his eyes for some clue as to what he was thinking, but his focus was on Kari.

"Carol's right, Kari; the other bottles were all marked with a number seven and contained, as we all now know after Tyler's report yesterday, the deadly poison aconite." Eric gave Tyler a reproachful look, then picked up the bottle, opened it, and spilled the contents out onto the console. "This however," he said, rubbing the salt between his fingers, "is simply a bottle of bath salts, a very nice bottle in fact, and quite harmless." Eric glanced over at me. "Quite nice," he added. I caught a slight twitch at the side of his mouth and resisted the urge to smile. I sat down and looked away. "I suspect, Kari, that you know where it came from."

"Me?" Kari's eyebrows arched as she peered over the top of her designer glasses at Eric. "Why would I know?"

"Because," Tyler said, "I found it in your office last night when I was looking for a cigarette. It was in a box under your desk."

"My desk." Kari sat upright. Her chin dropped, her mouth forming a perfect letter O as her eyes clicked from Tyler to the bottle and back to Eric. Suddenly it came to her. "Oh, my gosh. I forgot all about it. Is it connected to the murders?"

"Let's just say, it's why Agent Langdon's here," Tyler said. "You see when I phoned last night and told him about the bottle of Lavender Lush I'd found at the station—exactly as the FBI asked us all to do—I'm afraid my call wasn't particularly well received." Tyler paused and, tilting his head in Eric's direction, rolled his eyes. "It seems Agent Langdon didn't care for the way we handled our report of the murders in North Hollywood yesterday, but they had a break in the case. They've discovered where the bottles of bath salts have come from." My eyes met Eric's. "I suggested that since he had news and believes our reports have upset the public, perhaps he'd like to come by the station for a little air time of his own. Of course it didn't hurt that I told him you'd be doing the interview, Carol."

Tyler looked at me and smiled smugly.

I nearly laughed out loud. Tyler's premeditated slip about the poison yesterday had put KCHC front and center for news about the murders, factual or otherwise. No other station in town had even come close to the coverage we'd given the story. He had successfully created a media storm. Our call lines were being flooded with worried and panicked listeners, and Tyler was loving every minute of it. What better choice would the FBI have than to address the issue via our airwaves, where they could instantly reach the largest, most misinformed audience in the marketplace?

"Sixty seconds, Ms. Rhodes."

Tyler nodded for me to sit next to him then instructed Kari to open the show, explaining to her fans the discovery of the bath salts and introducing Agent Langdon. "After that let Carol take the interview. That work for you, Agent Langdon?"

Eric nodded.

I sat down and reached into my bag and took out the stack of photos I'd been carrying around with me from Sam's condo. Gently placing them on the console in front of me, I folded my hands over them. I wanted Eric to know I knew something about the bottles as well. Eric eyes glanced curiously at the pile then back at me. *What's this?* I wished I could've have had a few moments with Eric alone, briefed him on my findings and particularly Misty's strange call last night, but I had no choice. We were live and about to go on the air. I smiled and waited for my cue.

"Welcome back, darlings! You're listening to the Kari Rhodes Show, and friends, before we begin, let me share with you that during the station break my programming director, Tyler Hunt, came to me with shocking news. He found a bottle of Lavender Lush—exactly like that the FBI issued a warning about yesterday—in my office! I can't tell you how shaken I am. To think that I had, in my possession, a bottle of these very same bath salts—or frighteningly similar anyway—to those used in the Hollywood Bathtub Murders. Thank goodness the FBI informs me there was no poison in my bottle. But to think that I have been that close, or perhaps could have even been a target myself, is chilling."

The three of us exchanged a look. Even in the midst of breaking news concerning a mass murder investigation Kari had found a way to make it about her before finally turning the show over to me.

I thanked Kari and adjusted my headset.

"Agent Langdon, I understand you're here this morning

because you've had a break in the case. Some good news, that you've discovered the original distribution point for the bath salts."

"We have, Carol. But before we begin I'd like to say I know there's been a lot of concern, particularly with some of your listeners, that the FBI's played down the threat to the general public and held back vital information." Eric glanced dismissively over at Tyler. "I'd like to restate that we've confirmed the bottles of Lavender Lush were never available at any retail location, and that we feel confident the general public was never in any danger. We take threats like this very seriously."

I could feel Tyler's elbow in my side. A sharp jab, a subtle reminder to stay focused. He expected tough questions. If I didn't ask, he would.

"However, Agent, after yesterday's grim discovery of the two bodies in North Hollywood, there is a concern the general public could be in danger. We know one of the victims, Heather Broderick, was an employee of the ACT Agency, but what about the other victim, the young man Miss Broderick was with? Has the FBI been able to determine who he was?"

Tyler leaned back and crossed his arms, his legs wrapped around the stool.

"His name was Michael Sanford, and you're right, Mr. Sanford was not affiliated with the ACT Agency. He was a twenty-one year-old college student from Cal State Northridge who appears to have been in the wrong place at the wrong time. After yesterday's press conference we received information identifying the bottle of bath salts as a party favor, given out at a birthday party for Ms. Pepper Millhouse. We believe Miss Broderick brought the bottle of Lavender Lush #7 home with her after attending the party for her former employer last December and was using it last night to celebrate with her friend, Mr. Sanford. We found an open bottle of champagne by the tub in addition to the bath salts."

I closed my eyes momentarily. I could imagine the scene. This so easily could have been Eric and me. The champagne, the celebration, the bath. I pushed forward.

"The information, identifying the bath salts as party favors for Ms. Millhouse, where did it come from?"

"I can only say it came from a source close to the investigation, someone who has asked to remain anonymous."

I had no doubt Eric's source was Sarah Millhouse. I knew it wasn't Misty. If she'd talked to Eric last night she would have told me. What worried me was that Sarah had Eric's ear and I knew she'd be pointing a finger at her sister. I needed to tread lightly.

"May we assume then, Agent, that this unidentified source has also provided you with a guest list for the party, and that those persons who attended have been contacted concerning the possibility they may have in their possession a bottle of the poisonous bath salts?"

"You may, but—"

"Then it's possible, isn't it, that those guests who attended the party, like Samantha Millhouse, may have gone home with a bottle of the poisonous bath salts and not known it."

"It is. However—"

I couldn't let Eric finish; I needed to make a point. If I could cast the least amount of doubt onto Sam she might come out of this interview sounding less like a serial killer and more like the victim I believed she was. I jumped in with another question. "But in Samantha case's, the police found the bottle at her home and arrested her. Is that correct?"

"I believe there was other evidence that led to her arrest. However, Carol, I'm not here to comment on the investigation concerning Samantha Millhouse. I am here to focus on the missing bottles of bath salts. It's important for your listeners to know that, because of the nature of Hollywood, party gifts, like these, are often re-gifted. It's very possible someone may have unknowingly received a bottle of the bath salts and will try to use them. So once again, we're asking for the public's help, to be on the lookout for bottles of bath salts like that we found yesterday."

Eric continued to describe the bottles of Lavender Lush while I looked down at the photos in front of me, lifting my hand slightly to get a better look. I had what I needed. I glanced back at Eric.

"Do we know exactly how many bottles there may be?"

"We have a guest list of one hundred and thirty. As for how many bottles were marked with a number seven and may be poisonous, we don't know."

"Does the FBI know where the bottles came from? I mean before the party? Who might have had access?"

"We're talking to a number of different people."

"Suspects perhaps?"

Eric smiled.

"Let's just say, persons of interest."

"In addition to Samantha Millhouse, then?"

I slid the stack of photos across the desk. On top was a picture of Misty and Sarah standing by the gift table with bottles of Lavender Lush clearly evident from inside the clear plastic gift bags.

Eric glanced down at the picture, then back at me, a look of surprise on his face.

"Again, I can't comment."

I thanked Eric and finished the interview, recapping the FBI's request that the public remain on the lookout for missing bottles of Lavender Lush. Tyler looked at me and smiled. I knew Tyler couldn't find fault with my interview. I'd asked the tough questions, and I'd survived his intimidating jab in the ribs. The question was, had my relationship?

Eric stood up, tossed his headphone onto the console, then leaned over and whispered in my ear. "We need to talk, Carol. Now."

CHAPTER 18

I wasn't at all certain how this *talk* was going to go, or for that matter exactly what it was Eric wanted to speak to me about. Was this going to be a conversation concerning my investigation techniques? Or perhaps something of a more personal nature—and dammit if it were—why hadn't he called last night?

Walking to the car several steps ahead of Eric, I convinced myself this was going to be the big brush off. Maybe Tyler was right about media and law enforcement. We don't mix. On a good day there might be some mutual admiration between us, but inevitably there would be a line drawn in the sand and we would stand and look at one another like we existed in parallel universes. *I should just turn around and tell him to forget it.* I quickened my pace. And then the sky opened up and the rain started to come down like sharp needles. Eric put his arm around me, the warmth of his body against mine. We jogged toward the car, dodging rain drops. Any other time this might have been a romantic chase through a rain shower, but now it felt oddly different, worrisome. I held my purse over my head, trying to keep my hair from looking like it was plastered to my face—if this was going to be the big breakup I wanted to at least look good. Reaching the car, he smiled and opened the door.

I got in.

I watched though the windshield as he ran around to the driver's side. Tall, trim, good looking. My stomach turned. I hadn't had a lot of luck with romantic relationships. I was tone deaf when it came to understanding the typical female role. But with Eric I was beginning to think that I was capable of harmonizing and liking it. *Dammit, why couldn't we make this work?*

Eric took a seat behind the wheel and, glancing over his shoulder, pulled out of the parking space reserved for the station's VIP visitors.

I took a deep breath and looked out the window.

"I'm sorry I didn't call last night," he said.

A burning sensation started behind my eyes. I squeezed them shut. I didn't want this case to come between us.

"It's been non-stop since we found those kids yesterday," he said.

"I'm surprised you agreed to Tyler's interview."

"I didn't." Eric glanced over at me and winked. "I agreed to be interviewed by you."

I felt a small twinge of relief. In that small gesture I knew if there were any issues between us he'd tabled them.

"I need to ask you about those pictures. Where did you get them?"

"Let's just say someone you know wanted me to find them."

"Misty?"

"She called last night. I was at Sam's, getting food for the cat, when I came across them. She told me the bottles of Lavender Lush are all hers. You know that, right?"

We stopped for a light. Eric looked over at me, "Like I said, we need to talk. You got time for lunch?"

I've never met Burt Marx. In fact, the only time I'd ever heard about him was when his daughter Amber accused her father of Pepper's murder. Beyond that, I knew nothing. But Eric did and evidently so did the FBI. In fact, the man had quite a dossier.

According to Eric, Burt was a conscientious objector the FBI had lost interest in years ago. In the sixties, he had been an antiwar protester, a grassroots organizer of peace marches. The report said Burt and a group of free loving hippies had settled in Topanga

Canyon where they established a commune called The Village. Ultimately, the group did little more than show up at peace rallies, sing protest songs and smoke a little pot. Eventually, the FBI closed its file.

"Not many members of the Village are still around. Save for Burt. Most moved on, cut their hair, got married, had families and went on to teach, write, or climb corporate ladders somewhere."

"Most?"

"I'll let Burt explain. He runs a small restaurant along with an organic food co-op in the canyon. Food's pretty good. You'll like it."

Burt's Place wasn't easy to spot, particularly in the rain. If Eric hadn't known the location we probably would have driven right by. The road through Topanga Canyon is steep, narrow and twisted, populated by the occasional little hamlet of small cabins and shops all looking like they'd promise a lot in the way of peace and tranquility, but not much in the way of parking.

Halfway up the canyon a fruit stand advertised locally grown organic foods and a crudely made sign pointed in the direction of the café. We parked alongside the road. It was still raining. Eric got out, ran around to my side of the car and opened the door. Holding his coat over my head and with his arm around me we ran beneath tree branches, dodging puddles as we hopscotched across an old bridge to the restaurant.

"You're back." A voice hollered from beyond the porch where we stood beneath a wooden overhang, shaking the rain from our clothes.

I looked up to see a man emerging from a small forest of trees that encircled an old cabin, maybe three hundred feet from where we stood. He waved, one arm over his head and smiled.

This had to be Burt Marx. He looked exactly as I had imagined, a sixty-something, aging ex-hippy with a graying ponytail. He was tall, slim and wearing a worn, vintage Bob Dylan t-shirt, torn jeans, sandals and a weather beaten old bucket hat to protect him from the rain.

"I figured when I heard 'bout those bodies yesterday that you'd be back." Burt stepped up on to the porch, took his hat off and shook the rain from the brim.

"I'm not here about that," Eric said, "unless maybe you know something you're not sharing?"

"Don't know anything more than what I already told you." Burt stomped his feet on the mat then opened the door to the café. A set of cowbells rang as we entered.

The café had a rustic charm about it. Despite the gray skies outside, windows from a high beamed ceiling and overlooking the creek bed gave the room both light and sound. I could hear the creek bubbling as we entered. It looked like a small hunting lodge, warm and inviting with its wood floors and a river rock fireplace. A peace symbol made from the same stones from the river had been crafted into the mantle. A dozen roughhewn tables and chairs filled the room. On the center of each was a small vase with colorful wild flowers.

"Who's this?" Burt asked.

"Carol, meet Burt." Eric handled the introductions. "Burt, this is Carol Childs. She's the reporter who broke the story about Pepper Millhouse's murder."

"Wasn't me who did it." Burt looked at me then nodded toward a table in the corner. "Believe me, I had plenty of reason. Your friend here knows that."

"She's not here about you, Burt. Seems the two of you have someone in common. I thought maybe you might be the best person to explain the connection."

Picking up a couple of menus, Burt led us to a table in the corner that overlooked the creek. "I'll put some water on for tea. Your girlfriend here looks cold and could probably use one of our special brews. May take a while. Go ahead and make yourselves at home. Have a look around if ya like. Lots of history on these walls."

We were just about to sit down when Eric's cell rang. He glanced at the caller ID then walked away, looking serious. I sat down at the table alone. It was a work of art with wood burned peace symbols and names from the past. With my index finger I began tracing the names and wondering about the faces that might have gone with them. Heather, Moonbeam, Joy, Sage, Misty.

Misty?

So this was the connection. The reason Eric wanted me to meet Burt. I looked over at Eric. He'd moved across the room and stood with the phone pressed to his ear, his eyes focused on the creek bed below. Whoever was on the other end of the line had his attention. I got up and started to study the photos that lined the wall, a black and white history of the Village's former occupants.

There were pictures of members of the commune, all of them young with their hair long and wearing beads, bellbottoms and headbands. In some they were standing around a campfire, in others, a group of girls, wearing nothing more than beads and a smile, posed naked for the camera. In all of them they were flashing peace symbols. I moved along the wall, over to the cash register, where there were more recent photos of the Marx family. One of Burt with his wife, April, looked like it had been taken on their wedding day. She was in a white cotton caftan and obviously very pregnant. Burt was easily twenty years her senior and wearing a white beaded shirt, a full beard and what looked like the same pair of sandals he had on now. But even with the obvious age difference, they appeared happy.

Next to their wedding photo another picture showed Amber with her mother and father kayaking on what looked like a family vacation. There were no photos of Amber alone, no signed fan photos or publicity shots like those in the small stores and specialty shops in Hollywood. Here there were only family photos, nothing to indicate that this was the former homestead of the famous Amber Marx. In the pictures she looked like a normal kid hanging out with her folks.

From across the room I could hear Eric finishing up his call. The look on his face said the news wasn't good. We both returned to the table.

"Kim LaSalle just called the police. She was listening to the Kari Rhodes show this morning and remembered bringing home a bottle of bath salts from Pepper's party. It's Lavender Lush and it's marked with the number seven."

"Kim LaSalle was a target?" I hadn't expected that. I looked down at the creek bed. "I actually thought she might even be behind the murders." I shared with Eric how Kim, months ago, had tried to go after Pepper with a knife, and how Sam had covered up the story, claiming Kim was suffering from an addiction to pain pills. "You think if Kim was targeted, that Tyler's theory about the number seven might be right?"

"It could be. With five deaths and Kim LaSalle finding another poisonous bottle this morning, I'm open to thinking a lot of things before another body shows up dead."

"Including that Misty Dawn might be involved?"

Eric shook his head.

"Sorry to disappoint you, but no. We talked to Misty again early this morning. She told me about your conversation last night. She wants to help, Carol. I know she's spooky, but she's no more guilty of product tampering than the makers of Tylenol were back in the eighties. Plus she'd have nothing to gain by poisoning the very people that promoted her. It'd ruin her business."

"But they were Misty's bottles."

"We know the bottles of bath salts belonged to Misty. We also know that on the afternoon of Pepper's party, Samantha called her sister and asked her to drive out to Santa Clarita where Misty was working on the set of *The Sorcerer's Daughter*. She asked her to pick up the bottles. Seems Misty had called Sam and told her she was running late, and was afraid she wouldn't be able to get to the party on time. So Sarah picked up the bottles and dropped them by the agency. They were in her office all afternoon. Sam's prints are all over them."

"So, then Sarah did have access. She could have done it."

Eric shook his head and rolled his eyes. I could read his expression before he spoke.

"I doubt Sarah's IQ is as high as her body temperature. Barely normal. The woman's just not bright enough to have pulled this off.

Whoever did this was smart. It took planning and lots of patience."

I glanced back out the creek bed. So far Eric had dismissed my two prime suspects. I didn't agree with him. In my mind, Sarah, Misty and maybe Andrew were all in this together, but I could see it was going to take more than a hunch on my part to convince him.

"What if all these murders aren't related? What if Heather Broderick and her boyfriend were an accident?"

"Go on." Eric folded his arms across his chest and leaned back in the chair.

"I keep thinking about the pictures I took from Sam's place. The party, the people, there's something there." I pulled the stack of photos from my bag and began dealing them out like playing cards on the table, pointing to each as I spoke. "Look. In all of these photos, Pepper Millhouse is surrounded by friends and clients. Here she's with her business partners, Adel and Helen. Here she's with her nieces, Sam and Sarah, and over here it's Pepper with her favorite clients, Kim LaSalle, Amber Marx and Clarissa St. Clair. But where's Heather Broderick? There's only one shot in all these pictures with Heather in it, and she's not with Pepper, not in any of them. She's by herself, alone by the gift table." I pushed the photo of Heather Broderick closer to him.

"So what are you saying?"

"I'm saying I don't think Heather Broderick was a target any more than her friend Michael Sanford. He wasn't connected to the agency and Heather wasn't a major player. Certainly not like Pepper and her business partners. She was a nobody. Out of this whole pile, there's only one picture of her. And in it, she's alone, standing by the gift table, looking more like the hired help than a guest. If you ask me, I think she took a gift bag home with her that was meant for someone else."

Eric's eyes met mine and held steady. I felt a flash of heat pass between us before he looked back at the photos.

"Whoever's been targeting the agency had no reason to go after Heather. She was too low on the totem pole. If someone really wanted to hurt the ACT Agency, they'd go after Pepper, Adel,

Helen, Sam, and maybe some of the talent, like Kim LaSalle."

"Carol, the District Attorney's not going to agree Sam's a victim. As far as he's concerned, she's been arrested on three, very possibly five, murder charges and he's looking to make it stick." Eric stared down at the photos, "However, there is another possibility." He spun the photos around for me to see. "There's one person who's not in any of these, but who's very involved in the agency."

"Who?"

"Andrew Reese."

I stared at the pictures in front of me like I was looking at them for the first time. Andrew Reese wasn't in a single one. But he had to have been at Pepper's party. He was far too involved in the day-to-day activities of the agency not to be.

"You're right. He was also the one who reported Heather Broderick hadn't come into work, and he had to have been at the agency when Sarah brought the bottles by."

Why hadn't I thought of Andrew before? He wasn't just Sarah's lackey. He was close to both sisters and no doubt knew about Misty and her magic potions, and when Sam was arrested it was Andrew who called Sarah to come back to the agency to help out.

Moments later, Burt returned with a basket of warmed croissants, wrapped in a red checkered cloth napkin and a pot of freshly brewed tea, still steaming.

"So, you want to know about Misty, do you?"

I nodded as he placed the basket on the table.

"Real free spirit that one. She was part of the original clan who settled with us here in the Village, back in the sixties. Came out of nowhere, driving up the canyon in this flower painted VW van with peace symbols and signs all over it. Said she was selling love potions. Kind of like the song, maybe you remember."

"Love Potion #9?" I looked at Eric, my eyes wide, the voice in my head screaming so loud, he had to know what I was thinking. Clearly Misty had escalated from love potions to death salts.

"Even back then some people thought she might be a witch. She claims to be a seer, says she hears voices. She's always been a bit odd with all her herbs and potions. Fact is, I think she's a little crazy." He laughed slightly as he put a set of utensils down in front of us then stood back from the table. "But she can make a believer out of you. Her predictions are right on. Told me years ago a young nymph would be the love of my life. Said I'd meet her by the creek bed and we'd live together in the light and then one day she'd disappear 'neath the dark waters."

"And that's what happened?"

"Just like she said it would. One day this beautiful young woman was standing barefoot on the rocks in the middle of the creek bed, right there." He pointed out the window to the river. "I remember it like yesterday. Sun was out, not like today. I think she'd been rock hopping up the canyon. Her back was to me and she had this long wavy blond hair, down to her hips that framed her figure. I'll never forget it. She was bathed in this golden light and when she turned and looked at me, those emerald eyes of hers, they were mesmerizing."

"Where did she come from?"

"Don't know, a groupie maybe. She wanted to know all about the village, who lived here, what happened, that kind of thing. I used to get a lot of that around here and I'd chase 'em off. I became pretty much of a hermit after everyone moved on. Didn't want the interference, but April was different. We got married not long after that." Burt turned away from the window and nodded to Eric. "Better watch out, Agent, Misty may still have some of that love potion round; certainly changed my life."

Eric laughed nervously, reached for one of the croissants and started to butter it.

I switched the conversation. We hadn't come to talk about love potions.

"And what about your daughter, was she close to Misty, too?"

"Since before she was born. You see, once April found out she was pregnant she begged Misty to read for her. She wanted to know all about the baby. I didn't think much about it, but looking back I think she was worried something might be wrong. Misty convinced her she'd be fine. That the child she was carrying was special. April got it in her head that meant Amber was destined to be a big star, and she started asking Misty to introduce her to her Hollywood friends. After that they were inseparable."

I glanced back in the direction of the family photos above the cash register. In all of them Amber looked like any other child, a bit precocious, always posing for the camera, but absent was the flash of Hollywood. She was just another kid.

"I'm afraid I didn't agree with all of that. The business made me uncomfortable. Next thing I know Misty's introduced my wife to Pepper Millhouse, my daughter's got a contract and she's off to Hollywood. I should have stopped it long ago, but I couldn't. Far as I'm concerned, Pepper Millhouse and her crowd got exactly what they deserved."

"And Misty? You blame her?"

"I can't blame Misty. She was there for Amber after April died. Thank goodness, too. I wasn't much good after the accident, and when Pepper led the charge to steal my daughter from me I was happy Misty was around. She's like family. But if I had it to do over again, believe me, Amber never would have left home in the first place. I blame Hollywood for the loss of my daughter, not Misty."

Burt set the tray down on the table and turned to look at the creek.

"I'm sorry to ask, Burt, but how did your wife die?"

"Drowned," he said flatly.

"Drowned?" I glanced at Eric. *Drowned?* "And Misty, she never warned you that your wife was in danger?"

"Misty told me later she tried to tell my wife she saw darkness all around her. But if April knew, she didn't tell me. Looking back, Misty knew all along. It was exactly as she said it would be. One day April would return to the waters. She had predicted it."

I was uncomfortable talking about Misty and her premonitions, particularly her vision of darkness. A chill ran down my back. Without realizing it I wrapped my arms around myself and began brushing my shoulders with my hands, then catching my actions, I stopped abruptly.

"Did April drown here?" I glanced down at the creek.

"No, we were on vacation, in Mexico." Burt looked away from the window, abruptly. "I'm sorry, I really don't like to talk much about it. It was an accident."

I decided it best to switch the subject.

"What do you know about monkshood?" I asked.

Burt put the tea pot down on the table and began wiping his hands on the dish towel. "You think Misty did it, don't you?"

"I'm just asking questions. The bottles of bath salts were hers."

"Let me tell you, Misty's a good person. Years ago she and I both took an oath. I suppose Eric told you. I'm a conscientious objector. So is she. Neither of us believes in violence or in doing physical harm. I didn't care for Pepper Millhouse, and I didn't really know her business partners, but Misty couldn't have done this." He paused and looked back out at the creek. "Unless—"

I looked at Eric then back to Burt. "Unless what, Burt?"

"Unless, she was experimenting with a new batch of bath salts and it was accidental. She fancied herself some kind of herbal-pharmacologist. She was always mixing up remedies. It's possible she might have mixed in the monkshood like the Chinese do with this tea here. She was into that. The Chinese dry it and blend it with a few other herbs to neutralize the poison. Supposedly it has great medicinal value. This here's called Fu-Tuz. I drink it for the chills. She could have made a mistake. She forgets things."

I glanced at Eric. *A mistake?* I knew Misty could get rattled. I'd seen it first hand, but didn't think was a mistake. This was all too premeditated. Whoever mixed the bottles of bath salts with monkshood and marked them with the number seven knew exactly what they were doing.

"You like a cup?" Burt picked up the pot and about to pour some, when Eric stopped him.

"I don't think so, Burt. It's getting late. I'm afraid we've taken up too much of your time already. Carol needs to get back to the station and I've got some more work to do. Maybe next time?"

Burt pulled the pot away, holding it next to him with both hands. "Like I told you, I wouldn't kill Pepper Millhouse. I don't believe in murder. But Pepper and her crowd aren't a big loss for this world far as I'm concerned."

CHAPTER 19

Between the rain and the slick canyon road leading from Burt's Place back toward the 101, Eric barely got me back to the radio station in time to start my evening shift. Traffic was stop and go, with a near solid stream of red taillights. And so was our conversation. If Eric had taken me to visit Burt Marx to settle my mind about Misty Dawn it was having the exact opposite effect. I now had more questions than ever about the woman, and as far as her relationship with Sarah Millhouse and Andrew Reese went, I hadn't even begun to connect the dots. I just knew there had to be some, and I was certain Eric thought so too.

"You don't really think Misty accidentally poisoned the bath salts, do you?" I glanced over at Eric. He was strangely quiet, his eyes focused intently on the traffic ahead. I started to prod. "Look, we know the bottles are hers. Burt says she mixes monkshood into her teas. She's probably got a stash of the stuff hidden away somewhere."

I was getting nothing back from Eric. He looked lost in his thoughts, miles away. Then half-joking and hoping for a response, I added, "Hey, maybe she's escalating from love potions to something more deadly? You know, a little more permanent than affairs of the heart."

Eric glanced over to me. His mind still elsewhere.

I persisted. "I think Sarah might be using Misty."

Again no response. Eric's eyes returned to the road ahead. We drove on another couple of rain-slicked miles in silence, and then,

"When this is over, I think we should set sail for Catalina. The island's beautiful this time of year."

I looked at him curiously. "You don't want to talk about the case?"

"I think we need to talk about what's really bothering you."

I sighed and looked out the window. *Now we're going to have the conversation? Dammit, I thought we'd moved beyond the need to discuss our relationship.* "Like what?" I asked.

"The other woman. Let's start there. I know she bothers you."

I closed my eyes, shook my head and bit my lip to keep from smiling. Eric's *other* woman is a sixty foot schooner called the Sea Mistress, a former drug smuggler's vessel he'd bought at auction.

"You know how I feel about her." I tossed the comment back. The very thought of Eric's Sea Mistress turned my stomach. From the first time I'd boarded her, or attempted to, I felt nauseous, my legs like rubber and I slipped from her deck. Eric had to fish me out of the water. I was a mess, sopping wet, my hair mixed with seaweed in stringy ringlets and I smelled of brackish seawater.

"I don't think you've given her a fair chance, and once we're done here it'd really be nice if we set sail for Catalina. Maybe make it a threesome?"

I laughed.

He smiled and reached over to squeeze my hand.

I sat back and looked out the window. There was no point in trying to discuss the case. For right now it was off limits, but at least I knew despite everything that had happened yesterday, we were back on an even keel.

"Perhaps I should ask Misty for something," I teased. "No doubt she's probably got a cure for seasickness in that bag of hers."

I waited for a response. Eric shook his head as though he were trying to dismiss the thought and said nothing. Then as we pulled into the parking lot he reached for my hand. "Carol, you and I, we can't talk about this case right now. You know that. It's an open investigation and we each have a job to do. I wanted to take you to lunch, to meet Burt and let him tell you about Misty. I thought it might help. But right now, I need to check something out alone. Okay?"

I kissed him lightly on the cheek. "I get it. You're worried I'll solve the case without you."

He laughed. "I'll call later."

I grabbed my bag and holding it over my head ran into the station. Tyler may have been right about reporters and the FBI, but he wasn't right about Eric and me. We could harmonize.

I brushed past the security guard, pushed through the station's double doors and dashed down the hallway toward the studio. In the background the start of the second quarter of the Lakers' game broadcast throughout the station. Screams from enthusiastic fans were bouncing off the walls. Kobe Bryant had just scored his third three-pointer. I swung into the news booth, dropped my wet bag at my feet and skimmed the news feed. There was no mention anywhere that Kim LaSalle had found another deadly bottle of Lavender Lush.

I considered buzzing Tyler, bringing him up to date on the news about Kim LaSalle, but I knew he'd be swamped with the responsibilities of the remote broadcast and an arena full of screaming fans. I breathed a little easier. With the game in full swing I was alone in the studio. I had better than thirty minutes to halftime and more than enough time to prepare for my newscast.

I rewrote the leads to a couple of national news stories and opted to green-light the news about Kim LaSalle finding a bottle of poisonous bath salts. Satisfied I had plenty of material and more than enough time for a cup of coffee I decided I'd head to the employees' lounge.

With Tyler out of my way, it would be a light night. I could relax. I'd have enough free time to call my son and maybe even do a little online research concerning herbal remedies for seasickness. Much as I looked forward to time with Eric, the idea of a day at sea caused my stomach to flip-flop.

I stood up, stretched and caught my reflection in the tinted glass between the small news booth and the adjacent studio. There in the dark window, looming from within my own image was the shadow of another figure. I wasn't alone.

I stepped forward, placing my hand on the windowpane and stared into the empty studio. The dim red light above the microphone flickered, as though an object had passed through it. For a moment I thought I was seeing a ghost. I froze. A dark silhouette wearing a scarf and a beaded necklace appeared to be asleep, actually snoring, her round shoulders rising and lowering like waves, behind the console.

"Misty?" I tapped on the glass. She jerked awake, her head like a bobble doll, appeared disoriented, then stared back at me.

"Oh, you're here, finally. I've been waiting for you."

"What are you doing here?" I stepped back from the glass. How could Misty possibly have gotten into the studio? It's not like KCHC is some rinky-dink little station. It's a state of the art facility, surrounded by twelve foot high walls and twenty-four seven security. I considered pressing the small emergency call button beneath the console to alert the guard. But Misty was on to me.

"You don't need to bother with that. Your security guard knows I'm here. He let me in. Sweet fellow by the way. He and I've become quite good friends. I think his name is Jake, or James, or something like that. I forget, but he remembered me from the other night. We agreed it was just too cold and wet to wait outside, so he let me in. I told him you were expecting me. You got my message, right?"

"Message?" I picked up my bag, rifled through it and checked my phone. There was nothing. I held it up against the glass for her to see. "It says no new messages. Satisfied?"

"Oh, my dear, you still don't get it, do you? You mean to tell me I haven't crossed your mind at all? Not once the entire day?"

I tossed my phone back into my bag.

"You might consider using a phone, Misty. It's what most people do. I'm afraid this really isn't a good—"

"Time?" Misty stepped forward and put her hand on the glass, directly opposite where mine had been. In the dim light I could see her cloudy white eyes looking back at me. Glowing. "I'm afraid when it comes to things like this there's never a good time. But just give me a few minutes. I have information that can help your friend Sam. It's urgent."

My stomach tightened at the mention of Sam's name and I drew back from the glass and pointed toward the exit. "Fine, meet me outside the studio."

Without a word I headed down the hallway toward the employee's kitchenette with Misty following behind me. Despite the broadcast of the Lakers game in the background the sound of Misty's jewelry jangling and that of her moccasins as she shuffled behind me was all I heard.

When we got to the doorway of the employees' lounge, I stopped and pointed to a corner table. With my back pressed up against the wall I held my breath as she passed in front of me. She was dressed in a long skirt, a loose fitting shirt and shawl. Over one shoulder she was carrying a large canvas bag that she clung to like a security blanket, and in her hands she held a bouquet of long stemmed blue flowers wrapped in newspaper. Irises? Hydrangea? I hoped they weren't monkshood.

"So how is it you think you can help Sam?" I watched as she squeezed in behind the table, leaning on the chair like an old lady for balance then sat down.

"Aren't you going to offer me some hot water for tea?" She exhaled as she placed the flowers on the table then took the bag from her shoulder as though its contents might be heavy and set it on the floor beside her. "I'd like a cup first. Will you join me?"

"No, I was about to have coffee." I moved toward the kitchen counter and reached for the coffee pot. "I'll stick with that, thanks."

"Suit yourself, but I'll need water. Please?" She reached down into her bag and took out a small cup and several small baggies full of twigs, seeds and earth colored powders, similar to those she'd brought with her last time and then proceeded to line them all up on that table. I didn't want to think what might be in those bags.

"Oh, and these here are for you." Unwrapping the long stems

from the newspaper, she leaned forward and waved them inches from my face. "Beautiful, aren't they? You know what they're called?"

"No. I'm afraid I don't." I veered away from the flowers, stooping to avoid them as I reached for her cup on the table. Then turning my back to her defensively I began filling the cup with hot water from the insta-tap. My quick reaction caused her to laugh.

"Oh, of course you do. They're gladiolas, from my garden." She sat down, laying the flowers on the table in front of her. "Beautiful, aren't they? But that's not what you thought, is it?"

Cautiously I leaned in, placing her cup back on the table, then turned around to fill my own cup with coffee.

"I think you know what I thought," I said.

"That these are monkshood? Oh, Carol, don't worry. Burt told me all about your visit this afternoon. I'm well aware how guilty you think I am."

I turned back to face her, the coffee pot still in my hand. She stopped talking while she fixed her tea. I watched as she methodically patted each of the small baggies in front of her as though she was feeling, not looking, for its contents and finding what she liked, opened it, took a pinch from inside and sprinkled it into her cup. Then pushing her frizzy gray-blonde hair from her face, she blew over her tea and began slowly turning the cup several times before taking a long sip.

"Your mind's been working overtime trying to figure out if, like Burt said, it could have been an accident, or if maybe I actually did it. A mystery, isn't it? And yet, here I am. Odd, even if I do say so myself. I mean if I was the guilty party, the murderess so to speak, I'd hardly be here trying to help Sam, now would I? By the way, did you know Burt and April lost a baby six months before she died? Crib death. It nearly killed Burt."

I stopped pouring coffee into my cup and stared at her. I had no idea there had been a baby.

"Not surprising you didn't hear. Not a hint of it in the tabloids, or any media, for that matter. Pepper kept it quiet. It's what she did. Strange, isn't it? All the junk she managed to pitch about her clients that ended up on the front page, and not a word about the sudden death of Amber's little brother. I have to say, the woman had power and she used it to bury this story. Not so much as a blimp on the radar. But the entire family was devastated. They were just getting back on their feet when Burt took the family on vacation to Mexico and April drowned."

"You're telling me you had no idea? With all your psychic powers or whatever you want to call them, you didn't know about the baby? Or that April would die?"

"It's not always possible to decipher between emotion and energy. I was too close, and when I'm involved like I was with them, things get clouded."

"I'm not sure I understand. What do you mean emotion and energy?"

"Sometimes I hear voices, sometimes it's a feeling I get when I'm with someone or read about something. Like with the young coed at the university. I didn't know her, but heard about her missing and one day when I was working in the garden I just knew. I started to feel her presence. I know it sounds strange, but in truth it's a power we all have. Most people just don't listen. You have to appreciate that the universe is all energy, either positive or negative.

"When I meet someone I can feel that energy. Like with you. It's positive. There's this glow about you, but then there's also a dark energy moving around you. It concerns me. Perhaps it's because you're working the case or because whoever did these murders is somehow very close to you."

"You gals okay?" Jake, the security guard, stood at the door with a big smile on his face. In his hand was a brownie. "Just checking. And thanks, Misty, for these." He nodded to her, and taking a bite of the chocolate bar, added, "Better 'n my wife makes, but that's just 'tween you and me, right?"

"Anytime, Luv."

I looked at her. "You bribed him!"

"He was bribable. What do want me to say? I needed to see you."

I waited until Jake left. I shudder to think what might be in those brownies. Jake looked awfully happy.

"You know what I think?" I still had the coffee pot in my hand and gripped it more firmly as I spoke. Not that I intended to throw it, but I felt a little more secure with something between us, just in case she didn't like what I was about to say. "You're right. I do think the person responsible for the murders is close to me. I think it's you, Misty, and I don't believe it was an accident. Not after watching you blend your tea. You may be foolish and forgetful, but you're not stupid. You're much too careful when it comes to your precious herbs."

"You're quite observant, Carol. If you could only be so trusting, perhaps you'd understand that's why I'm here."

"I think you're here and following me around because you're trying to feed me facts to throw me off. Or maybe it's because you didn't act alone, that you're involved with Sarah and Andrew and you're trying to get close to me to find out what I know. I don't know for sure. I haven't figured it all out yet, but I'm going to. You can count on it."

"Oh, Carol, you're much too dramatic."

"Am I?"

"Think about it, Dear. Why would I want to kill Pepper Millhouse and those two darling little old lady business partners of hers? They gave me my break in Hollywood. To them I was Mystic Misty, Psychic to the Stars. You think I'd undo that? Pepper Millhouse and I may have had our differences, but she took care of those who could make money for the agency, and over the years I made plenty of money for her. Plus, I brought her Amber Marx, and when she needed someone to look after Amber, I was there. Believe me, we understood one another. She's the reason I've got the job as consultant on *The Sorcerer's Daughter*."

I looked at the clock. It was getting late. I'd already lost the opportunity to call my son and wish him good night.

"Look, you said you had something that would help Sam. What is it?"

"Well, that's just it. I've been trying to call Sam's attorney. What's his name?"

"Mr. King." I shook my head. How on earth could a psychic have such a terrible memory?

"Yes, Mr. King. But it seems I'm unable to rouse him."

"Okay, stop. Wait a minute." I put my hands up to stop her from rattling on about Mr. King. "Are you telling me you tried to actually *call* Mr. King?" I asked, pantomiming a phone to my ear. "I mean really call him, on the phone?"

"Why, of course. You could hardly expect an attorney to understand transcendental communication. I'm afraid that kind of thing is way over their heads. They're just not capable."

"Misty." Again I put my hand up to stop her. "The reason you were calling Mr. King, was because...?" I prompted her, trying to hurry her along. I was due on the air in ten minutes.

"He's ill. I couldn't get hold of him. He's under the weather. At least that's what his assistant tells me. Odd way of phrasing it, don't you think? Under the weather. It makes one sound like they're standing beneath a black cloud. Oh, but it's nothing so serious, least not with him, just a nasty cold, although I do think it's pneumonia, the walking variety, mild, but miserable."

"I see." I glanced again at the clock. If nothing else I at least knew now why Mr. King had not returned any of my calls.

"But I do have a solution."

"What's that?"

"Ginger tea and almonds."

"Misty," I said pointedly. "Let's stick to the reason you're here. Just what is it you wanted to share with Mr. King that would help Sam?"

"Why, her allergies of course. The girl's allergic. Desperately."

"I don't understand. Why are Sam's allergies of any significance to her defense?"

"Because Samantha Millhouse is highly allergic to flowers!

And monkshood, just like these flowers here, is a flowering plant."
She picked up the bundle of flowers on the table in front of her and
shook them. "If she's exposed to any type of pollen her eyes swell
up terribly. There's absolutely no way she could have dried and
chopped up the monkshood and mixed it in with the bath salts."

"And how do you know about Sam's allergies?"

"I've known it for years. When I first met Sam she had tears
running down her face. Her nose was red, her eyes puffy. Poor girl
looked a mess. I thought perhaps it was something Pepper had said.
Believe me Pepper's words can cut tears quicker than a thunder
storm brings rain. But when I asked, she said Pepper had ordered
her to have fresh flowers in the office every day. It wasn't enough
for her to have them delivered. She wanted Sam to actually arrange
them and distribute them throughout the agency. Her aunt knew
she was allergic. It was torture. Pepper even knew the exact types of
flowering plants Sam should avoid but still she insisted. She wanted
fresh chrysanthemums and daisies in her office every morning."

I put the coffee pot down and took a sip of my coffee. Maybe
Misty did have a point. Sam never had fresh flowers around the
condo. She couldn't have made up the bottles of Lavender Lush
without coming into contact with the flowering plant. It made
sense. I made a mental note to mention this to Mr. King soon as
possible.

"Oh, and by the way, Carol, I bought you something."

"Me?"

"Yes, just a little something you might need." Misty reached
into the pocket of her skirt, pulled out a small pink sachet and
motioned for me to come forward. She must have seen the
uncertainty in my face and fanned away any concern, shaking her
head as she waved her hand in front on her as she spoke. "Oh, for
heaven's sake, please, I'm not about to hurt you. This is for you and
your young agent friend. A gift."

Putting my coffee down on the counter I stepped forward
tentatively. "What kind of gift?"

"Love potions. Something a girl should never be without."

Then, taking my wrist, she pressed the sachet into my hand.

"Why would I need this?" I stopped myself. I wasn't about to enter into a conversation about love potions with some self-touted psychic. I pushed the pouch back in her direction.

"They'll help keep that mistress of his at bay." She held my hand tight.

I closed my eyes and shook my head. "Misty, there's no mistress, and that's not why you're here. I'm not seeking your guidance. I don't need your help."

"Of course you do. Laugh if you like, but I'd hate to see him go sailing off into the sunset. Keep it, just in case. You'll be happy you did, and if it works you'll be back for something else for that little problem you have when you go sailing." Then taking the pouch from my hand, she shoved it into my pocket.

I wasn't happy that Misty was able to jump into my private thoughts. I had no idea exactly how it was she that did it, but I wasn't about to argue with her about love potions or about why I might or might not need them. "How about we stick to the bath salts, shall we? Tell me what you know about them."

"Like I told you before. I made them, but not the poisonous ones from the party, accidently or otherwise." She shook a finger at me as though to shame me for the thought she knew I was thinking. "Why would I do that? I wouldn't have a following if I did that, now would I?"

"But still, *you* made up the bath salts for Pepper's party?"

"Of course I did. Lavender Lush. It's one of my best lines."

"That's not why I'm asking, Misty. I need to know what happened to the bath salts after you made them up."

Misty exhaled. She was obviously annoyed at me. "You already know. It's like I told the FBI. I called Sam and told her I was running late. That I didn't think I'd be able to get the bottles to her in time. She suggested I leave them for her sister to pick up."

"And as far as you know, Sarah picked them up?"

"Oh no." Misty put her cup down on the table abruptly. I watched as the color in her face drained and she stood up.

Hurriedly she started to shove things back into her bag.

"What's the matter?"

She grabbed my wrist, and holding it tight, looked me in the eyes. "There's still a dark shadow around you. I had hoped I removed it, but I didn't. You need to be careful, particularly around water."

Dropping my wrist, she turned to go. I reached to grab her, putting my hands on her shoulders. I wanted her to face me. I wanted answers. I wasn't about to let her walk out the door without an explanation. She shrugged and my hands slipped from her shoulders. She was surprisingly strong.

"You need to remember this." She turned and looked at me again, her face stony white. "No matter what happens, Carol, time is simply energy. It's never solid. It's fluid and faced with danger; there are elements, or fractions of time, when your energy can change the course of fate. You can do that. Trust me."

I had no idea what Misty was talking about. It was as though one minute she was lucid, or as lucid as Misty could possibly be and the next she was doing some type of psychic reading, or warning. I wasn't sure. She shoved the flowers into my hands and turned to go.

"You'll have to excuse me. I need to go."

I stood there with the flowers in my hand and a very uneasy feeling something terrible was about to happen. I watched as she walked away, her long skirt slowly swaying down the hallway, her beads jangling, until she disappeared through the double doors and into the lobby and there was no longer any sight or sound of her in the building.

CHAPTER 20

By the time I got home I was too keyed up to close my eyes and afraid that if I did I might wake and find Misty Dawn sitting at the foot of my bed. The thought unnerved me. I fixed myself a cup of hot chocolate, something to steady my nerves, and crept upstairs to check on Charlie. The moonlight, slipping softly through the blinds above his bed, illuminated the room. It was the perfect picture of peace and tranquility. He was asleep, beneath posters of super heroes and football stars, school books neatly piled on his desk next to the bed, and Bossypants snuggled at his feet. All was well. I straightened the blankets on the bed and lightly kissed the tips of my fingers and pressed them to his head, then went to my room.

But I couldn't kick the feeling that there was a shadowy presence around me, or the memory of Misty's odd premonition that I could change the course of fate and soon might be asked to do so. Before this was over I was going to get to the bottom of Misty Dawn, but right now—after everything that had happened today—I was going to start by finding out what I could about Sarah Millhouse and Andrew Reese. I fluffed the pillows on the bed and grabbed my laptop. If I couldn't sleep, I could at least do research.

I began by Googling Sarah Millhouse and found a few publicity shots for a less than stellar acting career and a brief bio indicating she was the niece of Pepper Millhouse. Nothing I didn't already know. I moved on to Andrew Reese. His LinkedIn profile indicated he'd graduated USC with a degree in business and been active in Thespians International and was currently listed as an up and coming executive with the ACT Agency. Nothing new there either. I continued to query him under a pseudonym I'd seen listed in his bio, Drew Reese, and hit pay dirt. A small article from the campus newspaper indicated Drew Reese and some fraternity brothers had once been suspected of hacking into the university's computer system and changing grades. However, the case was never brought to trial, and all charges against the boys were dropped. *Interesting.* I then Googled Misty Dawn. There were numerous listings for her, dating all the way back to the sixties, but nothing earlier. All of them said the same thing: former flower child, psychic, mystic to the stars and sometimes clairvoyant who had successfully worked with the FBI on more than one occasion. I then moved on to monkshood, and what I found there made my skin crawl.

Monkshood, also known as the assassins' plant of choice, or killer plant, had over two hundred and fifty different species from which the poison aconite can be easily derived. In addition to being highly toxic, it was, just like Burt Marx had said, used by the Chinese as an herbal remedy for a number of ailments, anything from the chills to cancer. It was also thought to be hallucinogenic. Witches believed it could make them fly. I started to wonder if perhaps Misty had slipped something into my coffee last night. Maybe I had fantasized everything, particularly her warning. I leaned my head back against the pillows and closed my eyes. I tried to sleep and finally gave up around six o'clock. Grabbing my slippers and robe I headed downstairs, made myself a cup of strong coffee and went to the front door for the newspaper.

The headline stopped me cold. *Star Finds Bottle of Deadly Bath Salts.* It tied Kim LaSalle's find of the poisonous bath salts to that of the other Hollywood Bathtub Murders and then went on to suggest that it was very likely Ms. LaSalle was the sixth intended victim. The article also identified Andrew Reese as the acting head of the ACT Agency and quoted him saying there was definitely "bad blood" between Kim LaSalle and Samantha Millhouse. He blamed Sam for having Kim committed unnecessarily to a rehab facility after a recent "incident" between the two inside the agency. The details of which he said he just couldn't get into, citing client confidentiality. Also included in the story was the fact that Sam's fingerprints had been found on all the poisonous bottles of bath salts and that it was well known among industry insiders that Samantha Millhouse had a contentious relationship with her aunt and her aunt's business partners, frequently referring to them as "old hacks." I didn't like any of it.

I returned to the kitchen, sat down at the table and stared at my coffee cup. I was trying to sort out this morning's headlines and Misty's surprise visit to the radio station last night when my son came bounding into the room with all the enthusiasm of a half-grown pup.

"Boo!" He put his hand on my shoulder, jarring me from my reverie then wandered over to the refrigerator. "What's wrong, Mom? You look like you just saw a ghost."

I didn't want to tell him that I thought I had. That I was worried a psychic named Misty Dawn might be stalking me and had surprised me in the studio last night.

"You feed the cat?" I asked.

"Fed, watered and changed his box."

Charlie stood leaning in front of an open refrigerator door, air conditioning the room, his attention drawn to the cellphone in his hand.

"Hey mister, breakfast, remember?"

He took a hardboiled egg from the refrigerator and stuffed it in his pocket, then grabbed an apple and put it in the other, all the while never taking his eyes of his cell. "Gotta run. Coach called an early morning meeting with the team."

I stood up and handed him his notebook. "Don't forget your jacket. It's cold outside."

He bussed me a kiss on the side of my cheek and headed out the backdoor, then stopped suddenly, his attention once again drawn to his phone. "Hey, guess who just tweeted? Amber Marx!"

"I would have preferred it be your coach."

"Mom!" He looked at me like I was from another planet. *Didn't I get it? Amber Marx was hot.* Of course I got it. My son was at that awkward age, a pubescent teen, with posters of superheroes plastered across his bedroom walls, while beneath his bed were stashes of my Victoria Secret catalogues. I understood all too well just how impressionable he was and I didn't like it.

"She's got a big party at the beach this weekend. Can I go?"

"Not going to happen, Buddy. You're with your dad this weekend. And make sure to take that phone out of your back pocket and turn it off while you're in school. Last week you butt-dialed me during your physics class. Twice."

"Yeah, yeah." He winked at me, held the cellphone up over his head and waved goodbye as he headed out the door. "Sure thing. Don't worry, Mom."

I was glad Charlie wasn't old enough to drive. I reminded myself that, God willing, he'd outgrow his infatuation with Amber Marx. Besides, he had a game tonight and I knew his dad would keep him busy this weekend. There was no way he'd have time to do a beach party. That was one worry I could put aside.

I glanced up at the clock. It wasn't too early to try Mr. King. I wanted to tell him what Misty Dawn had said about Sam's allergies. It was the smallest of hopes but after reading this morning's paper, she needed everything we could get right now to help with her defense.

The phone rang just once before someone answered.

"Hello?"

I barely recognized the voice. "Mr. King? You sound awful. Are you okay?"

King cleared his throat, the sound of it like a cement mixer. Misty was right, he was miserable. He struggled between coughing spells to tell me he had a cold and had been in and out of the office.

"Hit me like a son of a bitch." He started to hack again.

I waited until the spasm passed, then explained how Misty Dawn had surprised me at the radio station the night before.

"Believe me if I thought witches were real, I'd swear she was one. I can't imagine how she knows the things so does, but I do know this, the woman's stalking me." A vision of her from last night sitting in the darkened studio sent a chill down my back. "Anyway, she says she's been trying to reach you. She has information she believes will help Sam."

King started to cough again.

"And she suggested ginger tea and almonds for your cold. I got the feeling she'd be happy to come by and make a house call. If I was you I'd look out."

"Why? You jealous?"

I laughed. Even sick, King's libido was still in play, if only in jest.

"That's not why I called. She said Sam couldn't possibly have poisoned Pepper; she's highly allergic to flowers."

"Really?" His voice cracked. I could tell he was struggling to speak. "I'll remember not to bring flowers next time I visit her in jail."

"You don't get it. This isn't funny. Monkshood is a flowering plant. Sam couldn't possibly have handled it, even with gloves. She's too allergic."

"I'll give it some thought. But, I'm afraid Sam's got bigger problems right now. We got another will."

I wasn't certain if I was hearing him correctly. "Another will? What do you mean, *another* will?"

"Pepper's housekeeper, Arminta Gutierrez, claims she's had it in her possession since before Pepper's death. She says Pepper made it out right after she filed the current will with Mr. Matteson. Said Pepper came home, thought about it and wanted to change everything to reward her housekeeper for being so helpful. Evidently she felt bad about her situation with the baby."

"Baby? What baby?"

King cleared his throat again. I waited until he felt strong enough to speak clearly.

"I spoke with Matteson yesterday, but only briefly. I'm only operating at about fifty percent. He says Miss Gutierrez has a son, an illegitimate baby with one of Pepper's clients, Dek de Convero. Pepper hushed it up. And according to Miss Gutierrez before Pepper died, she told her she was leaving the guest cottage to her and everything else to Sarah Millhouse, cutting out Sam entirely."

"I don't believe it. You're telling me Mr. Matteson didn't know anything about this until yesterday?"

"That's what he's saying."

"And Sarah, you don't think she knew?"

"Matteson's claiming Sarah's surprised and didn't know anything about the existence of a second will. Arminta showed it to her a couple days ago, and Sarah convinced Arminta to take it to Matteson to check out. He sent over a copy to me this morning. He'll be sending over a copy to the prosecutor as well. I've put in calls to both of them now."

"But I don't understand. Won't this be good for Sam?"

"The prosecution will spin it. In fact, the date on it is curious. It appears Pepper wrote it the day after she visited Matteson's office to file the last will. They'll use that to get Matteson to say how fickle Pepper was. That she was always going back and forth on things. Claiming Sam may have suspected her aunt would change the will and killed her before she thought she could do it."

"But what about witnesses? There had to be someone who knew she had another will, someone other than the maid."

"That's just it. There are two signatures on the will, as is required, but one of the signatories is dead. Helen Howard. It appears she signed the will the day she died. It was probably the last thing she did."

"If she did it at all. Sarah probably forged it. Maybe even got a little help from her friend Andrew Reese." From the news story I'd read last night, I knew Andrew had some experience with faking documents.

"We'll check into that."

"And the other signature?"

"Clarissa St. Clair. And she's on her way to Spain as we speak. It looks like we'll have to wait until she lands to get a statement from her. In the meantime, I'm wasting my voice here. I have to talk to the District Attorney and go see Sam. She doesn't know any of this yet. We'll talk later."

I wondered as I hung up the phone if Clarissa's signature might have been forged as well, or if she even knew what she had signed. From everything I had seen at the radio station when both she and Amber were together, there was very little they did without supervision. The girl might have signed the document and never known what she'd signed. I was anxious to talk to Clarissa. I couldn't wait for her plane to land.

CHAPTER 21

Millhouse Manor is less than fifteen minutes from Sam's condo. I know because Sam told me. Her aunt had insisted when she bought her place that it be no more than a quarter of an hour away. And on numerous occasions I believe the Queen of Mean actually tested it out, making certain that no matter what the hour, Sam could actually be on her doorstep within the required time frame. I'm sure Pepper had Sam's cell on speed dial. I got used to seeing Sam leave at all hours of the night with a pint of Ben and Jerry's, her aunt's favorite, in one hand and a handful of contracts in the other. Despite the many stories Sam would share with me about her aunt and the descriptions of her home, I'd never been inside.

I stood on the doorstep beneath a large arched entry and rang the bell. According to Sam, her aunt had bought the mid-century English manor in the early seventies and had done little to it other than to maintain the integrity of the architecture and christen it with her own last name. Clearly the fact that Millhouse Manor had not gone the way of many of the more modern, oversized McMansions in the area was part of its charm. While waiting, I could hear voices mixed with squeals of laughter and footsteps coming to the door. It sounded like that of a small child running and an adult in close pursuit.

"Mi hijo." There was giggling, then two pairs of dark eyes peered back at me from behind the heavy mahogany door as it opened.

"Arminta? Are you Arminta Gutierrez?" I asked.

The woman pulled the small child closer to her. The chubby

cheeked little boy stretched out his hand, opening and closing his fingers. "Hola, hola," he squealed, as though he wanted to grab me.

"Sí," she answered softly, her head pulled back slightly from the door, the expression on her face suspicious.

"I'm Carol Childs. I'm a reporter for KCHC. I'm also Samantha Millhouse's friend. I have a few questions for you regarding Pepper Millhouse."

Arminta sighed. Holding the baby tightly she opened the door all the way. "Pasa adelante. Come in please."

I stepped inside. It took me a moment to take in the room. Morning light beamed in from the windows beneath large cathedral ceilings and onto the hardwood floors, giving the space a warm, almost celestial look. A baby's blanket had been set down on the floor in the center of the room, building blocks and soft plushy toys were scattered everywhere.

"Dios Mío. Oh, my God!" She backed further into the room. "Crees que soy culpable."

"Aminta, please, could you speak English?" She looked like a frightened animal standing in the center of the entry, her eyes frozen on mine. I felt badly for her and softened my voice. "I'm sorry. My Spanish is not so good."

"You think I did it, don't you?" She squeezed the baby closer to her, whispering in his ear.

I looked at her, stunned. Of all the possible scenarios I'd never considered Pepper's housekeeper to be the murderer.

"No," I said.

"Because Ms. Sarah, she make me do it."

"Make you do what?"

"Take the will to Señor Matteson." Arminta turned and walked ahead of me into the great room where she placed the baby on the floor in front of a large over-stuffed chair, then stood with her arms wrapped about herself and stared at me.

"Please, Arminta, sit down."

Like an obedient servant, Arminta nodded then sat cross legged on the floor in front of her son.

"It's going to be okay, Arminta." I stooped down next to her. Without looking at me, she picked up a stuffed animal, held it for the baby to see, then smiled and cooed at the infant. "I just need you to tell me about the will. Did Sarah tell you the will was a fake? Un falso?"

"No." She shook her head and, refusing to look at me, continued to play with her son. "She tell me Ms. Pepper want to help me and she has paper that can make it so. That I need to take this paper to—I don't know how you say. El abogado."

"Attorney," I said.

"Si, attorney, and that this paper say I can live here, in the guesthouse with my son."

"And what else did she say?"

"That I need to tell this attorney that Ms. Pepper gave me this paper before she died, and not to lose it. That it is her Last Will and Testament."

"And is it?"

"I don't know. Ms. Sarah said if I didn't do it that she would tell Miss LaSalle about my son. That he is," she put her hands softly on the baby's ears and whispered, "Mr. de Convero's baby. She says she will send me back to Columbia, and I'd never see my baby again." Arminta pulled her son into her lap and scooted away from me.

I put my hand on her shoulder. "It's going to be okay, Arminta. Nobody's going to hurt you or the baby. I promise."

Things were starting to fall into place. It was obvious to me the will was a fake. Sarah had made the whole thing up and was blackmailing Arminta, maybe with Andrew's help. But they weren't going to get away with it any more than they were going to get away with murder.

"When did Sarah bring you the will?"

"After the police find those other bodies. Like Ms. Pepper in the bathtub." Arminta's eyes looked strained. She'd clearly been holding this secret to herself for some time and was very worried.

"You mean, Heather Broderick and her boyfriend?"

"Si. She was furioso."

"Furious."

"Like a crazy woman. And now Miss Sam is in jail and everybody thinking she killed her aunt. But Miss Sam didn't kill Pepper. I know that. I don't know what to do."

"You can help me, Arminta, that's what you can do. I know Sam didn't kill her aunt, but I need to prove it, and I think maybe you can help me find who did."

"I don't know. I try to think, but Ms. Pepper, she had a lot of people who not like her."

"Okay, but maybe you know more than you think. The night of Pepper's birthday, who brought the bottles of bath salts into the house?"

"Miss Sam. She came with Mr. Reese, and he carried them into the house for her and gave them to Miss Broderick. She was in charge of the gift table. Later, I take the bath salts upstairs to Ms. Pepper's bath where I always put her things. But I didn't do it. I swear."

Arminta started to cry. I reached over and put my hand on her shoulder again. "It's okay, Arminta. I believe you."

"If Miss Sarah thinks I talked to anyone, she'll send me back to Columbia, and I'll lose my son."

"Nobody's going to send you back to Columbia." I squeezed her shoulder. "I promise, but you can't talk to anybody about this. Not yet. Promise me you won't."

CHAPTER 22

I needed to talk to Sam. After meeting with Arminta I was convinced she was being blackmailed by Sarah Millhouse, and that Andrew Reese was involved as well. I felt certain the two had found a way to tap into Misty's stash of Lavender Lush—either with or without her knowledge—and poison enough of the bottles to knock off the senior members of the ACT Agency and very possibly Heather Broderick and her boyfriend. If there were other planned poisonings, I didn't know. Not yet anyway. The only thing I knew for certain was Sarah was trying to pin the murders on Sam. It was an elaborate plot, most of it still swirling around in my mind like soup. But I knew I was onto something. I just had to prove it, and I hoped talking with Sam would help me do that.

I met Mr. King outside the Metropolitan Detention Center in downtown Los Angeles, a facility that houses both male and female prisoners awaiting trial. He was wearing a beige trench coat and when he saw me, held his hand up in front of his face.

"Don't get too close." He coughed into his handkerchief.

I kept my distance and walked ahead of him into the building. Inside a security guard smiled at me as I stripped off my heels, threw my purse and jacket onto the conveyer belt, then proceeded through the scanning device.

"I'm pretty sure Sarah's blackmailing Pepper's housekeeper, and that's not all..."

I glanced back at King. He was struggling with his overcoat and had stopped as though his mind and body could not possibly work at the same moment. His cold was really getting the best of him; he looked pale, his nose red and bulbous.

"No? What else?" he asked.

"Sam wasn't the only one with access to the bath salts. Sarah and Andrew Reese both had contact the day of Pepper's party. Sarah picked them up from Misty and brought them to the agency. Then Andrew and Sam brought them to Pepper's party. The common denominator here being Andrew."

King looked at me wearily, took a handkerchief from his pocket, blew his nose then hurriedly stuffed it back into his jacket. "And you know this, how?"

"I have my sources, but it's good isn't it? I mean that puts both Sarah and Andrew alone with the bath salts and she, or they, could have easily tampered with them."

King coughed and shook his head, indicating now was not the time for me to be going on about my theories, then grabbed his coat off the conveyor belt. Once through security a guard greeted us and directed us to follow him into a small, green windowless room. He nodded to a metal table, and King and I took a seat and waited. We both watched as the door closed slowly behind the guard, and with it all contact to the outside world. I thought I'd suffocate for lack of fresh air. The cold concrete walls felt like they were closing in on me.

Ordinarily prisoners held in the Metropolitan Detention Center were there for no more than forty-eight hours before either being brought before the court or transferred to the county jail. But King had pulled strings to keep Sam in what was considered the lesser offensive of the institutions. He described it as kind of a purgatory, or hell-light by comparison. I shuddered to think what was going on behind the walls, the sheer number of people jammed together in overcrowded dormitories with nothing to do but wait and wonder. It had to be torture.

Finally, outside our small room I could hear the heavy sound of boots in the hallway. A guard appeared at the door with Sam at her side, her feet shackled together, her hands cuffed behind her. She was dressed in an orange prison jumpsuit, her dark hair pulled back into a ponytail. She looked gaunt with circles beneath her eyes, but surprisingly resilient, her posture much more confident than when I had last seen her in court.

She smiled at me as she entered the room, shuffling awkwardly next to the guard as they approached the table. King and I stood while the guard released her ankle chains then handcuffs and allowed her to sit down.

"So what do you think?" Sam raised hands in question. "You like the orange? It's the new black, you know. Everybody's wearing it."

I smiled and waited until her jailer had left the room.

"Personally, I prefer the black." I pulled the chair out across from her and sat down.

King remained standing. "Ladies, you'll pardon me if I remind you we're not here to discuss the latest fashion trend."

"Oh, and I thought you were here to tell me the DA was dropping the charges." Sam rubbed her wrists. "How silly of me. It's hard to believe after all my sister's humiliating accusations that the District Attorney would actually find enough evidence to charge me with anything—other than the misfortune of having a twin sister who's so obviously jealous of my success."

"What they've found, Ms. Millhouse, is enough to concern me that the DA has a very probable case against you."

Sam crossed her arms and stared coolly back at King.

"And it's not just the bottle of poisoned bath salts from beneath your bathroom cabinet, but a plastic bag containing bits and pieces of dried monkshood." King paused as though he were waiting for a response from Sam, and when none came, he continued. "That and rubber gloves, boots, and a mortar and pestle. All of which they will say you used to cut the poison you put inside those bottles of Lavender Lush. Plus, they also found a black felt pen, in your office. They believe it matches that used to mark the poisonous bottles with a number seven before you placed them inside party bags for your intended victims. And they've got your fingerprints on all the bottles."

Sam started to laugh.

"Of course they've got my prints on the bottles. Why wouldn't they? I did a count of the bottles before I took them to the party. If I had made a mistake and didn't have enough Pepper would have had my head."

I nodded at King, then leaned across the table and put my hand on Sam's arm.

"Look, Sam, I know Misty made up the bottles; she told me last night they were hers. She came to the radio station." Her eyes met mine. I could see the questions starting to form in her head. "I also know you called Sarah the day of the party and asked her to pick up the bottles."

"What did Misty tell you?"

"She said you couldn't have done it. That you're allergic to flowering plants."

King looked anxiously down at the file he brought with him and began flipping through the pages, then finding what he was looking for, held it up.

"I'm afraid that's not going to help, Carol. The DA will refer to the materials removed from Ms. Millhouse's medicine cabinet. I've got a complete inventory here." He held up the list. "They'll say it looked like a pharmacy. It shows here you had three, four, five different bottles of antihistamines in your medicine cabinet. They'll convince a jury you were stocking up on them."

Sam shook her head. "A person can't have allergy medication? Several different brands?"

"I'm afraid it gets worse. The prosecution's also prepared to bring forth a table full of witnesses who will say that on the night of the Silver Screen Awards you actually threatened to shoot your aunt."

"Pretended to shoot her! Like this. " Sam clasped her hands together, her index fingers pointed at King, like a make believe pistol. I could tell she was getting agitated. "And believe me any one of those people would love to have shot my aunt. Why aren't they under investigation?"

"And, Sam, they have a witness who will say you were at your aunt's house the day of the awards show. Her housekeeper Arminta Gutierrez will testify that you came by and went upstairs to your aunt's bedroom, alone."

"My aunt called and asked me to bring Amber Marx by. She wanted to talk to her before the show. We all suspected Amber would win for Best Supporting Actress and Pepper wanted to congratulate her privately. I went upstairs to borrow a shawl. It was cold. My aunt suggested I might want wear it later that night."

"The DA will say you made up an excuse to get upstairs. You wanted to make certain the bath salts were next to the tub, that you were familiar with your aunt's routine, that at the end of the day she liked to soak in a warm bath and you moved the poisoned bath salts where she'd find them. He'll say you were growing impatient, that since Pepper's birthday party only two of your intended targets had died, and you wanted to rush things along. We'll of course deny it, but this, along with the fact you've had some serious financial problems and were very aware of your aunt's financial assets, goes to building a case against you, Sam."

Sam looked down at the table and sighed. She looked as though she was weighing the evidence against her and not liking the odds. I felt the need to say something hopeful.

"But what they don't have," I said, "is any real witnesses. Someone who can say they actually saw Sam tamper with the bath salts. That's got to mean something."

"What they do have are emails that Sam's former assistant, Andrew Reese, turned over to the police. One particularly damaging, where the subject line reads, *Time to Kill off the Deadwood.*"

"That's ridiculous." Sam leaned back her chair and crossed her arms. I was hoping that she'd deny it, that maybe Andrew Reese had trumped up a bunch of phony emails—a task for which I knew he was accomplished—but she continued as though it were a pesky nuisance, hardly a matter of consequence. "That particular email was in response to our last board meeting. I told them we needed to cut the deadwood and move on. I certainly didn't mean to kill them. We needed to clean house at the agency. It's no secret our top management was getting old. They were in bed by eight o'clock at night in a town where you need to be out and about at all hours. Adel used be sharp as a tack. Once she knew everybody, but these days she did well to remember her middle name. And Helen, she hadn't been involved in anything more than selecting the new office furniture in ages. The lion's share of the work was falling on my aunt. She was making mistakes, she was exhausted and ill-tempered, and I caught the flak for it all. Something had to be done."

"That makes sense to me. You should read some of the emails I get, particularly those from Tyler." On more than one occasion I'd wanted to tell him to go and take a flying leap off of KCHC's antenna. I nodded at King in agreement.

"I'm afraid that's not the only reason we needed to talk today. Mr. Matteson says there's another will."

Sam looked away, shook her head and exhaled quickly, kind of a half laugh. "Let me guess, it leaves everything to my sister."

"Not quite," I said. "It leaves Millhouse Manor and the agency to your sister, but the guesthouse goes to Arminta."

"Really?" For the first time, I caught a look surprise on Sam's face.

"I spoke with Arminta this morning, Sam. She said Sarah presented her with the will and told her to give it to Matteson. I think Sarah's blackmailing her."

"You think?" Sam turned her head to me, her eyes wide. She had to know the will was bogus.

"Arminta's panicked," I said. "She believes Sarah's going to have her deported and take her son away."

"And you're concerned the prosecution will use this new will against me as well?" Sam turned to King.

"It goes to motive. They'll say you were worried Pepper would make out another will. That she was vocal about it and you wanted to make sure she was dead before she could."

"Right, and just what else does the prosecution have, Mr. King?" Sam looked up at him, shaking her head.

"The police found an airline ticket in your office, along with travel brochures to some pretty exotic places."

"Oh, yes. The travel brochures. I almost forgot."

"Can you explain it?"

"I was working a lot of long hours. I got lonely. It's hard to meet people when your work's so all consuming, and Andrew Reese and I started fooling around. It was nothing serious, kind of friends with benefits type of thing. We teased about getting away, taking a trip together. He'd bring in travel brochures and we'd talk about how great it'd be to go to a beach somewhere. But it was just some silly form of escape. It was a joke."

"Pretty serious joke, particularly since he didn't waste any time switching loyalties and teaming up with your sister right after your arrest."

"What can I say? Andrew was looking for a leg up in the industry any way he could get it. If I wasn't around, my sister could be. I'm not surprised; he's not stupid."

"How surprised would you be to learn that your sister's framing you, Sam?" I asked. "Or that your sister plotted with Andrew to take over the agency and killed your aunt and her business partners? Maybe because she was angry she'd been let go and blamed you. We could build a case. Maybe even tie-in that Sarah was jealous of Heather Broderick and killed her as well. The prosecution's looking at that possibility with you right now. We could act first."

"You mean accuse them?"

"Look, Sam." I leaned across the table, my hand on her arm. "I know Sarah had access to the bath salts. She brought them to your office."

I looked at King. We waited for her to respond.

"I asked her to. Misty was running late and I couldn't do it. Between work, the party, and Pepper, I didn't have time. So I called Sarah and asked if she'd drive out to the set of *The Sorcerer's*

Daughter. She was always looking for an excuse to get on the set. I knew she'd go. She picked up the bath salts along with Amber. I needed Amber back in time for an interview with a new tutor. It was no big deal."

"And Andrew Reese, he also had access to the bottles, before the two of you took them to the party?" King asked.

"I asked Andrew to help unload them and make up the goodie bags. I was busy working on a contract with my aunt so it was a while before I was able to get back to the office. I spot checked the bottles and told Andrew to go ahead and put them in my car."

King took a handkerchief from his pocket, blew his nose loudly then putting it back, moved from the wall to the table, and sat down.

"Sam, I'm not going to lie to you. The evidence here is mounting up, and it doesn't look good."

"It's all circumstantial. Like Carol said, they've got nothing, no one who can say I put the poison in those bottles, which by the way, I didn't do."

"That may be, and you may not put much faith in their circumstantial evidence, but let me remind you, you're not sitting behind these bars because the DA doesn't think he can use what he's got to prove you're guilty. The fact is they've got a case and enough evidence, circumstantial and otherwise, to not only keep you behind bars the rest of your life, but very possibly execute you."

Sam blanched. What little color she had left in her face drained away. She grimaced then clenched her jaw.

"This is crazy. Why doesn't anyone think I'm as much of a victim as the rest of them? Like Kim LaSalle or Heather Broderick? I brought home the same bottle of bath salts. You think I knew they were poisonous?"

"That might work for us, Sam, if the police hadn't found any other evidence inside your home and your office, and if you hadn't been so vocal about your feelings concerning your aunt."

"Since when is free speech a crime?" Sam asked.

"Sam, you need to get on the offense here. Simply saying 'I

didn't do it' isn't going get you out of jail."

"She's right. We need to come up with an alternative theory." King glanced at me. "That someone else, maybe someone close to your aunt and the agency, someone with a score to settle maybe, might have done this. You must have some ideas?"

"You're asking me to point my finger at someone?" Sam shook her head as though she couldn't believe it. "My aunt had enemies. It could have been anyone. Or maybe this is like the Tylenol murders. The press has been all over that, haven't they, Carol? I heard them discussing it on the news. The FBI never did find who did those murders. Maybe this will be like that, a mystery."

"Big difference, Sam. The Tylenol murders were random. The prosecutor's not going to believe that and neither is the public. All our victims here were all working at the ACT Agency. Everyone believes the victims were targeted, deliberately sought out, by someone with a score to settle. Someone with a lot to gain."

"No." Sam shook her head. "I'm not going to do it."

"Sam, you need to at least consider—"

"No!" she screamed at me. "She didn't do it. She didn't know what she was doing and I'm not pointing a finger at her."

"Her?" I looked at King and back to Sam. "Who, Sam? Your sister, Sarah? Misty? Did she do it?"

Sam stood up and yelled to the guard that she was ready to leave. King and I watched while the guard reentered the room, replacing Sam's handcuffs and shackles. She shuffled towards the door then stopped and looked back at us both.

"I know a thing or two about the law, Mr. King. I'm not stupid. You're an excellent lawyer, and you hate to lose, particularly a case as high profile as this one. That's why I hired you. You're going to have to find a better way."

CHAPTER 23

I was thirty minutes from work and due in the studio in fifteen. I called Tyler, got his voicemail and high-tailed it down the freeway from the jail to the radio station. I knew he'd cover for me. There would be hell to pay for my tardiness, but I figured it'd be worth it when he learned about the second will and even better that I had proof Sarah was blackmailing Pepper's housekeeper.

I pulled into the parking lot, raced into the station and was halfway down the hall on my way to Tyler's office when he came rushing out, his head buried in a news story. We bumped shoulders in the doorway.

"Carol, get this on the air, now."

He pressed the wire copy into my hands, my eyes skimmed the news, my stomach knotting as I read. I looked back into his eyes, searching for some mistake.

"Go!" he yelled.

Crushing the copy to my chest I turned around and hurried back down the hall to the studio. Kari immediately stopped pacing behind the console as I entered. Her eyes followed me to the news booth as she continued her broadcast. I wasn't due on the air for another twenty minutes. With my hands shaking I put the headphone on my ears and adjusted the mic.

"Kari, I'm sorry to interrupt your show. We've just received word that Clarissa St. Clair has died. She passed away on a flight to Spain this afternoon. An airline spokesperson is reporting that Miss St. Clair was found dead shortly after the crew served breakfast prior to landing in Barcelona, Spain."

Kari sat motionless, stunned, her eyes pinched shut. There was an audible silence. I waited for her to say something, but white noise filled my headphones. I stared back into the studio. Just forty-eight hours ago Clarissa was here. I could still see her with Amber Marx, sharing photos and exchanging makeup while they waited impatiently for Sarah to finish up her interview. I wondered if I'd ever get that picture out of my head.

With Kari clearly at a loss for words, I filled in as best I could with what little information I was able to pull up from my computer. Outside the studio window members of the staff began to gather with looks of shock and disbelief on their faces as they listened.

"The nineteen-year-old starlet, who just two days ago joined us here in the studio at KCHC to promote her upcoming movie, *The Lady in White*, was booked on World Air's redeye flight to Spain. At this time we are still awaiting further details concerning the cause of death. Her family has been notified and a spokesman for the airline says a coroner will need to examine the body before it can be released and returned to the U.S. for burial."

I finished the story, stood up, and started to leave. I needed fresh air, anything that would wash the vision I had of Clarissa crashed dead over her food tray. Kari was already on the line talking with someone. She looked up at me and punched the two-way between our studios. "I've got Sarah Millhouse on the line. She thinks it was an allergic reaction: peanuts. You want to stay?"

I shook my head. Clarissa St. Clair's death wasn't an accident. No matter how Sarah Millhouse would try to spin it, I knew it couldn't be. The girl was barely nineteen.

"The FBI contacted us first thing this morning..." Sarah's voice sounded strained. A little too rehearsed, I thought. "We're all devastated by the news. This is tragic. Totally unexpected. We knew Clarissa was highly allergic to peanuts. We're thinking it might have been that. We always checked ahead when she traveled and she carried an injectable with her, epinephrine for emergencies. Beyond that we just don't know what happened. If I could, Kari, I would like to make a statement." She paused, then proceeded with what I thought sounded like canned copy. "Clarissa St. Clair was a wonderfully talented young actress who will be deeply missed not only by her fans but by those of us who knew her personally…"

I couldn't listen. I got up and walked out.

Tyler met me at the studio door. "Follow me."

CHAPTER 24

I squeezed into Tyler's vintage red MG, a convertible with about as much room for my long legs as a coach seat on a cheap airline, and held on for dear life. With no explanation as to where we were going, or why, Tyler tore out of the parking lot. We sailed west down Pico Boulevard and were a good mile from the station before he hollered something in my direction. I could scarcely hear him.

"What?" With the wind whipping through my hair and the loud vibrations from the motor, I was only able to pick up about every third word, something about the station doing a remote at the pier in Santa Monica.

"...tomorrow night...you coming?"

"No!" I yelled.

Tyler swerved to miss a cyclist. I crouched down into the seat, holding my hair tight into a ponytail with one hand and bracing myself with the other as we slipped beneath a red light. If this was Tyler's attempt to clear my head of Clarissa's death I could think of a hundred better ways.

"Probably too hip for you anyway." He put the car into over drive and we continued west, toward the pier, with nothing but the sound of the wind and the roar of the MG's engine between us.

"I need to check something for tomorrow's remote. Thought we might split a bucket of shrimp."

Tyler downshifted, turning right onto Ocean Boulevard, the sound of the engine giving way to squawks of low flying seagulls and waves lapping the beach. The pier stretched out into the ocean, sparkling with sunshine, like an old fashioned boardwalk. Atop of its wooden structure vendors, restaurants and rides, including a century old carousel with hand painted horses and a huge Ferris wheel looked out over the water like a giant eye. I sat up as we approached. The smell of hot buttered popcorn and fresh salt air refreshed me.

Tyler parked the car and like a grasshopper with his skinny legs jumped out and bounded down the pier as though he was late for an appointment. He was a good thirty feet ahead of me before I caught up to him.

"We're setting up at Papa Shrimp's for the broadcast. You know why, right?"

I nodded. I didn't care about tomorrow night. My mind was still back in the studio, thinking about Sarah Millhouse and Clarissa. I could do without the small talk.

"Route 66 celebration. Twenty-four hundred and forty-eight miles from Chicago to LA. Sweet, don't you think? Doesn't actually end here though, but who's gonna know? Going to hang a sign right here tomorrow night." He hit a post with the flat of his hand as he sauntered ahead of me toward the restaurant. "Hope you're hungry, 'cause I'm starved."

I sat down in the booth across from Tyler and buried myself in the menu, my thoughts miles away. Tyler tapped impatiently on the tabletop, like he was playing the drums, I could feel his eyes penetrating the space between us. Then he grabbed the menu from my hand.

"You look like you could use a drink, and right now, you're not on the clock. Talk to me. What's going on?"

Tyler signaled to the waiter to bring two beers and ordered a bucket of shrimp.

I leaned up against the red Naugahyde booth and folded my arms in front of me. It was hard to know where to begin. I explained a second will had surfaced and that I'd spent the morning talking with Pepper's housekeeper and then Sam at the county jail.

"I'm convinced Sarah's blackmailing Arminta. As for the bath salts, I'm swimming in theories. I know Misty made up the bottles, but I'm not certain she knowingly poisoned them. She might have even done it accidentally. But what I can't shake is the feeling that Sarah and Andrew are involved, and--"

"And what?" Tyler coaxed.

"Sam knows something. I'm sure of it. She almost said as much, but then she stopped talking. King's worried. He thinks the prosecutor's got a good case and he wants to start proposing alternative theories. But Sam won't even entertain the idea. And now with Clarissa's death, I don't know what to think."

The waiter hastily put two icy cold beers down in front of us.

Tyler grabbed one and took a long swig then leaned back against the booth.

"You know exactly what happened with Clarissa. It's what everybody's thinking. Trouble is you're too close and don't want to see it." That stung. Tyler was right. I didn't want to think Sam could have possibly murdered Clarissa. "And if I had anyone else I thought could handle the story I'd take you off it. But the fact of the matter is I don't."

"Do I take that as a compliment?" I was about to pick up the beer and toast Tyler, when he interrupted.

"You know me better than that. I don't give compliments, not for doing your job anyway. But right now, because of your so-called friendship with Samantha Millhouse, you're probably the only reporter in town who's not just reiterating what the FBI and the court's telling us. You're actually investigating, asking the right questions. I like that. But I also think maybe you need to ask a few questions of yourself."

"Like?" I gestured with the bottle toward Tyler.

"All this time, Carol, haven't you had the slightest doubt about Sam? That maybe it might be just be a little too convenient for her to have you as a friend?"

"Oh, come on, Tyler, she's my neighbor. It's not like she sought me out. What are you saying? You think she set me up, or something?"

"Didn't you ever wonder why Sam didn't have an attorney of

her own? Her aunt ran a very large, successful talent agency and yet, when she needed a lawyer she asked you for a recommendation."

"She was distraught. She didn't expect to be arrested. Suddenly the police show up and she reached out to me. I merely suggested King. He's the best, you know that."

"Maybe, but what about the fact that the morning her aunt died she showed up on your doorstep?"

"She wanted to borrow my phone. Her cell died." I couldn't believe Tyler was asking such obvious questions.

"She didn't have a landline?"

"Lots of people don't these days. She didn't need one. It was expensive."

"And you don't think for one minute that maybe her knocking on your door that morning was planned?"

"No. I don't. Not at all. Damn it, Tyler, the woman's been in my home a hundred times, looks in on Charlie when I work late, tipped me off to news stories. We're friends."

"Exactly, Carol. You're friends. She's been good to you. In fact, maybe if you hadn't been friends, you might not have had access to some of the insider news you've been privy to, and if you hadn't, I might never have hired you to sit the news desk during Kari's show. Sam's given you some hot leads. No doubt helped you out."

"What are you saying? You think she's using me? That she's guilty?"

"What I think doesn't matter. It's your story, Carol. Just make sure you're covering it and not letting your personal relationships interfere."

"I think I'm quite capable of separating the two." I was about to get into a lecture of my own when the waiter brought a bucket of shrimp and a basket of curly fries and slapped them on the table. My phone rang. I excused myself and took the call. It was King.

"What's up?"

"I just got a call from Sam. She wants to talk. But I'm sicker than a dog and headed home."

"Does she know about Clarissa? That she's dead?"

King coughed and struggled to clear his throat. "I couldn't get into it on the phone and can't see her today. I'm too sick to think straight. I'll call you later."

I hung up and returned to the table. Tyler had a bib beneath his chin and had plowed into the bucket of popcorn shrimp and curly fries. He looked at me, licking his greasy fingers, like a kid who'd been caught with his hand in the cookie jar. Guilty pleasures.

"You want some?"

"No." My stomach was too tight to think of food. "That was King. Sam wants to talk."

Tyler popped a shrimp in his mouth and wiped his hands on his bib. "You know what I think? I think your friend wants to make a deal."

CHAPTER 25

The news of Clarissa's death was overwhelming. All around town mourners were holding candlelight vigils in her memory. With no word yet as to the official cause there was panic and speculation among her fans. Even the late night news was dovetailing reports of Clarissa's death with that of the Hollywood murders. The connection was obvious and speculation among viewers growing. TV crews combed the streets of Hollywood filming groups of her followers along Sunset Boulevard and standing in front of the Chinese Theater, formerly Grauman's. Most held signs and photos of her, some chanted and called for an investigation into her death, while others stood with tears in their eyes, holding tight to one another with a look of disbelief on their faces.

I was working the evening shift when Eric called. He told me the FBI had just received word from investigators in Spain that Clarissa's death was being ruled a homicide.

"Was she poisoned?" I asked. I was already certain of the answer.

"Looks like it. Once we got word of her death we asked for a medical examiner there to check into the possibility. They found suspicious looking teabags on her meal cart. It appears she carried them onboard with her."

"I'm not surprised. And I'll bet they found traces of aconite in them."

"The forensics guys there say they were laced with it. We're still waiting on an autopsy, but we know what they'll find."

I closed my eyes. I could see Clarissa and Amber sitting in the studio. She was so young, so vibrant. "It's official then. Clarissa St. Clair was murdered, and there's a connection to the other killings."

"I can't comment on a connection, Carol. Not officially, anyway. Only that Clarissa St. Clair's death was not by natural causes. She died under suspicious circumstances. But if it helps, you can say that an unidentified source close to the investigation has indicated there's been a break in the case. That it's believed Ms. St. Clair's death may be linked to that of other victims within the ACT Agency, and that the FBI is expected to be making an announcement shortly."

"Good. I'll take that for now, but I want an exclusive on this later."

Eric laughed softly. I could imagine the warmth of his breath on my ear. "But there's something else, Carol." I could hear concern in his voice.

I paused.

"Misty was right; you're a little closer to all this than I'm comfortable with. Tuck yourself in safe tonight and we'll talk in the morning. We should have everything tied up by then."

"I knew it!" I stood up and cradled the phone closer to my ear. "She is involved."

"I didn't say that, Carol. But just the same, you should go home and lock your doors. You'll be fine."

"I'm going to be glad when this is over." I closed my eyes and imagined us together. "I've been thinking we owe each other a long, luxurious soak in the tub without worrying about poisonous bath salts."

He chuckled. "Believe me, that's been on my mind, too."

I hung up the phone and refocused my energies. I could think about Eric later; right now I had a report to file. By ten p.m., news that Clarissa St. Clair's death was a homicide was my lead story.

"An unidentified source close to the investigation believes there is a link between the young actress's death and the recent Hollywood Bathtub Murders. An announcement is expected shortly."

The phone lines lit up, which surprised me, since my report fell in the middle of the late evening sports talk show. Hardly primetime, but the Dynamic Sports Duo of Dan and Deb were thrilled. Suddenly they were fielding the calls about something other than the Lakers' recent losing streak and with no game to report on and the sudden news that the FBI believed Clarissa's death to be a homicide, they opened the phone lines to callers.

Off the air, Dan thanked me. "We haven't had a criminal case like this since OJ. You mind hanging out in the studio awhile? In case we have any questions?"

Reluctantly, I agreed. They recapped the case, play-by-play, like a football game; beginning with Pepper's death and that of her business partners, then putting the ball down the field, connecting the bath salts to the young couple in North Hollywood and ending with a field goal, the suspicious circumstances surrounding Clarissa's death.

"And those two sisters, you think they're innocent? With that much money sitting on the table, I wouldn't be surprised if either of 'em did it."

I was about to leave the studio when Deb said she had a private caller on the line.

"She wants to talk to you. I'll transfer it. We've had about all the fun we can take. We're going to have to get back to sports talk."

At first I didn't recognize the voice. It was soft, high pitched, almost kitten like.

"Carol, I'm so sorry, I don't know who else to call. I need to talk to someone and… do you mind?"

"Amber?"

"I heard you on the air. I don't have anyone to talk to."

She sounded frightened, scared, childlike, very different than the self-indulgent teenager I'd seen at the station just days before.

"I used to talk to my mother when bad things happened." She sniffed. She sounded as though she might be sobbing, then paused and blew her nose. "But she's not here anymore. I can't talk to her. I miss her a lot. She was always good with scary things."

I couldn't help but feel for her. Everywhere she turned her world was crumbling. "What would she do, Amber? Tell me."

"When I'd have a nightmare we used to play a game. She told me her mother did the same thing with her. She'd sit with her arm around me and we'd sing a song. Then she would pluck the bad thoughts from my head with her fingers and blow them away with a kiss so they couldn't come back."

I could tell she was in a dark place, and it worried me.

"You really miss her, don't you?"

She sighed.

"Kim LaSalle was my mom in my last movie. Did you see it? For a while I wanted her to be my mom for real. She's pretty. But she hates kids. She told her husband she'd never have any, and once when I saw her at the commissary she totally freaked out when I called her Mom. She said I should never do that. That her name was Kim or Miss LaSalle."

Amber sounded like a little kid who'd come home from school after a bad day and needed to know the world was still a safe place. She was pulling at my maternal heart strings. I didn't trust this girl, but I couldn't turn my back on her.

She was all alone on what was probably one of the worst days of her life, and I knew she had several—with the loss of a baby brother and her mother—how could she not sound crazy? I did my best to soothe her. I figured no kid should be alone at a time like this.

"You know, I saw pictures of your mom. Sam had them at her house. They were from a party at Pepper's home, couple years ago. You look a lot like her."

"I wish...I wish she was here now." Her voice was ragged. She sniffed as though she was trying to hold back a sea of tears then blew her noise again.

"Are you okay?"

"It's hard. Everybody's gone... Pepper, Clarissa, my mother, they're all dead. It's not supposed to be like this. I know it's not. It's 'sposed to be like in the movies. In the end it's all okay. Everybody goes home happy. That's how it's got to be. Happy. We have to be happy."

She wasn't making any sense, between her garbled speech and reference to the movies I wondered if she'd been drinking, or maybe using drugs.

"Amber, I'm worried about you. Do you want me to call someone?"

There was a long silence. All I could hear was her ragged breathing, as though she were trembling.

"Maybe you should talk to your father?"

"No!" She screamed into the phone. "Not him. Absolutely not. He never wanted me to be a star. And if I go home, he'll never let me leave. Ever."

"Okay, maybe there's someone else."

I couldn't think of who I might call. Certainly not Sarah, Andrew, or Misty. If Eric was close to an arrest, I was pretty sure they'd be unavailable, and I didn't know anyone else at the agency to call.

"There's no one. I just needed to talk to you. That's all."

"But—"

"It could have been me, you know."

"What do you mean, it could have been you?"

"Clarissa... she and I did a lot of things together. I could have been the one."

"Amber, you can't think like that, please don't—"

"No. It should have been me."

"Don't blame yourself."

"You don't get it. Nobody got it. They wanted me for *Lady in White*. I was the one right for the role. But Adel and Helen, they convinced Pepper it should be Clarissa, 'cause she was older. So they pitched her. And now they've killed her."

"Killed her? Amber you're not making any sense. Who killed her?"

"They did. They killed Clarissa."

"Sarah and Misty? You think they killed Clarissa?"

"I don't trust them. Not any of them, particularly Misty. She's a witch, I know it. She has all kinds of poisons and potions in that bag of hers."

I didn't want to tell her I had the same fear. That I was certain Misty was involved.

"They like her on the set, 'cause she knows about such things, but I know she's there to watch over me. Sam and Sarah want her to. But they don't need to worry, I'm emancipated now. The judge said so. I'm responsible for myself."

I wondered if maybe I should go get her. I could have her stay at the house with me, at least until tomorrow. "Amber, I could come get you."

"Why, you afraid I might hurt myself?"

I glanced at the emergency numbers taped to my computer screen. I could call the local police department and request a welfare check. But unless she was threatening suicide they wouldn't respond.

"You've been through a tremendous shock."

"Don't worry. I know how to take care of myself. I'll make myself something to drink. I'll be fine."

I glanced at the clock. It was getting late. I needed to check the newswire, but this wasn't a conversation I was ready to let go of, not yet. I felt like I was holding onto the hand of a non-swimmer who might be about to sink to the bottom of the pool.

"I've got a newscast coming up. Give me your number. I'll call you back."

She hesitated then reluctantly gave me her number.

"Thanks, Carol. You know Charlie's really lucky. You're easy to talk to. Be sure to tell him hello for me."

I hung up the phone. I felt bad for Amber but I wasn't happy she'd brought my son into the mix. I glanced at up at the clock. It was nearly eleven. I still had a little over an hour to go. I promised myself I'd call her back when I left the station and check in. If not me, who else would?

CHAPTER 26

I pulled out of the parking lot in my Jeep just after midnight. In my rearview mirror the radio towers appeared to glow luminescent beneath a full moon. In a near cloudless sky they cast a surreal shadow inside the car. I double checked the mirror, half expecting to see Misty sitting in my backseat, smiling back at me. It was empty, but I couldn't shake the feeling I wasn't alone.

I leaned back against the seat, confident Misty wouldn't be surprising me tonight. By now, if what I suspected was correct, Misty, Sarah and Andrew were busy answering questions for the FBI. I was confident based upon what Eric had told me on the phone an arrest was imminent. Soon this whole ugly affair would be behind me, Sam would be home and my world would be back to normal.

I picked up the phone and dialed Amber's number. I wanted to get back to her. I couldn't imagine being seventeen, losing my best friend and being totally alone. I dialed her number, but there was no answer. Concerned, my next call was to the local Santa Monica Police Department. I hoped I could get them to do a welfare check, stop by and see if she was okay. I explained who I was, that I had been talking with Amber Marx on the phone and was concerned about her safety.

"I don't know exactly where she lives, but maybe you could do a reverse directory lookup, or something. She's upset and I'm concerned about her."

"Did she threaten to kill herself?" The officer sounded impatient. Phones were ringing in background. I could tell he was prioritizing calls. I probably sounded like an over-wrought fan he could dismiss and move on.

"No, but she—"

"Lady, I'm sorry, if we knocked on the door of everybody who called to say they were upset we'd never get around to responding to those calls where we're really needed."

I knew he was right. Regretfully, I hung up the phone and drove the rest of the way home in silence. I didn't want to hear music and I couldn't stomach any more news, not tonight. I just wanted to let my mind rest, let the crazy thoughts that had been kicking around in my head since Sam first knocked on my door, escape. I wanted to believe this whole affair was finally going to be over—that Eric was right. The FBI would make arrests, and if the guilty parties were who I thought they were, Sarah, Misty and Andrew would soon be behind bars, and Sam would be freed.

Except deep down inside I knew it wasn't over, not yet.

I wanted to get home and hug my son. I wanted to hold his slim body against my own and never let go. That's what parents do when death takes someone so young. They hold on to their kids. But tonight was Friday and Charlie was with his dad for the weekend and instead of the commotion of a rambunctious teenager greeting me, I'd be alone.

Bossypants meowed as I entered the house. I suppose the cat considers that a kind of greeting, but it wasn't enough to take my mind off Clarissa's murder. I flipped on the light, tossed the mail on the kitchen counter and checked the cat's bowl for food. It was empty. I took the last of the kitty-kibble from the cabinet, and scratched him behind his ears.

"Don't get too comfy, fella, your mama's coming home real soon. I promise."

At least I knew there was some light at the end of tunnel.

Exhausted, I headed upstairs, kicked off my shoes and leaving a trail of clothes behind me, slipped beneath the covers. I turned on the TV. My eyes were so tired they'd barely focus. Nearly every station I tuned to was airing reruns of the news, recapping

Clarissa's untimely death. There was no escaping it. There were red carpet interviews, clips from her past films and comments from fans. I closed my eyes finally; thankfully sleep came.

CHAPTER 27

.

The next morning I went for a run along Mulholland Drive. I needed the fresh air to clear my head and the narrow twisting road offers spectacular views from the top of the mountain's back. On the city side, the ocean glistened like a diamond beneath the bright sunshine, while on the other the Santa Susana Mountains reigned like a strong barrier protecting the grid of the valley's streets below. I kept thinking as I ran, my heart pounding, how no one had protected Clarissa and how messed up Amber sounded when we last talked.

Slowing to a jog and with my breathing heavy, I came to a stop. I doubled over with a stitch in my side and tried to catch my breath. Something didn't feel right. I pulled my phone from pocket and checked to see if I had a call from Eric. There was no message. I had an uneasy feeling things had not gone as smoothly last night as I had hoped.

My next call went to Amber. I couldn't get her out of my mind. She had sounded so troubled and alone last night. I jogged back toward the Jeep, letting the phone ring in my ear as I ran. She didn't pick up. I thought if I only knew where she lived I would go by her house and do my own welfare check. But I didn't. Instead I rationalized if I couldn't get hold of Amber, at least I could talk to her father. The girl had to have someone. Maybe her father could get through to her. After all, a parent ought to know when their kid is going through hard times. I had to do something.

*   *   *

I stood in the doorway of Burt's café, certain I looked a wreck. I hadn't bothered to change out my sweats, and with my hair pulled back in a ponytail and baseball cap, I scarcely recognized myself. Burt did a double take. I wasn't sure if he didn't remember me, or from the surprised look on his face, if perhaps it was something else.

I stepped inside. Burt stood behind the cash register, a hand towel thrown over his shoulder, his arms folded across his chest as I approached.

"I need to talk to you about your daughter."

"Carol, right?"

I nodded.

"It's a free country. Go ahead." He stepped back from the register and leaned against the wood paneled wall.

"Clarissa St. Clair was murdered yesterday."

"I heard." He nodded and wiped his hands on the towel.

"I spoke with Amber last night. She called the radio station. She was pretty upset."

He stepped forward, opened the register door and looked down, as though he were about to take something out, then slammed it shut abruptly. His action startled me, but I didn't move. I held my ground. I reminded myself Burt was a conscientious objector; the idea he had a gun or might harm me was unlikely.

"I thought maybe you might try to call her."

Without a word, Burt nodded for me to follow. He led me to the corner table where Eric and I had sat before. The café was moderately busy. A waitress served a few weekenders lingering over brunch. Burt pulled up a chair opposite me and sat down.

"Amber can talk to me anytime. She knows how I feel."

"Teenagers can be tough. I know. I'm a parent, too, and if my son was in trouble I'd want someone to tell me."

"You can stop right there." Burt pointed his finger at me, put his elbows on the table and leaned over and looked me directly in the eye. "So what'd the FBI do, send you out here to start snooping around?"

"No, I came on my own."

I was startled. I had no idea Burt might think my visit was somehow related to the FBI. Eric was clear he didn't think Burt was a suspect. I thought he knew that. I hadn't expected any of this, certainly not this reaction.

"Or did you just think you'd come out on your own and test the waters, maybe tell me what I already know. Get a reaction, something for your news report. You reporters, you're all the same. Sell outs."

"No, really, that's not why I'm here."

"'Cause with my background—the whole radical sixties thing— believe me, I don't need the FBI snooping around in my personal life. Not anymore. So unless you've got something new to tell me, I think we're done here."

Burt's voice was loud. He screeched the chair across the floor as he got up from the table. Several of the diners looked in our direction. I grabbed his wrist.

"Wait! I didn't come here for anybody but Amber, and I really don't give a rat's ass about what the FBI knows or doesn't know about you—that's ancient history far as I'm concerned—and I'm certainly not out here snooping around for any dirt between you and your daughter. I'm here because she needs you, and I think if you reached out to her it would help."

Burt exhaled, his big shoulders heaving, then taking the dish towel he'd thrown over them he started to wipe his hands.

"Look, when I spoke to her last night, she sounded pretty low. I'm worried about her."

"You realize if she comes home, I won't let her leave again."

"If I'd been through what you have, with the death of your wife and son, I don't think I would either."

Pulling the chair back out, he sat down again. I thought I might be getting through to him. His eyes met mine then looked out the window toward the creek.

"Right there's where I buried Amber's mother and my son. Least that's where I scattered their ashes. Every time I look down there, I remember them. Just like that creek, they were two of a kind, always bubbling and full of life."

"I'm sorry for your loss."

"I suppose I should have seen it coming. Amber's mother April was never well."

"I thought you said she drowned? I didn't realize she was ill."

"April had some form of mental illness. I don't know what they call it exactly. Bipolar, schizophrenia, something like that; it made things difficult between us all. I should have seen it when we first met, but it's not always easy to spot. All I saw was a beautiful young girl who had hiked up the creek. She wanted to know all about the Village and what went on here in the sixties. She thought it was romantic and mysterious. Called it her Camelot in the Canyon. I thought she'd get her fill and leave but she stayed. Truth is, she captivated me. People like that, they have a power, almost mystical. She had me under her spell, although it wouldn't have been hard back then. The Village had disbanded, it was the eighties, the hippie movement was long over and here was this beautiful young woman who wanted to—"

His eyes started to mist over. I picked up the conversation.

"Who wanted to play Guinevere to your Lancelot?" I smiled, hoping to ease the pain of his memory.

"Something like that. Truth was, I should have been more curious about her. Where she came from, who she was. Maybe if I had, I would have seen the warning signs."

I glanced up at the wall at the black and white photos of their wedding.

"You looked happy."

"For a time. Unfortunately, April was delusional, easily upset and fragile. I thought if I could just take care of her, if it'd just been us, maybe it'd work out. But then she got pregnant. You'd think she was going to give birth to the second coming she was so excited. She was convinced Amber was going to be a star. Probably didn't help that Misty was around and would read for her, told her the baby was special. I should have said something, but she was happy and Misty was able to deal with her moods with her special teas and things. Before I knew it, she had Amber out to casting calls and doing commercials. Next thing Amber's got a contract and was doing movies. April was ecstatic."

"And you?"

"Didn't like it, not at all. I didn't want Amber growing up on some Hollywood set. That's how it was you know. One movie right after the other. Kid was always on the set, or she was off for lessons, or meeting with tutors. There was no sense of reality. That's no way to grow up. I wanted her here, rock hopping in the creek down there."

"And Amber? What did she want?"

"She loved it. Turn a camera on and she came to life, like a little pixie triggered by the lens. Then my wife got pregnant and Amber started to get resentful of her mother's time with the baby. I thought it'd pass, that it was just sibling rivalry, but I was wrong."

He clasped his hands together and began rubbing his knuckles as he stared down at the creek. His thoughts lost in the past.

"Kids can get jealous," I volunteered. "It takes time to adjust."

"We didn't get time." He looked at me, cutting me off before I could say any more, his eyes boring into mine. "After the baby was born April was despondent, depressed. I didn't know what to do. Misty tried her herbs, but nothing worked. She didn't rally, not like she did with Amber. I was worried. I'd seen these black moods before, and things with Amber, they just seemed to disintegrate. And then the baby died. Crib death." He said the words with such finality I didn't know what to say. I waited for him to go on.

"I knew I had to do something. I thought if maybe if we all went away together, took a vacation, it'd get better. So I planned a trip to Mexico. San Felipe. We used to go there when Amber was little. You ever been?"

I shook my head. I couldn't think of words to say that might help. So I just listened.

"It's beautiful. Big sandy beaches, long hot days. The night so black you can't see the shore from the sky, 'cept for the stars. And there are thousands of stars. So many you think you could touch them. I thought it was going to be fine. For the first time since the baby was born my wife started to smile again, and she and Amber were laughing together. During the day we rented wave runners and at night did campfires." He stopped rubbing his hands, opened his palms and stared at them. "And then April drowned."

He paused. Pain registered on his face. He closed his eyes, exhaled then bit down on his lips, his mouth closed. Then taking a deep breath, he completed the story.

"After my wife drowned, I wanted to take care of Amber. Have her come home, stop working. I wanted to keep her here where it was safe. She needed that, but Pepper Millhouse stepped in. Far as I'm concerned that woman and her agency got what they deserved. She said Amber was too big a star to stop. She had all kinds of contracts and couldn't just quit. She looked at my daughter like she was some cash-cow she couldn't afford to lose. She convinced Amber I'd smother her, that I was jealous of her success. Before I knew it she's filed for emancipation. I'm afraid I wasn't in much of position to fight it. I'd just lost my son and my wife."

I reached into my bag, found the small piece of paper I'd scribbled Amber's phone number on the night before and pressed into his hand. "Burt, your daughter needs you. Why don't you give her a call?" Giving his hand a squeeze I got up and left.

Later that morning I was in the shower when the phone rang. It was nearly noon. I grabbed my robe, and wrapped a towel around my wet head before answering.

"Houston, we have a problem." Eric's voice sounded tired. Things hadn't gone well.

"What happened?"

"Let's just say we spent the night talking and we don't have anything, at least not enough to arrest Sarah Millhouse or Andrew

Reese. Not yet anyway. We had to kick them loose this morning. I'm not sure if we'll ever be able to charge them with anything. We'll keep Andrew under surveillance, but I don't think we'll find anything on him and quite frankly, Sarah's like I said, just not smart enough to have pulled this off."

"What about Misty?"

"Misty." I could visualize Eric shaking his head. I knew before he answered he had nothing. "I wish there was a short way to describe my conversation. But you know better. She gave me a complete chemistry lesson on the healing properties of lavender, more than I needed to know. Plus I got a run down on the power of color. Which is, just in case you want to know, not just lavender, but magenta. It was chosen for its energy properties."

"She's not exactly what you'd call a woman of few words, is she?"

I sat down in front of my dressing table, took the towel from my head and began to finger comb my wet hair. "Could she have done it accidentally?"

"Maybe, but she swears she's extremely careful and that she's never used monkshood with the bath salts. Only with her teas and then only a trace amount. It's an elaborate process. You'll forgive me if I don't get into it."

I could tell it had been a long night. Eric's voice was scratchy, half an octave lower than usual. He sounded extremely tired.

"And Sarah? Could this dumb blonde act be a role?"

"Even if it is an act the only thing we have tying her to the bath salts is her picking them up from Misty the day of Pepper's party then taking them directly to Sam's office. Based upon the time she picked up and dropped off she wouldn't have had time to tamper with the bottles, or even switch them out for that matter. The box was sealed, her fingerprints aren't on any of the bottles and she was alone in the car."

"Alone? I don't think so." I surprised myself with the energy of my response. It was as though the words "alone in the car" had touched a nerve. Sam had told me how she'd ask Sarah to pick up the bottles of bath salts, but she'd also asked her another favor. "Sarah had Amber with her. Oh my God! It's Amber! It's got to be. Sarah took her back to the agency when she picked up the bottles. Amber had an appointment with a new tutor that afternoon and Sam didn't want her to miss it."

I was beginning to think I might have an idea what Sam was doing. She was protecting Amber.

"I don't know why I didn't think of it before. I've been so focused on Sarah and Andrew that it didn't even register. But it makes perfect sense. Misty had the bath salts with her on the set and Amber's with her nearly every day. She would have had plenty of time and opportunity, plus she's been studying witchcraft for years. It's part of her character as the sorcerer's daughter. By now she must know as much as Misty, maybe more."

I sat up and grabbed my comb and began combing my hair.

"And it would explain why Sam's been unwilling to point a finger at anyone. I thought it was her sister, but it's not. It's Amber. At first maybe Sam even thought Pepper's death was an accident. That's why she talked so big. She didn't think someone had really murdered Pepper. But at some point, after she was arrested, I think she figured it out, and she's been trying to protect Amber ever since. She probably even told Sarah, but she's afraid Sarah will say something, so she doesn't dare incriminate her. It's just like Sam to protect her people. She always bragged the big difference between herself and her aunt was that she believed in taking care of the talent."

"Protecting her people is a long shot from being an accessory to murder."

"I don't think Sam's believes she's an accessory. If anything, I think she believes she's helping Amber. It would explain why King called to tell me after Clarissa died that Sam wanted to cut a deal. I think that's when she figured it out, and I think Amber's father knows too."

"Whoa! That's a leap. You really think Burt Marx believes his daughter may have murdered six people, and is keeping it quiet?"

"I know he's worried. Amber called the station last night, right after I reported Clarissa's death to be a homicide. She sounded frightened and she wasn't making a lot of sense. She wanted to talk. She said she missed her mother. I was worried about her and I had to get off the phone for my next newscast. I called back when I left work and again this morning, but I couldn't reach her, so I went to see her father. Did you know Amber's mother suffered from mental illness?"

"He told you that?"

"He told me she was ill. I got the feeling she'd been emotionally unstable for a long time. He said he didn't know much about her, where she was from, her family, that kind of thing. The kind of questions you ask when you're curious about someone. Too bad the FBI doesn't have a file on her."

Eric laughed.

"Contrary to public opinion, Carol, we don't have files on everybody."

"Yes, but if you did, maybe we'd know something about her mental history. As it is, I'm pretty sure Burt knew something was wrong and was trying to cure her on his own. And knowing his relationship with Misty, probably even solicited some of her magic potions. Truth is, I think he's afraid we'll find out his daughter's suffering from the same mental disorder, and he'll lose her as well."

I stood up, threw the towel in the hamper and walked into the closet. With the phone tucked beneath my chin I started to look for something to wear.

"He said Amber and her mother hadn't been getting along. That after the baby died, things started to get strange between them. I suspect he thinks that might have even triggered Amber's illness."

"Did he say anything to indicate that his wife's drowning in Mexico might be other than accidental?"

I stopped sorting through my closet, my hand on a hanger, and stared at a shirt "You think Amber murdered her mother?"

"It'd be tough to prove."

"Yes, but it might explain why Burt had both of the bodies cremated! She may have killed her baby brother, too. He told me he spread their ashes in the creek behind the restaurant. Can you imagine, looking down there every day and knowing that?" I put the shirt on and pulled on a pair of slacks off the hanger. "I'll bet he wanted to make certain that if anyone like the FBI came snooping around they'd never know."

"You think Pepper Millhouse knew how sick Amber was, that she may have murdered her mother?" Eric asked.

"I'm not sure how much Pepper knew, but I think she thought she could control Amber. More importantly, she didn't want to lose a big star. Amber Marx was worth millions to Pepper Millhouse, both personally and to the agency. So she covered it up, made up a story that Amber's mother drowned while on a family vacation in Mexico. Then she convinced Amber her father wanted to isolate her from the world, take her away from the very thing she loved. Probably told her she'd never see a stage or studio again and that he'd end her career forever. It would explain the hostilities between Pepper and Burt and even more why Pepper never wanted Amber out of her sight."

"But if Amber Marx was suffering from a serious mental illness—enough so that she plotted out to kill six people—how is it no one saw it, or dared to report it?"

"I don't think anybody outside Pepper's inner circle, and by that I mean her business partners, Adel and Helen, knew anything about Amber's instabilities. If Sam knew she never mentioned it to me. Far as I knew the girl was just difficult, typical teenage girl angst, that kind of thing. All I know is what Sam told me: Amber was seldom alone; she had a handler with her always. Even after her emancipation from her father, Pepper made certain someone was with her. And Pepper would have squelched any story that might have shed a clue as to Amber's real trouble. There wasn't a word in any of the tabloids about her brother's death and very little about her mother's."

"But if Amber found out that Pepper and her business partners were growing concerned about her mental stability and wanted to rein her in—"

"Or that they pitched Clarissa for *Lady in White*—given her condition—she just may have decided to do something about it."

"Possibly." Eric said.

I put the phone down on a small dressing stool and set it to speaker while I finished putting my slacks on.

"What are you doing?"

"Getting dressed. We're going to get her, right?"

"We?" Eric paused, his demeanor suddenly professional, "*We* are not going anywhere. I'm going to a drive out to Santa Monica and have a talk with Amber."

"Humph," I responded, not happy with this shift back to his professional persona. "I'm not so sure I like being left out of the action."

"Sorry. This isn't a ride along. You and I'll talk later."

CHAPTER 28

I hung up the phone and stewed. Frustrated. If I couldn't accompany Eric to question Amber I could at least go back to work. I had an unsettled feeling in the pit of my stomach that there was something else. Something I had missed when I had last seen Amber with Clarissa at the station. Radio stations, particularly talk radio stations, keep a twenty-four hour digital recording of everything that's broadcast. Mostly it's used as a backup to verify the airing of commercials and sometimes the legal department needs it in the event someone on air may have slipped up and said something slanderous. But I wanted to listen to the last time Amber had been on station with Clarissa.

Fortunately, Saturday afternoons were quiet. I could have rolled a bowling ball through the dimly lit hallways and not hit anyone. Tyler was off with the KCHC's Street Team, preparing for tonight's big Pier Party, leaving an intern to man the news department. He scarcely looked up as I headed to the small recording studio where I could listen to Kari's show without being interrupted.

The show was exactly as I remembered it. Kari and Sarah chatting casually as though the two were sitting at a lunch counter. I could hear the clatter of Kari's coffee cup on the console and something else. I hit reverse and replayed the section several times. In the background I could hear giggling. I closed my eyes and listened harder, playing the scene back again in my head. Amber and Clarissa were sitting at the other end of the console, waiting to be interviewed. During the station break they had emptied their purses and like any teenage girls, the two were crouched over the cell phones, texting and exchanging makeup. Squeals of laughter, then Sarah got upset and told them to pick up their toys. At least I think that's the word she used. Toys. Amber was angry.

I stopped the recording, the sound of Clarissa's faint giggle still in my ears. I tried harder to remember the scene. Amber stood up. She was helping Clarissa put her things back into her bag: makeup, cell phone, wallet. They seemed to be talking about something; was it my imagination or did Amber stuff something in Clarissa's purse? Could that have been the teabags?

I was still sitting in the recording studio when my cell rang.

I knew better than to think it could be Eric. There was no way the FBI had wrapped the case this early. Even under the best of circumstances I wasn't expecting to hear from him much before midnight, and if I did, I figured he'd text first. Code 4 for all-clear, giving me a heads up he was about to finish and maybe come by. I glanced at the caller ID. It was blocked. I knew as I stared at the phone, feeling it vibrate in my hand, it was trouble. I debated whether or not to answer, then did.

"Hello?"

"Do you know where your son is?"

The blood in my veins went to ice.

"Who is this?"

"Carol, it's Sarah Millhouse. You need to listen to me. Your son is with Amber Marx."

"What?"

"She's upset. She's been calling all morning, using different phones. She's on the move, acting crazy. She wants me to get her a ticket to Spain. She thinks they're waiting for her to take Clarissa's role."

"What's all this got to do with my son?"

"All I know is that she told me Charlie's with her."

"Is this a joke? Cause if you're trying to get some payback for my reports concerning the murders I'll—"

"Don't threaten me, Carol, not now. Just call your son, okay? He's in danger."

Dial tone.

She hung up without saying another word. The dull sound droned in my ear like an emergency siren. Immediately I picked up the phone and called Charlie's dad. I could think of a lot of reasons why Sarah Millhouse might be harassing me, starting with the fact I was Sam's good friend and she knew I was on to her poor little sister act. But I couldn't believe she'd stoop so low as to use my son.

"Is Charlie with you?" I tried to hide the anxiety in my voice.

"No, why? Something wrong? He's at the beach with some buddies. He wanted to go down for KCHC's Pier Party to commemorate Route 66. He said you were fine with it. I figured you'd be there. Everything okay?"

"He's with Amber Marx."

"Really?" He laughed. "Not bad."

"This isn't funny, Robert. It's looking like she's a suspect in the Hollywood Murders."

"Oh come on, Carol. What is she, seventeen? I think you've been seeing a few too many of her movies."

I hated my ex at that moment. Reasoning with him had always been an issue. He constantly accused me of being overly dramatic.

"Look. This is serious. I need you to call him. He may be in danger."

"We're supposed to pick him up at ten p.m. I suppose we could pick him up a little early, but really—"

"Just call him, all right? And when you get hold of him, tell him he's got to ditch her and call me ASAP. I'm headed there now. This is no joke. He could be in trouble."

I hung up the phone and glanced up at the studio clock. It was six-fifteen.

My next call went to Eric and straight to voicemail. I left a message, my voice shaking with emotion. "Charlie's at the pier with Amber Marx. Call me when you get this. I'm headed there now."

Traffic to the beach on a Saturday night, particularly across town on the 10, can be a nightmare, a good hour's commute. But after years of playing beat the clock to get back to the radio station in time for a meeting or a broadcast I had an inside track, and it wasn't the freeway. There wasn't a surface street or back alley I didn't know. Driving white-knuckled with the steering wheel in one hand and my phone in the other I tried repeatedly to call Charlie. But there was no answer.

All I could think of as I zigzagged across the west side and flew the wrong way down a one-way alley was that Misty had warned me. *Death was all around me. Dammit, Charlie, why'd you go to the beach?*

I got to Santa Monica in the longest forty-five minutes in my life. It was dark as I pulled onto Ocean Boulevard and my phone started to ring. I nearly rear-ended the car in front of me. My cell registered the incoming call was from Charlie.

"Charlie? Charlie, can you hear me? Hello?"

He didn't answer. All I got was a mishmash of indecipherable noises: muffled conversations, laughter, the tinny sounds of music from the arcades and a barker yelling, "Ov'r here, Miss." And then the phone went dead. The call was lost.

Anxiously I redialed.

"Dammit, Charlie, you butt-dialed me. Pick up, please, pick up!" The call went directly to voicemail.

I did a U-turn. Pulled up in front of the Ivy Restaurant and tossed my keys to a valet. Without waiting for a receipt, I ran out in the middle of traffic, dodging cars like a maniac and stumbled up the pier's wooden steps.

Ahead of me crowds of people mobbed the boardwalk. I pushed through them, gripping the phone in my hand, bobbing my head above that of strangers, my eyes scanning the crowd. Charlie was here somewhere. I had to find him before Amber claimed him as her seventh victim.

I cut through a long line of people, families with little children waiting for the carousel ride, spilling popcorn as I bumped shoulders with their faceless bodies. I didn't see him anywhere.

I stood in the center of the pier, my heart pounding, sweat rolling down me. I was surrounded by people who blocked my view.

"Charlie!" I screamed, but my voice was drowned out by the rollercoaster as it thundered overhead, the clatter and vibration so loud it shook the pier beneath my feet. There was no way if my phone rang I could hear it. I gripped my cell harder, pleading for it to ring, but there was nothing. I stared at the screen. It was dark.

Desperate, I moved toward the side of pier and climbed up onto the narrow railing. Despite my fear of heights, I balanced myself against a lamp post and with a chilly breeze at my back, pushed the hair out of my face until I had an unobstructed view. Beneath a full January moon the old wooden pier stretched out above the black waters like a boulevard packed with partygoers, lit with happy lights and flagged with banners.

Standing on my toes, hoping to get a better signal, I held tight to the lamp post. I refused to give into my fear and look down at the dark waters below me. I held my phone up to the sky. Finally, it rang.

"Charlie?" I pressed the phone to my ear, anxious for his voice but instead I got more bits and pieces of an almost indecipherable conversation.

"When we first met I thought maybe you were older." It was Amber's light voice, although I could barely make out what she was saying. The signal kept fading in and out with the sound of the night breeze and the ocean beneath me. I put one hand over my ear and pressed the phone to the other, straining to hear. Somewhere in this crowd my son was walking with Amber Marx, maybe just feet away from me, totally unaware of the danger he was in. "...it's magic...you feel like you can fly..."

My heart started to pound. I must have had a thousand conversations with Charlie about the dangers of drugs. I felt helpless as I listened to Amber offering my son something that would make him feel like he could fly. All I could do was pray. *God, Charlie, don't be stupid.*

I yelled back into the phone. "Dammit, Charlie, pick up, now!"

Again there was no answer. The only thing I could hear were the sounds of their feet scuffing the pier's wooden planks and the faint sound of music in the background. I struggled to make out from which direction the music was coming. It wasn't the old-world waltz music like that coming from the carousel but a more tinny sound like that of an organ grinder. I stood up on my tiptoes. *Where is it?*

And then I saw him. The organ grinder with his monkey was standing directly in front of the radio station's remote booth next to Papa Shrimp's. I jumped down from railing, weaving through the crowd, bumping shoulders and nearly tripping over small children. I was almost there when a hand grabbed me from behind.

"Carol! What are you doing here?"

I spun around to find myself face to face with Eric. He obviously hadn't received my message. "It's Charlie!" I screamed. "He's here. He's with Amber."

Eric nodded to two other agents, dressed in FBI windbreakers. They each appeared to be scanning the crowd, one talking into his phone.

"It's going to be okay." He put his hand on my shoulder and looked me in the eye. I wanted to believe him. "We'll find them."

"Charlie's phone's been auto dialing. I could hear them talking and the music from an organ grinder." I was breathing hard, the words tumbling from my mouth. I pointed toward a crowd surrounding an odd looking man with a top hat and a monkey with a tambourine. "They've got to be over there."

"No, we've got a sighting. They're in line for the Ferris wheel." The agent on the phone nodded to the giant wheel, lit with thousands of colored lights. Without a word to me, Eric and the two agents started running in the direction of the big ride.

I stared up at the wheel, unable to move. Its glittered lights formed a kaleidoscope of patterns against the nighttime sky as it began to move. I strained to see if Charlie was onboard, scanning each of the cars for their faces. Then I saw them, Charlie sitting up straight next to Amber, his arm around her shoulder. She was dressed in a brown bomber jacket, the hem of her yellow skirt floating with the breeze as the gondola began to rise above the pier.

My eyes followed the car up into the sky, and as I did I felt a familiar presence behind me. I turned to see Misty Dawn.

"What are you doing here?"

"Sarah called me, right after she got off the phone with you. She's worried about Amber and I called your Agent Langdon and told him Amber was at the pier. So here we are, all of us. Just as it should be."

She smiled and stepped aside. Behind her was Sarah, with her eyes focused on the wheel, she approached me and whispered. "She's in character, Carol. She's not dealing with reality."

"What do you mean character?" I snapped.

Overhead Amber was leaning out over the safety bar, waving her arms to the crowd below like a bird about to take flight.

"Oh my God! Look at her, she thinks she can fly." I looked at Misty and her cool, cloudy blue eyes appeared to almost glow in the dark as she stared up at them. "I heard them on the phone saying she could fly."

"You're certain she said fly?" Misty asked.

I nodded.

"It's the witches' brew." Misty leaned closer to me. "She's made some."

"She's shape shifting," Sarah added.

"What do mean, shape shifting?"

Sarah answered, glancing over at Misty. "She's doing a scene from *The Sorcerer's Daughter*."

"What scene?" I asked.

"The death scene." They answered in unison, each putting an arm around my shoulder as we stood and watched beneath the big wheel.

My eyes were riveted on the gondola. Amber was now even more animated as she waved to the crowd below. Her yellow skirt billowed in the breeze revealing her long, slim alabaster legs. Charlie reached for her but she twisted away, tossing her long curls over her shoulder as she turned her back to the crowd and faced him. The car started to swing erratically. Charlie was pushed back into his seat. Then gripping one of the handholds, Amber turned back to the crowd and slipped a leg over the safety bar. As though she were oblivious to the danger she climbed out of the car until she was standing in her small white ballerina slippers on the step outside the gondola.

Below the wheel couples and families with children waiting in line looked up, stopped eating their popcorn and began pointing up in the air and yelling.

"Look that's Amber Marx! Hey, that's Amber! What's she doing? Are they filming something?"

Almost simultaneously the attendant beneath the big wheel grabbed a bullhorn and began yelling.

"Sit down! You have to sit down. Sit!"

An emergency alarm blared. The attendant hit a button and the big wheel groaned to a stop. Instantly the kaleidoscope of multi-colored lights was snuffed out, plunging the wheel into darkness, leaving the gondolas to swing silently in the black sky.

I pushed through the crowd, bumping bodies twice my size with Misty and Sarah at my side, until we were directly beneath the ride. Search lights that had been used to call attention to the Pier Party re-focused on the gondola, spotlighting Amber as she teetered on the step outside the gondola, now thirteen stories above the pier.

I grabbed Misty's hand, the scene before me quickly going from bad to worse. Charlie was standing up, his body braced against the side wall of the gondola, gripping the handhold as he reached for Amber.

Suddenly the car jerked, pitching forward violently. Charlie fell, his legs slipping out beneath him. Holding tight to the strap above his head his body hung, halfway suspended over the guard rail, fighting the pull of gravity and certain death. Then another sudden lurch and with the car swinging back into a neutral position, Charlie twisted with the motion, regaining his balance. Eric seized the bullhorn from the attendant.

"Charlie, this is Agent Langdon with FBI. Can you hear me? I need you to stay seated."

Eric turned to the agent next to him.

"Call the fire department. We're going to need a ladder, and get an ambulance out here, fast."

Charlie didn't move. His hand remained outstretched to Amber.

Eric tried again. "Listen to me, Charlie, the car you're in, it's not balanced. It's too dangerous for you to be standing up. You need to sit down."

Charlie wasn't responding. He leaned farther out of the car, holding tight to the hand hold. He was begging Amber to come to him, reaching for her.

She refused and gripping the safety strap high above her head she took one foot off the gondola. Like an acrobat she pirouetted out of his reach, brushing the tips of his fingers with her free hand as her yellow skirt swirled about her.

The crowd gasped.

Charlie lurched forward again. Grasping for her. This time he nearly doubled over the safety bar headfirst before catching his balance.

My heart stopped.

I turned away. I couldn't watch. I was certain Amber was going to jump and take Charlie with her.

Misty whispered in my ear. "Remember what I told you, Carol, your energy can change the course of fate."

"What are you talking about?" I pushed her away and stared up at Charlie. He was white with fear, gripping the bar in front of him. "I don't need your crazy hocus pocus tricks or your black magic. I need my son to be safe."

She stepped back and put her hand on my shoulder, the weight of it oddly heavy for her thin fingers. "I know you don't believe in me, but you do believe in your son. He's done this exact thing dozens of times. He's a natural athlete."

I looked at her, a crazy old lady with glassy white cataracts staring back at me. Around us, the crowd was growing like a feeding frenzy of sharks waiting for someone to fall.

"What are you talking about? He's never done anything like this."

"Of course he has, Carol. Think about it." Her voice was soft and soothing. "That old tree in your courtyard. He's climbed it, straight up to the top, dozens of times. The last time he did you sent him out to rescue the cat so you could talk to Sam."

I don't know how she knew about my conversation with Sam, or Charlie's rescue of Bossypants, but the fact she did momentarily caused me to glance away from the big wheel and into her eyes.

As I did, I felt a strange sense of calm come over me and a separation from the angst of the crowd around us. It was though it was just the two of us. Her voice almost hypnotic.

"You don't have to believe in me. But trust your son. He can do this."

She took my hand and placing it on her chest, told me to block out the negative energy around me, to concentrate solely on her voice.

"Breathe with me. See him in your mind, talking calmly to Amber, just like he did the cat. She'll respond."

I didn't have a choice. I couldn't bear to look at the scene in front of me another moment. I was certain Charlie was going to fall. Trembling, I closed my eyes and clenched Misty's hand in my own.

"Breathe for me. Slow and steady. In and out. Match the rhythm of my breath. Let my energy guide you."

I did as she instructed. I took a deep breath. Every fiber of my body was shaking, but I didn't dare open my eyes. I had to replace the vision in front of me. I needed to see Charlie, healthy and happy, walking into the kitchen, the cat under his arm with that big goofy smile on his face.

"That's right. Breathe deep."

My breathing was ragged, choppy.

"Slow it down a bit, and when you breathe out I want you to visualize the cat. See him in the tree, listening to Charlie. Nod for me when you have that picture in your mind."

I nodded.

I could see Bossypants curled up in a ball on a branch above Charlie's head.

"Good. Now can you hear the cat?"

I shook my head. Around me the noise of the crowd broke my concentration. I could hear the fire trucks and ambulance on the pier behind me. People talking. I was distracted.

"Try again, Carol. Stay calm. If you're calm, he'll be calm. We don't want him reacting to all this nervous energy. Block everything else out."

Squeezing my eyes shut I forced myself to recreate the scene until I could see Bossypants in the tree. He was just beyond Charlie's reach. Charlie stretched farther, his slim arm reaching for him. *Here kitty-kitty.* The cat resisted, pulling back. He looked as though he might spring from the tree at any moment. A fall would be fatal. Then coaxing him gently the cat inched toward him, purring softy.

"Ah!" A gasp from the crowd broke my concentration. I was too afraid to open my eyes. I gripped Misty's hand. *Did they fall?*

"He's got her, Carol. You can open your eyes. He's okay."

Within moments the lights on the big wheel lit up. A kaleidoscope of patterns flashed, lighting up the nighttime sky as the gondolas slowly started back to their load position. I didn't take my eyes off Charlie, not for an instant. He sat with his back straight up against the chair, the color drained from his face. Amber appeared to be talking. Her lips moving, Charlie's head barely nodding. He had one arm over her shoulder and his free hand firmly gripped her upper arm. He looked as though he was afraid to let go.

Eric turned to the crowd. Photographers had now joined a growing group of curiosity seekers. He asked them all to step back. A camera flashed in front of him. He palmed the lens with his hand.

"This is a federal investigation, not a photo shoot. I need you all to back up." The photographer grumbled, turned his back and then shot a quick photo of Amber just before the car arrived at the loading bay.

I waited with Sarah and Misty, our hands clasped together, as the car descended. Eric stepped forward and took Amber from Charlie. She looked deranged, her hair tangled and matted against her head. Gently he cuffed her then handed her over to one of the other agents. The crowd parted as she passed before us, her face hidden beneath the agent's jacket, as he led her to the waiting ambulance. Within minutes the EMTs slammed the doors, red lights flashed and the fire engine and emergency response unit vacated the scene.

For a moment I couldn't see beyond Eric's broad shoulders. I wanted to run up beneath the wheel and grab Charlie, but Misty held me back. Then Eric turned slightly and I could see them both. Eric put one hand on Charlie's shoulder and another on his head. He appeared to be looking into his eyes, asking questions. I couldn't hear what they were saying. All I could see was Charlie shaking his head and Eric tousling Charlie's sandy blonde hair affectionately. Then with his arm around my son, Eric led him back to me.

"He's fine, just a little shaken up. Why don't you both go grab something to eat? I need to check on Amber."

CHAPTER 29

I put my arms around Charlie and hugged him close. With his cool face pressed against my own I could feel his skinny frame through his sweatshirt, his heart pounding. I kissed his cheek. I could taste the salt air on his skin. His hair was damp with fear.

"You okay?"

He nodded, his head shaking involuntarily. "She confessed, Mom. She killed Clarissa. She killed them all."

"I know. We need to talk."

Pulling his hoodie up over his head and with one arm around his slim waist I led Charlie away from crowd beneath the big wheel. I wanted to protect his identity from curious onlookers and paparazzi surrounding us. Charlie looked pale. With his arms tightly crossed in front of him and his eyes downcast, we walked away. Away from what I feared may have been Misty's premonition. We walked away from the darkness of death and toward the music, toward the tinny sounds of the organ grinder and the waltz of the carousel, toward the smell of popcorn and laughter. Toward life. I wanted to feel the fresh sea air in our faces and the pier's rough-hewn wooden planks beneath our feet.

"How about we get out of here, find some place quiet to eat? Maybe go across the street for Mexican?" I didn't care what it was. I wanted to get as far away from the pier as possible.

"Yeah, sure."

We quickened our pace and were halfway down the pier towards the entrance when I recognized Charlie's dad and his wife. They were walking in our direction. Rob was pushing a baby carriage and Stephanie had another toddler in tow. They appeared oblivious to anything but each other, totally ignoring the exit of the fire department's big hook and ladder truck, until it honked alerting them to its presence as it passed slowly by. Only then did my ex look up.

"Hey there Buddy, how you doing?"

Charlie looked at me and smiled. My ex had missed the excitement. We both knew his father was going to have trouble believing the story. Not until it showed up on the late night news would he accept that Charlie had actually rescued Amber Marx from a near fatal fall.

"You ready to go? Your mom said you came down here to see Amber Marx." He winked at me. *He's growing up, Carol.* "Big party, huh?"

I was about to say something, tell him this wasn't just a big party, but that he very nearly lost his son, when I heard someone calling my name.

"Hey, Carol, wait up."

I turned to see Tyler running toward me.

"That your son up there?" Tyler was panting, out of breath. "I thought I recognized him with Amber Marx. Lucky kid. You okay?"

My ex looked at Charlie. He had no idea what Tyler was talking about. He put his hand on the back of Charlie's neck and rubbed it. With his thumb he pushed the hair from his collar as though he were looking for evidence of some amorous affair, lipstick perhaps?

"He's fine." I pushed my ex's hand away from Charlie's neck and I shot him a look. *We'll talk later.* Then I turned to Tyler. "We were just going to grab a bite across the street."

"Actually, Carol, I was hoping I could get you to come with me. We're broadcasting live from Papa Shrimp's. We were covering the party when the ruckus started up and someone yelled jumper. I look up and see Amber Marx standing on top of the Ferris wheel and the crowd below is going wild. Girl looks like she's about to take a header, and then I see what looks like your son leaning out over the gondola pulling her back in. Since you're the only one who knows what just went down, how about it? You up for an interview? You too, kid?"

My ex looked at me quizzically. I shrugged my shoulders. *Hey, I told you.*

There was an awkward silence. Tyler looked at me then back at my ex, and, realizing he had interrupted a family moment, attempted an apology. "Sorry to bother you like this, but that's quite the kid you've got there. You must be real proud. That was some rescue."

I smiled at Charlie.

"I'll do the interview. You can explain the rest of it to your dad. Best it come from you anyway." Then turning to my ex, I added, "And next time your son tells you he wants to go to the beach alone at night, call me."

I followed Tyler back to Papa Shrimp's. Outside the restaurant KCHC's promotional team was busy handing out keychains, t-shirts and autographed photos of the on-air staff. Directly inside the front door, cozied up in a corner of the restaurant's curio shop, was the station's portable studio.

Tyler patched us into KCHC's Dynamic Duo, Dan and Deb, and handed me a headset. I listened as they took cell calls from anxious listeners who had just witnessed Amber's dramatic rescue, describing her lithe body, hanging in the air like a Cirque de Soleil performer, a dancing ballerina, luminescent against the black sky, one hundred and fifty feet above the pier.

Some suggested this was a suicide attempt, based upon the death of her best friend, Clarissa St. Clair. Others were convinced this was just another Hollywood promotional stunt, something for her new movie, *The Sorcerer's Daughter.* Interpretations of the event, unlike my own thoughts, were all over the board.

I knew Amber was the killer. I was certain of it, but as to how much I could report on the air without verification of the evidence was going to be tricky. In the public's eye she wasn't a suspect. She hadn't been charged with anything, and right now she looked more like a victim than a villain. I was glad Tyler was doing the interview and I could gauge my response to his questions without revealing everything I knew. I took a deep breath and waited for Tyler to open.

"Folks, I'm sitting here inside Papa Shrimp's with the mother of the young man who moments ago dramatically rescued Amber Marx from certain death, and who I'm proud to say, coincidentally happens to be our own KCHC reporter, Carol Childs. He's a real hero, Carol. Am I embarrassing you?"

I glared at Tyler. *Where are you going with this?*

"You think I'm exaggerating? For those just joining us, let me say, it was Carol's son, Charlie, who risked his own life to save Amber Marx from a near fatal fall, and let me add, it looked touch and go for a moment. Carol, were you surprised?"

My throat tightened.

With his hand waving for me to respond, he continued. "Come on, Carol, tell us what you know. Was this a suicide attempt, or as some of our listeners have suggested, a promotional stunt? Something to hype Amber's next film?"

I cleared my throat.

"I can say with absolute certainty I don't believe this was a stunt of any kind."

"Then you were surprised to see your son, leaning outside the gondola, nearly falling himself, while attempting to save Amber Marx?"

I paused, closed my eyes and exhaled.

"It's a vision I'd rather not relive. But no, I had no idea."

"Excuse me, but do you mean to say that you had no idea he'd be here, or that Amber was in such a state? I mean, it was you who broke the news last night about Clarissa St. Clair's death, her good friend. Do you think that might have put her over the edge?"

"I don't know, Tyler. I can only say that I spoke with Amber last night after my broadcast. She called the station to talk. She sounded distraught and overwhelmed; I was worried about her."

"Did you think she was suicidal?"

"I was concerned that she was alone and depressed, yes, but

suicidal, no. We talked and she assured me before we got off the phone she was fine."

"And yet, suddenly she's here and with your son, and so are you."

"Right." I exhaled. "And believe me no one is more shocked than I am. Late this afternoon I got a call from a source close to Amber who told me she was at the pier and that my son, Charlie, was with her."

Tyler scribbled "who" on a yellow pad with a big question mark and shoved it in my direction.

I shook my head. *Don't ask.* I wasn't ready to get into it with Sarah Millhouse. I still had my doubts about her role, but now was not the time.

"Is there any reason to believe your son and Miss Marx were involved?

"No. Absolutely not. My son's a fan. Like a lot of kids. I know he saw a tweet from Amber Marx earlier in the week informing him about the Pier Party. He was down here with friends. Their meeting was accidental. I don't know anything more than that."

Even as I said it I wondered, *was I right?* Was it accidental? Or had Amber fixated on me, like she had Kim LaSalle, because she missed her mother? Maybe she wanted to hurt me through my son. I didn't know.

"Lucky for Amber she met Charlie. That was quite some rescue. You must be pretty proud."

"On the contrary, Tyler, I'm overwhelmed. Seeing Charlie up there like that is something I'll never forget it. No mother would."

"So let's get serious. If this wasn't a publicity stunt, Carol, do you think there's a connection to the death of Clarissa St. Clair and possibly the Hollywood murders?"

"I'm afraid there's a lot we don't know yet, Tyler. The only thing we know for certain is that Amber Marx was taken tonight by ambulance to the UCLA Medical Center for observation, and until the FBI has had a chance to question Miss Marx, it's too early to say what charges, if any, may be filed. I suppose we'll have to—"

"Stay tuned." Tyler interrupted, putting his hand on top of mine. The station was about to commercial break. "Carol, I think our listeners know that for the most accurate and up to date information on the Hollywood Murders and Amber Marx's near fatal fall and the story behind it, KCHC is their number one choice."

CHAPTER 30

Sunday morning I was sitting at the kitchen counter. I was still in my robe, sipping my coffee, and trying to wipe the vision of Charlie standing up on top of the Ferris wheel from my mind, when the doorbell rang. It was Eric, smiling apologetically, holding his phone in his hand. He was wearing the same clothes he had on last night, sans the FBI windbreaker. His shirt wrinkled, the collar open, his hair mussed like he'd finger-combed it as he came up the walk.

"I would have called, but my phone died."

"I've heard that line before." I smiled and opened the door. He was a welcome sight. "In fact, I think that's how this whole affair with Sam got started. She stood right there and said the same thing."

He laughed and stepped inside.

"I thought about going back to the marina, to my Sea Mistress, but I wanted to see you."

"I'm glad you did. I'd hate to think she had something to offer I didn't." I stepped closer and put my arms around his neck, then kissed him. We held each other, letting the exhaustion from last night drain from our bodies.

"How'd it go with Amber?"

"It was one of the stranger nights of my career." He glanced around the room then back at me. "We alone?"

"Unless you count the cat; he's slinking around here somewhere."

"I was actually more interested in Charlie. How's he doing this morning?"

"He went home with his dad. It was his weekend. But after last night, I don't think he's much of a fan of Amber Marx anymore. I suspect those days are over."

"I'd imagine so."

I suggested coffee and led the way to the kitchen, listening as Eric told me about Amber.

"She was in and out of things last night, not exactly coherent. At least not a hundred percent. At times I thought she was playing a role. She kept talking about a script, maybe from one of her movies. Her conversation, her persona, it was all over the place. Everything changed about her: facial expressions, posture, speech. I've never seen anything like it."

I handed him a cup of coffee and we sat down at the kitchen table.

"That's how she sounded the last time I talked to her. She called the station and I barely recognized her voice. At times I thought it was like talking to a small child. Then she'd change the subject and I'd have no idea what she was talking about, or even recognize her voice."

"The doctors who examined her said she probably hadn't slept in days, and that may have triggered this latest episode."

"So the doctors think there may have been others?" I wondered how long this had been going on.

"They wouldn't get into it with us. Not specifics anyway. But they admitted her. Initially they described it as a schizophrenic episode, that she's been suffering from bipolar disorder and had lost touch with reality. According to the docs the symptoms, hallucinations, delusions, thought disorders, they can come and go. There are periods of normalcy and then suddenly they're off into a world of their own." He took a sip of coffee. He looked exhausted, his eyelids heavy. "But she did confess. She admitted to poisoning Pepper Millhouse and her business partners because she was afraid they didn't like her anymore. The old ladies, as she called them, didn't want her for *Lady in White,* and she killed Clarissa because she got the role."

"And what about Kim LaSalle, did she say she was also one of her targets?"

"She seemed to mix up Miss LaSalle with her mother. One minute she thought Kim LaSalle was her mother and the next she was talking about April Marx, as though the two were interchangeable in her mind. She kept jumping back and forth between Kim, her mother, her baby brother, Mexico, the drowning. Near as we can tell, Kim LaSalle was a target. I wouldn't be at all surprised if we don't find out she killed her mother, too, and that, just as you suspected, her father's known all along."

I stood up and grabbed my bag and pulled out my reporter's pad. Misty's pink sachet of love potions fell out onto the counter. I glanced quickly over at Eric to see if he had noticed. He was staring into his coffee cup, his mind elsewhere. I stuffed the sachets back into my robe's pocket. I didn't need them. After all, Eric hadn't gone back to his Sea Mistress, he was here with me. I sat back down and started taking notes. I was going to have to file a report soon and I wanted to make certain I had all the facts.

"And Heather Broderick? Did she say anything about her? Did she intend to kill her and her boyfriend?"

"I don't think Amber even knew Heather Broderick. Near as we can tell, both those deaths were unintended. In fact, it was exactly like you and I discussed at Burt's Place. According to Amber, the bottles she made up were for Pepper and her business partners, Kim LaSalle, Sam, and Sarah."

"That's six victims. You think Clarissa had the seventh bottle?"

"We're checking Clarissa's apartment now. It's likely Clarissa took one of the poisonous bottles home the night of Pepper's party and never used it."

"And the closer it got to Clarissa's departure to Spain the more desperate Amber got. She had to come up with something else, something she knew Clarissa would use right away."

"You sound like you know something."

"I may have seen something. Yesterday, when you went to interview Amber, I went back to the radio station. I wanted to listen to Kari's last show with Amber and Clarissa. There was something about it that made me think I'd seen something. I thought if I replayed Kari's interview I might remember. And I did. It was during the station break. Kari was talking to Sarah and Amber and Clarissa were playing around with their cell phones. They had emptied their purses onto the console in front of them. It was full of makeup and what I thought was candy, only now I think it might have been the poisoned teabags. Sarah got upset the girls weren't paying attention and told them to pick up their toys. Amber was furious. She looked like she might be about to walk out, but Kari settled her down. I think she may have slipped the teabags, along with the cosmetics, into Clarissa's bag, right in front of me."

"The teabags our investigators found were small. They would have easily fit into the palm of Amber's hand."

"And they were wrapped in cellophane and tied with a lavender ribbon."

"What you're saying would match what Amber's told us. She admitted she slipped the teabags into Clarissa's bag right before she left for Spain. She told her they would be good for curing jet lag."

"And she got the poison from Misty, right?"

"Amber said she knew Misty carried a stash of dried herbs, including monkshood, around in that big bag of hers. She mixed the poison with the bath salts right on the set of *The Sorcerer's Daughter,* and nobody thought anything of it."

I wasn't surprised. Sam told me there was always a lot of down time between takes on the set. Amber could have been rehearsing or studying and no one would have noticed.

"But Misty must have suspected. Didn't she think it was odd the monkshood was missing?"

"That's just it. With monkshood you don't need much. Couple of teaspoons is all it takes. She said she shaved off the roots. Misty had stems of the stuff, and, as easily addled as she gets, I doubt she noticed."

"Her psychic abilities do seem to come and go, don't they?"

"You still think she's involved?"

"No. I think she's crazy, and like you said I don't understand how it is she seems to know what she knows. But I'll give you this, the woman's got something." I explained Misty's strange psychic prediction, her theories on energy and how she thought I could change the course of fate. "All I know is I'm glad she was with me last night. I was about to lose it and whether she did something or just helped me to remain calm, I don't know."

"None of us do, Carol. But you will be happy to know, Amber also admitted to planting a bag of monkshood outside Sam's front door. It was part of the evidence the police collected when they arrested her."

"I knew it!" I was on my feet, pacing the room. I explained to Eric that shortly after Pepper's murder I'd seen Amber on Sam's front porch.

"She was angry. They were yelling at one another. I was sure I saw her throw something into the bushes in front of Sam's place as she left." I walked over to the French doors and looked out at the patio. "Next thing I knew she was pushing past Charlie and me in a huff, and I was thinking how odd it was that she had on driving gloves. But it would make sense, wouldn't it?" I looked back at Eric. "I mean, if she had the poison with her she had to have gloves on, or she would have been poisoned, too."

Eric stood up and poured himself another cup of coffee. "You think Sam suspected Amber?"

"Maybe." I came back to the table and sat back down. I told him I knew Sam had called King after news of Clarissa's death had been broadcast. Maybe she'd figured it out by then. "Why?" I asked.

"Amber kept referring to a script. I'm wondering if maybe it was a script Sam had given her. That's what agents do, right? Get scripts into the hands of their clients for perspective work. Have them read it. See if they might be good for the role."

"Yes. So?"

"She said in the script she was just supposed to do the principals, but then the others got in the way. She needed to fix the problem. It wasn't just Pepper and the old ladies anymore. Kim,

Clarissa, Sarah and Sam, they all had to go. But most of all, she said she didn't trust Sam. She was afraid she'd betray her."

I got an uneasy feeling in the pit of my stomach.

"You still think Sam's guilty, don't you?"

"Let's just say I'm not so sure Samantha Millhouse is not involved."

"That's crazy. You just said she was one of Amber's intended victims. That Amber was afraid she'd betray her. I can't imagine why. Sam did everything for that girl. You can't possibly think Sam did this."

"I didn't say she did. I'm just wondering if she knew Amber was involved, and if so, when?"

I looked at Eric, our eyes locked.

"*If* she knew, and believe me I'm not agreeing she did, it was because Sam wanted to help Amber. Remember in the beginning Sam was saying all kinds of awful things about her aunt's death. She's got a big mouth and it wasn't smart. But at first we didn't know if it really was a murder. There was the possibility Misty might have accidentally poisoned the bath salts. I don't think Sam knew for certain it was Amber until after she was arrested, and then she wanted to protect her. Sam knew she hadn't killed anybody so she took the brunt of suspicion onto herself. To save Amber. She liked taking care of her people."

"Sam may have liked taking care of her people, but sitting in jail and watching the body count rise, at some point she had to start wondering if maybe this wasn't a good idea."

My mind went back to my last visit with Sam. She was confident King would get her off. Then Clarissa died and she called King and wanted to talk. That had to have been when she knew for certain it was Amber.

"So what's going to happen to Amber?"

"I'm not a lawyer, but I'd imagine Amber Marx will never see the inside of a courthouse, much less go to jail. After what I saw last night, she fits the classic criteria for someone who's criminally insane. For her the lines blur between fantasy and reality. She's clearly not competent to stand trial. It's likely she'll spend the rest of her life tucked away in a mental institution."

Eric's eyes looked heavy. He was struggling to keep them open. I got up and opened the door to the patio. It was nice outside, a beautiful sunny southern California day. Not a cloud in the sky. I suggested we get some fresh air and settled myself into a chair. Eric took the chaise lounge.

"So it's over?" I asked.

"For now, yes. With Amber confessing to the murders, and with the evidence we collected, we don't think there'll be any more poisonings. We've made contact with everyone who was at the party. We'll have all the bottles, including the one Clarissa took home, by the end of the day."

I put my note pad down.

"I guess I was wrong about Sarah and Andrew. They really weren't involved at all?"

Eric didn't answer.

"What's wrong?"

"Let's just say, sometimes things don't always wrap up quite as neatly as we like. But for now we believe we caught the person responsible for the Hollywood Bathtub Murders and the death of Clarissa St. Clair."

I excused myself and went inside. I called King, told him about Amber, then hung up and called the station. Tyler would be waiting for my report, and Amber's fans would want to know their star was in the hospital, alive and recovering. As for the charges of multiple murders, most would never accept that Amber Marx, Hollywood's sweetheart, could possibly have murdered her best friend, Clarissa St. Clair, along with five other people. I closed my report with news that the FBI believed Sarah and Samantha Millhouse and Kim LaSalle were likely other intended victims and the police believed they had found all the poisonous bottles of Lavender Lush #7.

When I returned to the patio, Eric was sound asleep.

CHAPTER 31

A week after the incident at the Santa Monica Pier, I was in the news booth waiting for Sam, Sarah, and Mr. King to join Kari for a special broadcast in the adjoining studio. All week long Tyler had been running promos hyping KCHC's coverage of Amber Marx's arrest and the Hollywood murders: *Don't miss KCHC's exclusive. The inside story of Amber Marx, Hollywood's sweetheart turned serial murderer...why there will never be a trial.*

I was growing impatient. Sam and I had yet to spend any time recapping the situation, and now that the case was considered closed Tyler had assigned me to other stories. Our day-by-day coverage had come down to Kari's special report. One final show, mostly for fans, so the station could wrap up loose ends and move on to the next big story.

Outside the studio window I watched as Sam, Sarah, and Mr. King chatted idly with Tyler Hunt, chewing up valuable time. It was hard to believe the two sisters were here together with King, acting so chummy, patting each other on the back, laughing. Their actions weren't befitting of their history. I wanted a few minutes alone with Sam. But I was stuck on the phone, getting an update on UCLA's waterless urinals story. *What a waste.* I couldn't break away. Finally, Tyler looked at his watch and, tapping King on the shoulder, pointed in the direction of the studio door. King came in first and Sam and Sarah, still talking, filed in behind. Sam waved to me, mouthed a silent hello then squared herself on the barstool. This was the first I had seen Sam since her release from jail. Once the charges against her had been officially dropped she called the station to tell me she was headed home. I felt victorious. Sam was free. This whole ugly mess was behind us.

"You're my first call, Carol. I don't have a lot of time, but I wanted to thank you. I couldn't have made it through without you. You've been—"

"Wait a minute," I stopped her mid-sentence. "I could use a quote for my noon report."

"How about...I'm looking forward to getting back to work and assuming my new position as head of the ACT Agency."

"Love it," I said.

I asked her to hold onto the line, until I could end my report. She apologized, said she had another call to make, more people she needed to thank. I understood. We agreed we would talk later. We had lots to catch up on.

Later that night I expected to see her. Grabbing Bossypants and a bottle of red wine I knocked on her door. There was nothing. No lights, no sound from the big screen TV, and when I peaked in the front window, no furniture.

Sam had moved out.

All week long there were voicemails, fragmented apologies for her sudden departure and excuses that things around the agency were *crazy busy*. Finally a text arrived suggesting lunch today after Kari's Show. Moments later, a second text, would I keep Bossypants? No explanation. I made reservations at the Palm, one of Sam's favorite restaurants. We had lots to talk about.

Kari, in full stage makeup, opened the show and in her usual flamboyant manner, gestured to each of her guests, introducing them as though her listening audience was actually in the studio with her.

I smiled at Sam. *Every business has its peacocks*. She smiled back.

"But, friends, before we begin, I need to say there is one person not with us in studio today who's informed me to expect they will be calling in with important news. And believe me when I say, everyone here, those listening at home and in their cars, is going to want to stay tuned to hear what our mystery caller has to say."

We all exchanged curious looks. *Who?*

The only person I could think of who'd been involved in the investigation and wasn't there was Eric, or perhaps, Misty. Eric was off with his Sea Mistress, exactly as Misty had predicted, sailing the high seas. With the case closed, Eric's use-it-or-lose-it vacation time demanded his leave, and it was highly unlikely he'd be calling. As for Misty, I didn't have a clue. I hadn't seen or spoken to her since that night on the pier.

Kari smiled coyly and continued with her opening statement, going on about how shocked she was Sunday morning to see Amber's picture on the front page of the *LA Times*.

"And not just the *Times*," she scolded, "but splashed across every tabloid in this country. None of us could escape it. Photos of her, clearly in a manic state standing on top of the Ferris wheel, threatening to jump." She rubbed her hands together and looked at King. "It just doesn't make any sense. That someone so dear to us all, could be so ill and now... Well, Mr. King, you're her lawyer, you tell us...what will happen to Amber Marx?"

King, still congested, cleared his throat.

"First, I'd like to begin by thanking your reporter, Carol Childs, for her work in uncovering information concerning Miss Marx's mental state and sharing it with the FBI. Had she not done so, things could have gone very differently, and Miss Marx might be wasting away in a jail cell, not getting the medical attention she needs. And secondly, I want to thank Samantha Millhouse and her sister, Sarah, for asking me to represent Amber. Sam was familiar with my work with the National Alliance on Mental Illness, and I'm pleased to be able to advise those closest to Amber on the best possible actions available to her."

I looked over at Sam. *You knew King?* She glanced away, refusing to make eye contact. I knew in that instant she had been lying to me.

Sam knew King all along. She knew about his involvement with the mentally disturbed, and she knew he worked for the station. She had probably heard him on the air and gambled I'd refer him to her. How convenient. And King? In all the excitement I'd forgotten when I explained the case to him that he told me he had known Pepper. "A gentleman never talks," he had said.

"Excuse me, Mr. King, I'm sorry to interrupt." Kari paused, her hand to her headset. "Our mystery caller is on the line. I believe she has something important she'd like to share."

"Thank you, Kari. My name is Misty Dawn, some of you may know me as the psychic to the stars or Mystic Misty, and while I'm here to make a prediction, I'd like to begin with an apology. Since Amber's rescue last week I've been with her father Burt Marx. He and I go way back. I felt I should be there for him. He's been greatly concerned and for good reason. Amber's mother had a long history of trouble with mental illness and he worried about his daughter constantly. He'd hoped Amber might never be affected but clearly she is, and I'm afraid, close as I was to the family, I didn't see it."

There was a silence in the studio that made my ears ache. Again our eyes clicked back and forth. *What possible prediction could Misty be about to make?*

With her elbows on the console, Kari leaned into the mic. "Just what is it you're predicting, Misty?"

"I may not be as good as I once was, my psychic powers seem to come and go these days, and it's compounded because Amber has multiple personalities. But I do know this case is not over. There will be more arrests."

King coughed, Sarah placed both hands over her chest (I wasn't sure if I didn't hear her gasp), and Sam stared stoically at Kari.

"Can you tell us who?" Kari asked.

"Unfortunately, I cannot. I can only say I'm devastated by these senseless murders and under the circumstances I have decided to retire. I will be terminating my contract with The ACT Agency immediately."

"Misty!" Sam, with her hands on the console, stood up and leaned into the mic. "Certainly after all these years you're not walking out? Not now."

"I'm sorry, Sam. My agreement was with your aunt. I've been in contact with her and under the present circumstances we both agree it'd be wise if I stepped away from the agency. At least for a short spell."

"What?" Sam sat down, disbelief written all over her face.

I squelched a laugh. I think everybody in the studio wondered if they'd heard her correctly.

Kari wrapped immediately with a station break. "On that note, folks, I think it's time for a word from our sponsor."

Prozac Oral for when life is overwhelming...

Misty's prediction was like a bomb had exploded in the studio. Stunned silence. Even the air felt heavy. I looked at King; he returned my gaze, and Sam whispered something in Sarah's ear then squeezed her hand. Nobody said another word until Kari came back on the air.

Kari opened with a few calls from her listeners, all of them commenting on Misty's prediction. Some saying they thought Misty Dawn was nuts, a sidewalk psychic from the sixties. Others wondered if perhaps while she admitted her clairvoyant powers may be fading, that she might be right, that Amber hadn't acted alone.

"What do you think, Mr. King? Did Amber Marx act alone?"

King cleared his throat. "I'm not in a position to comment, Kari, on what Misty Dawn does or doesn't believe. My job at this point is to do the best I can for my client, Miss Marx." He said it with such finality that Kari announced she'd take no further questions concerning Misty's prediction and turned the interview back to Amber's current mental state and her treatment.

"Okay, then, let's go back to Amber. Currently, she's at UCLA. Is that where she'll remain?"

King explained that at some point Amber would be transferred to a long-term facility for an indefinite period of time. That when she was taken into custody she was neither capable of understanding what she had done, or in any condition to comprehend what was happening to her.

Kari's eye shifted to Sam. "You had no idea, not an inkling, all this time that something was wrong?"

"Absolutely not." Sam shook her head. "You have to understand. Amber was my aunt's client and I was extremely busy with the agency. I had very little face time with her. I can only say my aunt loved Amber Marx and would have done anything for her. She's a remarkable young woman. We never thought she was capable of anything like this. Who would? We're all deeply troubled by what's happened."

"Actually, Kari," Sarah pulled the mic closer to her. "Sam and I've been discussing this. In hindsight we believe that if there was anything that might have triggered Amber's actions, it was likely the sudden death of her mother."

"And it was after her mother's death," Kari asked, "that Pepper began emancipation proceedings?"

"Yes, and we all did our best to become her second family." Sam went on about how busy the young actress was between her work on the set, special appearances and her studies. "We shadowed her as best we could. By that I mean, we had someone with her, close by, but we never wanted to appear overbearing."

"Then of course there was the party, Pepper's birthday." Kari looked over the top of her glasses at both sisters. "And we now know, according to evidence the FBI made available to us, Amber poisoned the bath salts given to seven of the guests at the party, including you, Sam, and you, too, Sarah. I imagine that had to make you both feel a bit uncomfortable."

Sam spoke up first. "Neither of us believes Amber really

understood what she was doing. For years she's been playing fantasy roles, her most recent being *The Sorcerer's Daughter*, involving witchcraft. We suspect somewhere along the line she lost touch with reality."

Sarah nodded in agreement. "And tragic as these awful murders have been, there's no way Amber intended to murder anyone."

Kari leaned back on the stool and crossed her arms.

"If I might go back a bit, Sarah, didn't you at one point actually accuse your sister?"

"I did. I was terribly upset over the death of my aunt and even more surprised at the reading of her will. When I realized she'd left everything to my sister, I snapped. I called the police and told them I thought she did it."

"Actually, Kari, it was a good thing." Sam grabbed her sister's hand and squeezed it. "If she hadn't, we might never have known that my aunt's business partners, Adel Powers and Helen Howard, had also been murdered. Fortunately the autopsy revealed exactly what it needed to and ultimately that we were all targets."

I looked at Sam. *You've been playing me. That's why you rang my bell the morning of Pepper's murder, why you wanted me to come with you to the reading of the will. You needed me.*

"So, you don't think your sister had anything to do with Pepper's death?"

"Goodness no. I was totally wrong to accuse her. I should never have done that."

"And yet, there was this issue of the second will..."

"If I might interrupt, Kari, I understand how my sister felt. I might have done the same thing under similar circumstances and manufactured a second will. Seems crazy, I know. But the truth is that my aunt was anything but fair. We called her the Queen of Mean. She pitted us against each other all the time. We never knew from day to day what mood she'd be in or who she'd prefer. The fact of the matter was, on any given day, my aunt's estate could just as easily have gone to my sister. Pepper was forever changing things."

"Seeing the two of you sitting here together today, smiling, makes me think you've buried the hatchet. Have you?"

"We decided it was for the best," Sarah said.

"And the two of you, you're back at the agency together?"

"We are." Sam answered.

"And Sarah, Andrew Reese, the young man who brought you back to the agency. Where is he?"

"Gone," both sisters answered simultaneously then laughed.

"For all we know by now he's probably on a beach somewhere," Sarah said. "I don't imagine he'll be coming back. I suppose he grew tired of Sam and me and decided the agency business just wasn't for him after all."

"Actually, Kari, if I might. Maybe it takes something like this to put things into perspective. If I've learned one thing from all of this, it's that life's short, and maybe spouting off like I have had a tendency to do—particularly like I did about my aunt—isn't always such a good idea."

"You think?" Kari laughed.

Sam didn't wait for the moment to pass. "I'm only going to say I never lied about my frustrations with my aunt or masked how I felt. She was, to say the least, a very difficult woman. Maybe I should have been a bit more circumspect in my opinions, but thank goodness, it's still not a crime in this country to say what you think. Isn't that right, Mr. King?" She paused, looked directly at me and then added, "And in the spirit of moving forward and putting the past behind us, I've asked Mr. King to help me draft a new agreement. I've created a living trust, adding my sister to what had been my aunt's estate. She's joining me at Millhouse Manor. It's big enough for us both. In fact, I've even decided to let my aunt's housekeeper, Arminta, live in the guest house with her son until such time she decides she no longer needs to, or wants to."

"Carol, I've not given you a chance to ask any questions, perhaps you have something?"

I looked directly at Sam. She knew it was Amber all along. She had used me to escalate the story to draw suspicion away from her.

It was all a ruse, even the war with her sister. All planned. But I couldn't say that on the air. I didn't have proof.

"When did you know it was Amber?"

"I think I started to figure it out after I heard about Clarissa's death. In jail you have time to think. Amber must have found out Pepper and her business partners had vetoed the idea of pitching her for *Lady in White*, and when Clarissa got the job it was too much for her. That's when she went off the deep end. I think Amber wanted to kill anybody associated with the agency. My sister and me included. She killed my aunt and her partners. She tried to kill Kim LaSalle and she succeeded with Clarissa. When I heard the news about Clarissa, I tried to call Mr. King from the jail but I couldn't get through to him. His assistant said he was home ill. Not that it mattered, they weren't about to let me out just because I thought I knew who the killer was. But eventually they would. They had to. I didn't do it, and then of course, Amber confessed."

"Were you surprised?" I was prepared to not believe her answer. I knew she was lying.

"I was, but awful as this is, Amber will finally get the help she needs. She never would have been able to do that with my aunt alive. Pepper never would have let her out of her contracts. Amber had two movies after *The Sorcerer's Daughter,* so taking time off wouldn't happen. It would have cost my aunt millions. That's the way Pepper was. She used people. If it'd been me, I would have cancelled those agreements and had her in treatment. Big difference between my aunt and me, I take care of my people." Sam pointed to her chest.

Take care of your people. The words soured in my ears. *Was I one of your people?*

"At least now," Sam added, "Amber will get the help she needs."

Kari leaned over the console and put her hand on Mr. King.

"And will she, Mr. King? Will Amber Marx ever get the help she needs?"

"I can't address the type of care Miss Marx will receive in the future or how effective it will be. Legally, I can say that at the time she carried out the murders she was clearly suffering from an acute form of mental illness over which she had no control. It's obvious she does not possess the ability to decipher reality from fantasy and therefore can't, and won't, stand trial. The DA realizes this and has agreed she be sentenced to a mental facility where she can receive the type of help she so desperately needs."

"Will she ever be considered cured?" Kari asked, "And if so, what will happen to her then?"

King sighed.

"I think for Amber's sake we can all consider her lucky. Our jails and prisons have become the insane asylums of yesteryear. Fortunately, Amber's been placed in a medical facility and not a jail. If at some point she is deemed sane and safe enough to rejoin society her case will be revisited, but until then, we just don't know."

"But it is possible, isn't it, that if her doctors no longer think she's a danger to herself or others, that eventually she might be released?" Kari asked.

"We have seen cases, like John Hinkley, who shot President Reagan, where he's been given temporary passes to visit home. Maybe one day, Amber will be allowed to visit her father. We just don't know."

Sam silently fist pumped her arm in the air. She looked jubilant, the smile tightly drawn across her face as she bowed her head. She'd won. Amber wouldn't be going to prison, she'd be getting the care she needed, and all because Sam took care of her people.

She had fixed it so that Amber would never get caught, and if she were, Sam made certain there was no connection to herself. The end result was exactly as Sam had predicted, a win-win. With Pepper Millhouse and her business partners out of the picture, Amber Marx had been neatly taken care of, and Sam was inheriting the agency she wanted.

I looked at her.

You did it. I don't know how, but I know you did. And somehow, I'll prove it.

I left the news booth before the end of the show. I didn't feel like lunch. I felt sick to my stomach. I told Tyler if Sam came looking for me to tell her I'd left early.

CHAPTER 32

Tyler refused to let me go to lunch. Grabbing his keys and a pack of cigarettes off his desk he pressed by me and said we needed to talk. I followed him, expecting another wild ride in his car out to the beach. Instead he took a left turn out of the news room and headed down the hall toward an emergency exit. He pushed through a heavy metal door that opened onto a smokers' porch, littered with cigarette butts, half empty cups of stale coffee, and furnished with cheap outdoor furniture. I wrapped my sweater around me and took a seat in one of the plastic lawn chairs while he leaned up against the gray cement brick wall and lit up.

"This case isn't over, Carol."

"Sam's lying. I'm not buying this new sister act. They're in this together and probably Andrew is too. I can't prove it but I'll bet you a year of doing nothing but traffic reports I'm right."

Tyler walked over to the table, pulled a chair out and sat down. "Sam used you, Carol. You were part of her plan. If Pepper's death was never disputed she was home free. And if it was discovered she'd been murdered, Sam knew you'd never believe she was guilty. Not for a minute. She needed you to fight for her, keep the light off of Amber Marx and onto a fictitious serial killer. In time, she figured it'd be an unsolved case, like the Tylenol murders."

I shook my head. I couldn't look at Tyler. "She got exactly what she wanted, the agency, Millhouse Manor and ultimately, Amber Marx her freedom. She planned the whole thing. She knew Amber was a time bomb. Pepper was going to use the girl until she was no good to her any more. I don't care what Sam said, Pepper and everybody else at the agency had to know Amber's father was worried about his daughter. Even I suspected that after interviewing him. Burt Marx knew Amber killed her mother and her baby brother. He wanted his daughter home so he could take care of her. But Sam used her. Amber was Sam's pawn. She used her to get everything she wanted."

"A pawn that went rogue, Carol." Tyler took a drag on his cigarette. "Sam may have intended to use Amber to kill Pepper Millhouse and her business partners but I doubt Sam planned on Amber taking out five people."

I knew he was right. Sam may have convinced Amber to make up the poisonous bath salts. She may have even told Amber it was all part of role she was playing for *The Sorcerer's Daughter*, but when Heather Broderick and her boyfriend showed up dead, and right after that Clarissa, Sam knew Amber had gone too far.

"They had to stop her," I said. "Up until then their plot was working. Sam had drawn just enough suspicion upon herself to get arrested. Nobody even thought of looking at Amber Marx. Sam knew King was an excellent lawyer. He'd find a way to get her out of jail, and the poisoning of Pepper Millhouse and her business partners would go unsolved or maybe considered to be accidental, a mistake on Misty's part."

I leaned back in the chair. It was the type of win-win scenario Sam liked to boast about. In the end, Sam got the agency, she settled with her sister and if Amber hadn't gone off the deep end she would have gone home and lived with her father, happily ever after. As it was now, Amber would get the psychological help she needed.

"But what I don't get, Tyler, is the second will. If Sam and her sister are in this together, why the second will?"

Tyler took a deep puff on his cigarette. "You're looking at it all wrong, Carol. Neither sister knew from day to day what her aunt planned to do. It was just like Sam said. Pepper Millhouse played them against each other. My guess is when Sam asked you to her aunt's office, she had no idea who her aunt might name as the beneficiary. Whatever happened, Sam and Sarah planned to play it out. They created enough of a ruckus to keep their dispute in the news for weeks. The public would side with one twin over the other. Convinced one of them murdered their aunt and the other was a victim. Your job was simply to report it, to keep the focus on one of the twins. As for the second will, you've heard the old expression, no honor among thieves."

I nodded.

"It's simple. Sarah and Andrew got scared. After Sam went to jail, suddenly there weren't just three murders, but five. They didn't expect that. My guess is nobody did. Sarah and Andrew started to worry if Sam went down for the murders Pepper's estate would end up in probate and they might never reap their reward. So Sarah phonies up a new will, blackmails Pepper's housekeeper and hopes for the best. Meanwhile, Sam sits tight. What else is she going to do? She knows her sister is not as strong as she is. She figures she'll straighten it out when she's released."

"Which is exactly what she did."

"And why Misty Dawn believes there'll still be more arrests." Tyler took a drag on the cigarette then blew smoke slowly from the side of his mouth. "But there's still something missing, connecting the three of them to the murders."

I thought back to my conversation with Eric right after Amber was arrested. He knew the case wasn't closed. He'd said as much, only I didn't want to hear it. Not then. Sam was coming home. She'd been vindicated. I didn't understand when he said, "Things didn't always wrap up quite as neatly as we like." But now I did, and my eyes were open.

"I can't think of what it would be. The police and FBI searched her place thoroughly. There wasn't much they didn't check or take with them, and now Sam's moved out. There's nothing left."

"There's always something. That's how cold cases are solved. You'll find it. 'Cause for you this case isn't over. It's personal."

*   *   *

A week later I was at my front door. It was late, past eleven p.m. From inside the house I heard the phone ringing. I had hopes it might be Eric, and grabbing what I thought were my keys I pulled them from inside my bag. Attached was Misty's small packet of love potions. The sachet's violet ribbon had wrapped itself around my keychain. Without thinking about it, I opened the door and hurried inside to get the phone.

I hadn't even said hello when the voice on the other end said, "I told you so."

"Misty?" I tossed my bag on the counter.

"If you'd used those love potions I gave you, that handsome young agent friend of yours might be with you tonight and not off with that mistress of his."

"It's not his mistress, Misty. It's his boat." I laughed to myself. Since the night on the pier I'd changed my mind about Misty. I was actually beginning to find her less worrisome and more oddly amusing.

"I know that." She giggled. "But that's not why I called. I've been talking to Pepper."

I sighed audibly. "And what did she have to say?" I still didn't believe in Misty's powers, but I was coming to understand when Misty got an idea she wanted me to think it was because she was communicating with her spirit world.

"You're close. Very close to finding the missing piece."

She paused. I paused. There was silence. Tyler had used the exact term "missing piece."

"Go on," I said.

"The piece will prove Sam, Sarah and Andrew were in this together."

I pushed the phone closer to my ear. "All three of them?"

"That's what Pepper thinks and so do I. But you mustn't worry. There's no dark aura around you this time. You're fine. You should relax, do a little light reading before you go to bed. See if it doesn't come to you." She giggled and hung up. I listened as the dial tone droned in my ear.

If I was close to finding the missing piece, Misty was right, it'd have to come to me. I was tired and wanted to go to bed. It had been a long day. I could think about Misty's premonition in the morning. I grabbed my bag off the counter, and whether it was the power of suggestion—or something else—I started looking around for something to take upstairs with me to read. On the coffee table was the script King had slapped in my hands the day of Sam's arrest. Something to keep me quiet. I'd forgotten all about it. I picked it up and was halfway up the stairs, my eyes scanning the cover page, when—

There, right in front of me, in my hands, was the missing piece. Exactly like Misty said it would be.

Written on the front cover of the script in light purple ink was a note.

Sam,

This is perfect for Amber.

Sarah

The title of the script: *Apprentice for Murder,* by Andrew Reese.

My eyes skimmed the synopsis on page two. A dark comedy about a young woman hired to murder her boss's employer. I turned around and went back down the stairs. I could sleep later. Now I had work to do.

NANCY COLE SILVERMAN

Nancy Cole Silverman credits her twenty-five years in news and talk radio for helping her to develop an ear for storytelling. But it wasn't until 2001 after she retired from news and copywriting that she was able to sit down and write fiction fulltime. Much of what Silverman writes about today she admits is pulled from events that were reported on from inside some of Los Angeles' busiest newsrooms where she spent the bulk of her career. In the last ten years she has written numerous short stories and novelettes. Today Silverman lives in Los Angeles with her husband, Bruce and two standard poodles.

Henery Press Mystery Books

And finally, before you go...
Here are a few other mysteries
you might enjoy:

KILLER IMAGE

Wendy Tyson

An Allison Campbell Mystery (#1)

As Philadelphia's premier image consultant, Allison Campbell helps others reinvent themselves, but her most successful transformation was her own after a scandal nearly ruined her. Now she moves in a world of powerful executives, wealthy, eccentric ex-wives and twisted ethics.

When Allison's latest Main Line client, the fifteen-year-old Goth daughter of a White House hopeful, is accused of the ritualistic murder of a local divorce attorney, Allison fights to prove her client's innocence when no one else will. But unraveling the truth brings specters from her own past. And in a place where image is everything, the ability to distinguish what's real from the facade may be the only thing that keeps Allison alive.

Available at booksellers nationwide and online

Visit www.henerypress.com for details

MALICIOUS MASQUERADE

Alan Cupp

A Carter Mays PI Novel (#1)

Chicago PI Carter Mays is thrust into a perilous masquerade when local rich girl Cindy Bedford hires him. Turns out her fiancé failed to show up on their wedding day, the same day millions of dollars are stolen from her father's company. While Carter takes the case, Cindy's father tries to find him his own way. With nasty secrets, hidden finances, and a trail of revenge, it's soon apparent no one is who they say they are.

Carter searches for the truth, but the situation grows more volatile as panic collides with vulnerability. Broken relationships and blurred loyalties turn deadly, fueled by past offenses and present vendettas in a quest to reveal the truth behind the masks before no one, including Carter, gets out alive.

Available at booksellers nationwide and online

Visit www.henerypress.com for details

DEATH BY BLUE WATER

Kait Carson

A Hayden Kent Mystery (#1)

Paralegal Hayden Kent knows first-hand that life in the Florida Keys can change from perfect to perilous in a heartbeat. When she discovers a man's body at 120' beneath the sea, she thinks she is witness to a tragic accident. She becomes the prime suspect when the victim is revealed to be the brother of the man who recently jilted her, and she has no alibi. A migraine stole Hayden's memory of the night of the death.

As the evidence mounts, she joins forces with an Officer Janice Kirby. Together the two women follow the clues that uncover criminal activities at the highest levels and put Hayden's life in jeopardy while she fights to stay free.

Available at booksellers nationwide and online

Visit www.henerypress.com for details

FATAL BRUSHSTROKE

Sybil Johnson

An Aurora Anderson Mystery (#1)

A dead body in her garden and a homicide detective on her doorstep...

Computer programmer and tole-painting enthusiast Aurora (Rory) Anderson doesn't envision finding either when she steps outside to investigate the frenzied yipping coming from her own back yard. After all, she lives in Vista Beach, a quiet California beach community where violent crime is rare and murder even rarer.

Suspicion falls on Rory when the body buried in her flowerbed turns out to be someone she knows—her tole-painting teacher, Hester Bouquet. Just two weeks before, Rory attended one of Hester's weekend seminars, an unpleasant experience she vowed never to repeat. As evidence piles up against Rory, she embarks on a quest to identify the killer and clear her name. Can Rory unearth the truth before she encounters her own brush with death?

Available at booksellers nationwide and online

Visit www.henerypress.com for details

CIRCLE OF INFLUENCE

Annette Dashofy

A Zoe Chambers Mystery (#1)

Zoe Chambers, paramedic and deputy coroner in rural Pennsylvania's tight-knit Vance Township, has been privy to a number of local secrets over the years, some of them her own. But secrets become explosive when a dead body is found in the Township Board President's abandoned car.

As a January blizzard rages, Zoe and Police Chief Pete Adams launch a desperate search for the killer, even if it means uncovering secrets that could not only destroy Zoe and Pete, but also those closest to them.

Available at booksellers nationwide and online

Visit www.henerypress.com for details

THE RED QUEEN'S RUN

Bourne Morris

A Meredith Solaris Mystery (#1)

A famous journalism dean is found dead at the bottom of a stairwell. Accident or murder? The police suspect members of the faculty who had engaged in fierce quarrels with the dean— distinguished scholars who were known to attack the dean like brutal schoolyard bullies. When Meredith "Red" Solaris is appointed interim dean, the faculty suspects are furious.

Will the beautiful red-haired professor be next? The case detective tries to protect her as he heads the investigation, but incoming threats lead him to believe Red's the next target for death.

Available at booksellers nationwide and online

Visit www.henerypress.com for details

16552401R00142

Made in the USA
San Bernardino, CA
09 November 2014